ELEVEN LITTLE PIGGIES

ELEVEN LITTLE PIGGIES

Elizabeth Gunn

This first world edition published 2012
in Great Britain and 2013 in the USA by
SEVERN HOUSE PUBLISHERS LTD of
19 Cedar Road, Sutton, Surrey, England, SM2 5DA.
Trade paperback edition first published
in Great Britain and the USA 2013 by
SEVERN HOUSE PUBLISHERS LTD

British Library Cataloguing in Publication Data

Gunn, Elizabeth, 1927-
  Eleven little piggies.
  1. Hines, Jake (Fictitious character)--Fiction.
  2. Police--Minnesota--Fiction. 3. Murder--
  Investigation--Fiction. 4. Families--Fiction. 5. Farms--
  Minnesota--Fiction. 6. Detective and mystery stories.
  I. Title
  813.6-dc23

ISBN-13: 978-0-7278-8236-3 (cased)
ISBN-13: 978-1-84751-463-9 (trade paper)

All Severn House titles are printed on acid-free paper.

Severn House Publishers support The Forest Stewardship Council [FSC],
the leading international forest certification organisation. All our titles that
are printed on Greenpeace-approved FSC-certified paper carry the FSC logo.

Typeset by Palimpsest Book Production Ltd.,
Falkirk, Stirlingshire, Scotland.
Printed and bound in Great Britain by
MPG Books Ltd., Bodmin, Cornwall.

ONE

'Whaddya say, Oz? My butt is frozen and the geese are gone.' The sun was as high in the sky as it was going to get this close to Thanksgiving, but inside our shooting blind it was so cold my shorts were stiff. I was thinking longingly about a hot cider laced with rum.

'We can't quit yet.' Ozzie Sullivan scanned the bright November sky above us, so cloudless and empty. 'I haven't got my limit.' He had two fat Canadian honkers in his bag as well as a snow goose and a pair of teal. But the state had raised the limit on Canadian geese a couple of years back to three and, haggling or hunting, Ozzie always tries to get all he can.

'You can have mine,' I said. I had bagged a Canada goose and a mallard, and had been thinking ruefully about the Thanksgiving turkeys we were committed to sharing with my mother-in-law and a roomful of Trudy's Swedish relatives in five days. Who wants leftovers from so many birds in one week? A guy could get cramps from that much stuffing.

'Come on,' I said. 'There goes the signal; the guides are closing the field to get ready for the afternoon customers.'

'I can't understand it,' Ozzie said, tossing empties into the cooler. 'We had great shooting early this morning but they sure thinned out later on.'

'Don't they always?'

'Well, usually. But all week long, guys have been coming into the bar so excited, telling me this part of the river was swarming with birds from morning to night. Everybody claimed they were bagging their limit.' We both have small farms near the dinky town of Mirium, forty miles north of Rutherford. Ozzie works as a bartender there in the winter to beef up his cash flow, and he and the other local sportsmen do a lot of competitive bragging.

'So they shot all the slow ones and now the fittest are frolicking on the Gulf Coast, just as Darwin predicted.' I disarmed my old

Remington 870 and put the shells back in the box, not really dissatisfied.

In fact, I didn't give a fiddler's fart where those birds had gone. I'd had six or seven good shots that morning and brought down two birds, about average for me. Now I could put my fleece mittens on over my shooting gloves and soon I would be indoors, letting my feet thaw while I nursed a hot toddy. My wife would be glad to hear she did not have to put up with the mess I can make getting a feathered creature ready to be roasted, and later on I would grill some brats to eat with the good beans she'd been baking all day.

I only came on this hunt because I like the occasional challenge of shooting at live game out of doors. I spend more than the required hours every year at the shooting range, staying qualified on the Glock 17 and the twelve-gauge Remington the Rutherford PD specifies for its officers. But going after live targets sharpens hand/eye coordination as no amount of blazing away at inert objects will do.

Dealing with the bloody remains of a day's hunt, though, always feels like a dubious reward to me. I mean, if my life depended on it, sure – if I had hungry little savages waiting in the tepee, I can clean a gizzard with the best of them. But as long as twenty-first-century grocers keep selling steaks and chops, I start asking myself as I pick out birdshot and pinfeathers: isn't this a pretty dim-witted way to get a meal? My idea of great *après*-hunt cuisine is burgers and beer, and I usually give my trophies away, if my hunting buddies will take them.

Ozzie Sullivan, on the other hand, is a passionate hunter and fisherman, and feels personally insulted when he doesn't get to feast on the flesh of his victims. He claims eating fresh game is what keeps Minnesota men so manly. His wife rolls her eyes up when she hears this and usually mutters something like, 'Yeah, man, and scaling fish can make their women look pretty butch, too'.

Angie thinks growing up in the country is good for her children, so she doesn't complain – much, usually – about Ozzie's barely profitable farming operation. But she works in town, bleaches her hair and wears fake fingernails with painted flags and sequins. Her deal with Ozzie is that he can have all the home-cooked wild-game dinners he wants as long as he's the home cook.

In a few minutes we had all our gear and the cooler ready to hoist out of the blind, and our game harvest laid out in front. We were in a bird-hunting area on the extreme north edge of Rutherford, just inside the city limits. It's run by a commercial guide service owned by two ex-marines, real hunting animals who can recite the breeding and feeding habits of North American waterfowl in their sleep. In mine, too, if they go on too long.

Their operation is a lazy hunter's dream – they rent the corn-field after the farmer's harvest is finished, dig two-seater pits amid the stubble and lay out nifty camouflage-speckled blinds that you just crawl into and zip up. They have hundreds of decoys and realistic bird calls to draw in the game, and strict rules of the field that keep the hunters from shooting each other. All their customers have to do is pay a guide fee, climb in and flip open the windows. Bunkered down in this coign of vantage, they're ready to stare out at decoys scattered in a stubble field for the next five hours.

'You call this recreation?' Trudy asked me the one time I took her along. She spent the first few minutes admiring the way the golden corn stubble shone against the fresh snow in the field, and then used her spotting scope to watch a noisy flight of crows fly in and out of a dead oak. She was a rock climber in those days, doing a lot of body wedging, belaying and other stuff I didn't want to hear about, bagging major peaks on her vacations. The entertainment component of hunting from a blind faded quickly for her. Not being one to tolerate boredom, she wrapped herself in an afghan and was soon engrossed in a paperback thriller she'd brought along. We were living together then but not yet married, and for the sake of the still-tentative relationship I never took her bird hunting again.

I don't do much hunting myself any more – with a house and a spouse, a demanding job and now a lively boy named Ben, there's never enough time. But Ozzie Sullivan won two tickets to this late-season half-day hunt in a raffle at his son's school. He intended to partner with his brother Dan, but then Dan got flu. So when Ozzie came looking for a substitute partner, I traded some favors with Trudy to free up a Saturday morning.

And when the first graceful shapes appeared, black against a dawn-streaked sky, and their wild cries sounded, I revived my inner savage and the emotional jolt he gets from the bird hunt. Besides the thrill of the chase, it's a unique intellectual exercise, deciding where in the sky to aim a shot so some part of it will intercept the body of a bird flying at unknown speed on an unpredictable trajectory. And for the satisfaction of occasionally guessing right – I knew at once when my first bird tumbled out of the sky – the risk of frostbite is a small price to pay.

We were in hog heaven for the first two hours, taking turns shooting at the flocks of birds that came to our decoys, high-fiving when one of us scored a hit. Then the birds, for reasons only they would ever know, went elsewhere, and for the last two hours I'd been ready to quit. Now I was beginning to like the other great feature of hunting here: we could be back out in Mirium with our guns oiled and put away in a little over an hour.

'Y'all ready to go?' Our guide was named Arlo, a self-styled 'big ol' brockle-faced Okie' who was part owner of the hunt. He zipped our shelter open and helped us muscle the cooler out. 'The van's there by the road, see? They'll take you back to the lot where your car's parked.' These people advertise a full-service hunt and even though we were free-loading that's what we were getting – everything organized, thought through, no effort spared to make our hunting day a pleasure.

It was colder, out of the blind, and there was a breeze. I zipped my coat up at the neck, put the hood up over my watch cap and pulled the drawstring tight.

'Looks like your partner needs some help, Arlo.' Ozzie pointed across the frozen field. One of the other guides stood by the farthest blind waving his arms. He yelled something my double-wrapped ears couldn't quite make out. 'What's he saying?' Ozzie wondered. 'He sounds kinda freaked.'

'Poor kid musta torn a hangnail, huh?' Arlo didn't even shift his gum, just went on chewing as he turned his pale gaze toward the signaling figure in the orange vest. This is the Hiawatha Valley Hunt Club, his stoical expression declared as he strode toward his noisy assistant; there will be no freaking on a Hiawatha Valley hunt.

I looked back a couple of times as we walked to our waiting transport, and saw that Arlo had intercepted his younger aide, who had joined two other men, probably clients from the looks of the gear they were carrying. On the far side of the farthest blind, the four stood talking, Arlo in a stiffly disapproving stance, looking down his long nose at his helper. The men with him waved their arms and pointed toward the fence. Barbed wire was stapled to hand-cut posts; it snaked through the trees and bushes that grew along the edge of the shooting field.

We reached the van, where our driver waited. He slid the big side door open and we loaded our gear. We were almost the last ones out of the field and the driver, impatient to be gone, had already strapped in and started the motor. As I slid the door closed, the driver's two-way radio beeped. He pulled it off his belt and answered while he looked back over his shoulder, beginning to back up one-handed. He stopped the vehicle as Arlo's voice, a little reedy and short-winded, said, 'Ask your passenger Jake Hines if he's carrying his cell phone.'

When he had me on the phone he said, softly, 'Can you come over here and help me a minute?'

'Sure. You want us to drive the van over?'

'No,' he said quickly. His voice was tense but low – the ultra-calm voice people use when they realize they're looking at a calamity but want you to know they are Still In Command. 'Will you please get out and walk over here by yourself? Tell the other people to wait in the van.'

'OK,' I said. 'What—'

His voice dropped again, almost to a whisper. 'I got a man down here—'

'Arlo,' I said, 'if one of your customers has had a hunting accident you should call nine-one-one right away.'

'I'm not sure this is an accident, Jake, and this man ain't my customer. He didn't rent no blind from me – I've never seen this fella before. He looks a little familiar, but – listen, if you'll quit talking, Jake' – he was doing all the talking – 'and come on over here' – his voice was cracking a little now – 'you'll see for yourself what the problem is.'

'What do you say it is?'

'That whoever this bozo is, he looks to me like he sure as hell is dead.'

TWO

'I'm going to be a little late,' I told Trudy an hour later. At the curb on the street side of the field, many vehicles were parking.

'You're already late,' she said. 'What else is new?'

'Didn't Ozzie call you? I asked him—'

I'd sent him home with a message for my wife when I saw what I had to do. My own call to Trudy had repeatedly been delayed by the blizzard of phone calls with which I had ruined a lot of Saturdays and summoned a crew.

'Yeah, Ozzie called as soon as he got home. So I wouldn't have to worry, he said. Then he bent my ear for fifteen minutes making it sound as crazy and ominous as possible. Somebody got shot?'

'Yes. And the guys who run this hunt,' I turned my back to them and muffled the phone with my hand, 'are very concerned, of course.'

'Why are you still there if it's a hunting accident? Isn't that something for the DNR?'

'It would be if I was sure it is an accident. But some things don't seem to quite add up.' Besides being a cop's wife she's a criminalist at the State crime lab, so I don't hesitate to share details with her. She'll be seeing it all on Monday anyway.

'Well, so, you've got a crew coming?'

'Yup. I can see them unloading now.' The street was filling up with detectives slamming doors, loading up with gear, calling out warnings as they took their first steps into the field.

A big snowstorm had blanketed this area two days earlier. A gusty wind overnight had piled it in little hummocks around the corn stubble, and today's low temperature froze the top layer. Every footstep broke through the rime ice with a crack and sank into inches of soft snow over patches of remnant ice from earlier storms. With miserable footing and a chance of frostbite for hands that needed to be bare for any tasks, there would be no need to urge this crew to work quickly.

'Soon as the People Crimes crew gets over here and I brief
Ray,' I told my mate, 'I'm out of here.'

'Good,' she said. 'How will you get home, though?'

'Dispatch located a social worker who has to visit a case in
Faribault,' I said. 'He'll drop me off.'

As she well knows, I have no business at a crime scene. I'm
head of Rutherford's police detectives; my job is to stay in the
station and tell people what to do. Of course, when a case comes
along like this one and gets in my face, I can hardly just walk
away. I was rehearsing that speech for the chief, who promoted
me to this job several years ago and still sometimes has to remind
me to stifle my fondness for field work.

The area around the body was being taped off by the street
patrolmen who'd arrived first. I'd done my best to protect the
crime scene till they got there, standing between the body and
the street and telling everyone who approached, 'Don't come any
closer, don't come any closer', like a recording stuck in an endless
loop.

I broke my own rule once briefly in the first few minutes. To
make sure Arlo's opinion of the downed man's condition was
correct, I crashed through the underbrush and squatted by the
victim, held two fingers behind his ear for a few seconds and
looked in his eyes. He had no pulse at all, and was very cold.
Besides that, he had that stony stillness, and the waxy pallor and
milky eyes of a body that had stopped breathing some time ago.
When I stood up I said, 'Yup,' to Arlo, who was standing nearby
looking as if he'd just passed a stone. 'Now we wait for the
coroner.'

'Come on,' Arlo said. 'You know he's dead.' He wanted me
to bag the victim up, call a meat wagon and get him out of here.
'No offense,' he said, 'but this is not good for business.'

'None taken,' I said, punching buttons on my phone, 'but rules
are rules.' He muttered something crude. I said, 'Pokey lives on
this side of town; he won't be long.'

I continued making phone calls while Arlo hopped around me
like a frustrated sparrow. You know how they never seem to be
content with the branch they're on? Arlo was jittering like that,
hopping from one foot to the other and emitting chirps of distress.
This was going to wreck his reputation, he said. His hunters sure

as hell didn't shoot this guy, he knew for a fact, so now why did
he have to get the penalty for carelessness he would never
commit? He actually asked me, 'Why is it cops aren't ever around
when you need them, and then they come down on the innocent
like a ton of bricks?'

I stopped dialing for a minute and said, 'I'm out here freezing
my ass off trying to help you. Now put a sock in it before I find
an infraction to write you up for.'

Working up to a nice argument with Arlo felt good for a few
seconds – I could feel my hands and feet start to warm up. But
there was a lot of work to be done, so I put a lid on my anger
and went back to dialing and talking. Arlo shut up and made do
with pacing and panting.

A few minutes later a noisy crew began unloading at the curb.
I looked across the field and said, 'Hey, here comes the lab team
from BCA. How'd they get here so fast?'

They pulled open the big doors on the back of their van and
swarmed across the field like ants. 'We were just finishing up
on an assault case in Owatonna when Saint Paul got your call,'
Tom Baines said. He's a Minnesota BCA photographer, so he
owns a large assortment of gloves with the ends cut off the
fingers. 'Dispatch decided to save some gas, so you're catching
us on the fly.' Baines is a bow-hunter who loves to talk about
his ability to follow spoor through trackless wilderness. I had a
pretty good idea what he'd think of a hunt like this one and was
hoping he'd keep his opinion to himself while he talked to the
hunt club people.

When Arlo first called me, I thought he was describing a simple
hunting accident, so I wasn't going to call the Bureau of Criminal
Apprehension. But after Arlo said over and over that there was no
way any of his hunters shot into that tree line where the body lay,
I'd decided to get the experts involved. When it comes to fingerprints and photography, St Paul has the latest machines and the
best-trained techies, and their DNA wizards are legendary.

Trudy's one of them. She used to work on these outreach crews
before she went full-time to the DNA lab, so I sympathize with
these lab scientists. They go out in all weather, day and night,
charged with bringing back precise information that may decide
a case later on.

Baines ducked under the tape first, to photograph the body from every angle before anyone else touched it. Holding up the tape for him and helping to pass his gear inside, I got another good look at it, and began to sort out my first impressions.

This man wasn't dressed as a sportsman. He wore green twill work pants, frayed at the cuffs, with long johns underneath, and four-buckle rubber overshoes. His cap was a plaid wool farmer's cap, with ear-flaps turned down and fastened with Velcro under his chin. He had leather gloves with wool liners, stuck in the pockets of his plaid wool jacket, and his bare hands were hard and thick with calluses.

He was lying between two trees, just inside the barbed-wire fence that separated this field from the one next to it. His body was easy enough to see now that I was close to it and knew where it was. Shielded by the underbrush of the fence line, and surrounded by a maze of animal prints and churned-up snow, it had not been visible from where we were shooting. Nobody had seen it, in fact, till the two men from the nearest blind began packing their camper to go home.

'Long, cold morning and we drank a lot of coffee,' the older one said. 'We decided to take a leak before we started the drive.'

'I didn't want to leave my pickup back there in the parking lot – I carry some pretty expensive tools in the lockbox. So Arlo let me drive it over here and park it nosed up to the tree line where I could keep an eye on it.' The younger of the two men, who on first impression looked baby-faced and playful, grew more serious and consequential as he talked. Now he looked a little embarrassed as he said, 'Tell you the truth, once we started shooting at birds I forgot all about my truck.

'But when we started loading up I opened the doors on both sides and they shielded us kind of like a little outdoor privy. I was just standing there in front of the Dodge, shaking off my willy, when I looked into the trees and that plaid cap suddenly kind of . . . *stood out*.' He shuddered. 'Boy, talk about your Kodak moments. I think my heart stopped. I stood and stared at that thing till I damn near froze my dick.' He nodded toward his partner. 'I said, "Whoa, Herman, is that what I think it is?"'

I asked them, 'You never saw anybody over here in the trees?'

'Never had any reason to look,' the older man said. 'Arlo made our allowable shooting range very clear before we started and there were plenty of birds there, coming up from the river, so we were busy watching for the next likely target. We never looked back here in the trees till it was time to load up.'

'It's odd,' I said. 'A farmer from the neighborhood would surely know about the bird hunting going on here – only an idiot would wander onto the range and get shot.'

'He did not get shot by anybody here, I'm telling you,' Arlo said. 'Our rules are crystal clear about lines of fire – these men just told you – absolutely no shooting except to the south and west, never back into the trees, and believe me, we check constantly.' He was very bristly and defensive, of course, feeling that his business was at stake.

Any one of the guns that had been used here this morning could have made the shot that had torn open the front of the dead man's coat – we all knew that. I had only taken one glance at the wound in his chest, which offhand looked to me like a close-range shot. But how could it be, if he was killed by one of the bird hunters? The nearest blind was fifty yards away at least.

Well, Pokey and the rest of the forensics team would give us, eventually, an educated guess about how far away the shooter had been. I was already dreading the inevitable conclusions at the end of this puzzle. The victim would have needed the arms of a gorilla to administer this shot himself – no way did this present as a suicide.

But here he was, in the field with the Hiawatha Valley hunt. So . . . *if one of Arlo's hunters didn't shoot him, who did?*

Ordinarily by the time a case reached this level of complexity I'd have called Chief McCafferty and shared some concerns. Beginning with: *This is starting to look like a complicated case where somebody might soon be talking about suing somebody, and a lot is going to depend on the physical evidence.*

I know it's Saturday afternoon, and the overtime budget is in ruins. But doesn't the need for speed and accuracy trump the need to save dollars?

However, the chief was skiing in Montana with his wife and

his three youngest children. It was a rare outing for them and I wanted to leave them alone to enjoy it. So I decided to use the assets I had at hand and figure out how to pay for them later.

'OK, let's roll the body so I can get some pictures of the back,' Baines said. 'I got all the other shots I need.'

'Better wait till Pokey's had his first look,' I said.

'Oh, crap,' Baines said, blowing on his hands. 'I stand around here much longer, he's going to have to decide if me or the victims' further along in rigor mortis.'

'Do some push-ups,' I said. 'He'll be here soon.'

And here he came now, slip-sliding across the wretched footing with his shoulder bag slapping against his hip, looking agile and interested.

Time never seems to lay a glove on Pokey. When I first met him, I was twenty pounds lighter, with no bags under my eyes. That was before Trudy, and long before Ben – for me, a different life. But Pokey hardly seems to have changed at all since then.

His name is Adrian Pokornoskovic, but nobody in the Rutherford Police Station can pronounce that, so we all call him Pokey. He comes from that embattled East European borderland where the citizens rarely knew, for most of the twentieth century, what to call their country. 'Germany, Russia, Ukraine, Poland . . .' he told me once. 'Whoever's lying to us today, we used to say.'

Now he manages his dermatology practice full-time and doubles when necessary as Hampsted County coroner. It works out all right given Rutherford's low crime rate – mostly he signs death certificates for old people in rest homes. He does have the occasional sudden-death-or-suicide puzzle to figure out, but this homicide, if it proves to be one, would be only his third this year – and the other two occurred in one case, back in June.

'What's this?' he said, looking around the field strewn with blood and feathers. 'Somebody get bored shooting ducks?' His youth on the run across Europe gave him that little cynical tic – working for the county hasn't dented his deeply entrenched suspicion of most of society's rules, and all of its rulemakers.

Recently I asked him, 'Pokey, haven't you noticed by now that you're *part of* the establishment?'

He'd looked embarrassed and kind of pawed at his sparse hair for a few enjoyable heartbeats before he said, 'Some science for police, is mostly for fun . . .' When I smiled at him, he said defiantly, 'Listen, Jake, you got to question everything that comes down from the top.'

'I do,' I said, 'including your attitude.'

'OK,' he said, 'smart ass,' and we'd finished eating lunch together in unruffled amiability. Pokey is angry, permanently and always, at The System, which he has reason to believe is rigged. To those nearest him, like me and other law enforcement types he encounters, and the girls in his office and his patients and especially his wife, Pokey is the soul of kindness and affability, never out of patience.

He appeared in particularly good spirits as he stood looking at the body and the ground surrounding it while the photographer took a few more shots. Then he ducked under the tape, knelt by the dead man and opened his bag. For Pokey, death is a beginning, not an ending, and he enjoys the journey from there to his own conclusions. He used a probe to take the temperature of the liver, shone a light in the eyes, looked at the hard, dirty fingertips and broken nails.

Ray Bailey, my Chief of People Crimes, had followed Pokey across the field and stood beside me now, ready to help if he was needed. I brought him up to date with details of the discovery. The gunshot wound in the chest he could see for himself. I told him the victim was not registered to shoot here and nobody knew who he was or where he belonged. He nodded, made a couple of notes in his tiny handwriting and said, 'I found all my crew. They'll be right along.' Ray's not a chatterer.

Pokey had unbuttoned the victims' jacket and shirt to look at the wound. It was about the size of a golf ball, and surrounded by a pattern of tiny bloody holes made by shot that had scattered out of the cartridge. He laid the clothes back down, stood up and looked down at the ground around the body.

'Lotta boot prints like this around him when you found him? Or just a few?' The scene was hopelessly compromised, churned by many feet.

The two hunters looked at each other, embarrassed. The younger one said, 'We never really looked.' Their faces said they didn't want to look at it now. Or even talk about it. They had come out to kill a few geese and wanted no part of dead humans.

'Pokey,' I said, 'most of these tracks aren't new – they were here when I first looked at the body.'

'Huh,' he said. 'Wonder why so many? There's just a pasture over there, right?'

'And a two-track, I think – a farm lane. I haven't had time to get over there yet.'

'Mmm. Lotta tracks,' Pokey said, sounding dissatisfied.

'Can we leave now?' the two hunters kept asking. 'We really need to get home.' To which Ray or I, whichever one they asked, invariably said something like, 'Just hang on here a little longer, please, till we sort a few things out.'

BCA guys were itching to take their samples and go, too; they were just waiting for the last of the pictures. So everybody looked happy when Pokey said, 'Guess you could roll him now,' pointing away from himself, toward the fence.

Ray and I stepped inside the tape. I took the head; Ray took the feet. The victim felt rigid and heavy as a log. When we rolled him onto his side the indentation from his big thick body stayed in the snow. A little blood and tissue clung in clumps in the snow where he had lain – much less than I'd expected to see.

There should have been quarts of blood, I thought, looking at the hole in his back – about twice the size of the one in front – and at the snow beneath him. And fragments of bone and tissue – where had it all gone?

Pokey looked down at the almost-clean hollow under the victim, twitched his nose like a rabbit, and made a tiny noise like, 'Hmmmp.'

A piece of bloody tissue, bright orange from the cold, fell off the body into the hollow. Shreds of his jacket and shirt hung off his back, soaked with blood and frozen stiff. A couple of nuggets of birdshot gleamed in the packed snow and, as I watched, another tiny metal fragment fell out of the jagged cavity.

'Can you two hold him right there while I get those?' Pokey asked us. He pulled a baggie out of a box and leaned in with tweezers, grunting with concentration as he plucked small pellets carefully out of the snow. The job was so nearly impossible, we all held our breath while his pincers grabbed the tiny pieces of slippery metal. When he had all three fragments we let out a collective sigh.

'Now me,' Baines said, and quickly got his pictures. He backed into a wild raspberry bush on his way out of the taped area, and treated us all to a master course in swearing as he freed his corduroys. As soon as he finished his tantrum he ran to join his teammates in the BCA van and they roared away.

Ray's crew had come across the field and stood outside the tape, waiting for marching orders. Ray nodded at them and went back to staring at the body we were holding. As Pokey pulled the torn garments aside to inspect the wound, Ray said, pointing at a back pocket, 'That looks like the outline of a wallet.'

'You want it? Here,' Pokey fished it out and handed it up.

'Funny,' I said. 'Never knew a farmer to carry his wallet in the field.'

'Me neither,' Ray said. 'Too easy to lose.' He was already rummaging through it, reading off cards. 'Owen Kester.' He looked around. 'Anybody know him?'

'Kester,' Arlo said. 'That's funny. Hey, I bet that's why he looks familiar. The guy I rent this field from is named Kester. He's a lawyer in town, though. But maybe they're related?'

'Let's find out,' Ray said. He gave the address to Rosie Doyle and said, 'Put that in your GPS and tell me how far away it is.' I expected her to trot back to her car but she just pulled out her smart phone and started cranking in numbers. Meantime, Ray handed Clint Maddox his iPad and asked him to see how many Kesters he could find on Google. Then he took Amy Nguyen a little aside and said 'Winnie . . .' which is what we all call her ever since the chief, after listening to her say 'Nguyen,' several times, introduced her to us all as 'Win'. It was some time before he figured out whether that was her first or last name, and while he was pondering we all started calling her Winnie.

'Winnie,' Ray said now, 'I want you to take these hunters for a little walk, get them to show you their pissing area—'

'Ah, boss, come on,' Winnie said, wincing. She has the courage of a lion running a marathon or, as she recently did, facing down a loaded gun in a raging river. But thanks to a strict upbringing by her super-tough grandmother, the boat lady who got the family here from Vietnam, she is much more demure than the average street cop.

'No, listen, you're perfect for this job, it'll throw 'em off their game a little,' Ray said. 'I want you to talk to them very sweet and polite till they show you their piss-holes in the snow. Then get all touchy-feely with your questions – insist they tell you exactly what they felt when they first saw it. Did they realize right away that they were looking at a dead man? If they say no, ask them what they thought was wrong? And why did they think that? Stuff like that.'

Winnie frowned. ' "Stuff like that" – what does that mean?'

'Feelings. Men don't like to talk about their feelings and the younger one especially wants to go home and bury this incident in several straight shots. See how he keeps blinking? He's afraid he's going to puke. I'm counting on you to get these guys to open up and talk about finding that body. First impressions are important! Keep your recorder on!'

Winnie went away looking as if he'd told her to eat a frog – but she went. She'd overcome long odds to get on the force; hardly anybody thought she had it in her to be a cop. But she spent five years as a by-the-book, spare-no-effort cop. Then she had to work extra hard to get assigned to investigations – petite and pretty, she fits nobody's image of the steely-eyed police detective. But she passed all the tests with scores so high they made her take some of them over (she scored even higher the second time). To keep this job she's worked so hard for, she'll follow orders, even the ones that make her grimace with distaste.

I had not observed Ray at work in the field for some time, and was impressed by his progress as a team leader. As a detective, he always had good focus and bulldog tenacity on a case, but when I was head of People Crimes and he was one of my detectives, he was a silent loner whose hardest task was telling me what he knew. The chief was dubious when I picked him to head the People Crimes section. He said, 'People aren't exactly his favorite thing, are they?'

'He's very smart and he never quits till he's found all there is to find,' I said. 'I think I can teach him to talk.'

Ray believed me when I told him communication was the key to success from here on. He's still quieter than the average sleuth, and gloomier-looking because he's a Bailey and Baileys have gloom in their DNA. But he's learned to tell his crew what he wants in simple sentences. And he never has any agenda – only a passion for facts you can take to the bank. So he runs a pretty happy ship. He needs one more investigator than he's got, and he knows I'll get one for him as soon as the chief can winkle out the funds from the tragedians on the city council.

'And Andy,' Ray said when Winnie was gone, 'why don't you mosey around in this tree line, and behind it in the field on the other side there, and see what you can find?'

'Like what?'

'Like the insides of a dead man or maybe a fresh casing for birdshot. Or a tire track or boot print good enough to make a casting, or any other sign of how this man got here. If you find any of those things give me a call and I'll send somebody to help you tape it off. You got gloves?'

'Sure,' Andy said, and trudged away. Andy Pittman, a tough and resourceful street cop for most of his twenty-seven years on the force, does not require much supervision.

'Here, I found him,' Rosie said, coming back with a map with the victims' house address on it. 'Less than three miles from here. Looks like it's in that section the city annexed a couple of years ago,' she said. 'The streets over there are mostly mapped but not built yet. They've even put some street signs out there, so the volunteer fire crews can find them if they need to. How much you bet me, though – it's going to be on a gravel road, used to be a county road and now it's just inside the city limits?'

'Why don't you go and find it,' Ray said, 'and have a talk with –' he turned to Clint – 'is there a Mrs Owen Kester?'

'Uh . . .' Clint whizzed back through a row of names, 'yes. Doris Kester, nee Kleinschmidt.'

'Probably one of those horsey Kleinschmidts that win all the trail rider classes at the fair,' he told Rosie. 'Go find her. Come back and tell me if we got the right Mrs Kester, and where she thinks her husband might be.'

'Do I have to tell her we think her husband's been shot?' She shook her head while she asked the question, willing him to say no. Red curls seized the opportunity to spring out of her cap and wave around.

'Um . . . should be two people for that.' He turned to Clint. 'You go with her.'

'Why me? I'm no good at that: I always cry if they do. Send Winnie.'

'She's busy with the pissers. You go – in fact, you drive so Rosie can take pictures on that smart phone. Here, give her my iPad – how about this, we're unwired for success! Take notes on that, Rosie. Wait, you got a picture of the victim?'

'Yes, Baines sent me a good one to my iPhone,' Rosie said.

'Good! Bring me back descriptions of everybody you find, and pictures, plenty of pictures. Fast as you can, please! We don't have much time left here; everything's starting to freeze!' He meant the body, which was, I could attest, stiff as a board.

Everybody had a job now except me, which was OK because my ride was suddenly double parked at the curb, calling on my cell phone to say, 'I'm late already, come right now!'

I said, 'Ray, give me a call later when you have time, will you?' and trotted toward the car that had a state seal on the door. After my first near-header, I slowed to a walk, schedules be damned. The colder the day got, the more that field resembled a skating rink covered in snowdrifts.

In the car, I called Trudy to say, 'Ride's here, I'm on my way.'

'Good. Benny's just waking up, so I'll feed him right away. And the beans are ready any time. Shall I start the grill?'

'I'll do it when I get there. Going to take me a while to thaw out anyway.'

'Thaw out, that's code for toddies, isn't it?'

'And canoodling, if you can put up with cold hands and a few feathers.'

'Ah, you're such a bad old bird.' Her giggle started warming me up, inappropriately, right there on the cold plastic seat covers belonging to an HHS guy with a thick casebook and an expression that said he ate small children for lunch. To be fair, I was raised in foster homes as a ward of this state, so all social workers look pretty ominous to me.

I felt like asking him if he owned any shotguns. But it was

his ride so I clammed up and began counting overtime hours. There was a woefully small balance left in the Rutherford PD emergency account. I used the rest of the trip to prepare a plea for help from the Mayor's slush fund, '. . . the third murder in six months, Your Honor . . .' If that didn't work, Rutherford investigators might be the next ones to discover that crime doesn't pay.

THREE

By the time Ray Bailey got around to calling me, I didn't much want to talk to him any more. I had enjoyed two rum punches, a large plate of brats and beans washed down with a couple of beers, and an hour of playing 'Whose ball is this?' with Ben. My son and I were both about ready for bed.

At nearly eight months, Ben was a round and happy babbler, guzzler, and waver of undifferentiated hellos and goodbyes. While this limited agenda had never seemed interesting when I observed it in other people's children, in Ben's chubby hands I found it intellectually complex and amusing. Besides the endless ball game we'd been playing all week, this month we were into 'This Little Piggy' big-time. Every night, watching Ben discover his hands and feet and learn to follow the ball with his eyes, I turned into a certifiable idiot who thought crawling on the floor making excited noises over ten pink toes and a small rubber ball was the best possible use of an evening.

I suppose I should admit that watching him learn new tricks wasn't all I enjoyed about playing with Ben. There was also the fact that at first sight of me, reliably, morning and evening, he wiggled ecstatically, crowed like a happy chicken, and grinned as if I'd brought him the best present he could possibly imagine just by showing up. I've never been anybody's hero before, and it's a little embarrassing how much I like it. In fact, when Ben looks at me that way I feel just about ready to strap on the cape and leap tall buildings.

Trudy handed the phone down to me and picked up the baby, saying, 'Ray sounds as if he needs to be burped. Maybe you better take this in the other room.' We were in the big open kitchen/family room where we spend most of our time. The dining room is for rare family gatherings like the Thanksgiving feast coming up, and the so-called living room keeps getting more and more like a home office. I turned on a light and took Ray's call in there.

'Well, the first thing to tell you,' he said, 'is that Andy found the victims' transportation. Five-year-old pickup parked on the two-track on the other side of this grove of trees. Keys in the ignition.'

'Registration?'

'In the glove box. Says the owner is Owen Kester; all the same information as his license.'

'Can you tell if he drove himself or—'

'I didn't see anything obvious, like blood. BCA crews were gone, so we just impounded the vehicle and had it wrapped and towed to the police lot. BCA's arranging the tow to Saint Paul.'

'OK. We should get good information from that baby.'

'Yeah. We were doing all right till about an hour after we found the pickup.' He sounded morose. 'But just when Rosie and Clint got back from the Kesters' farm wanting to tell me all about it, I got a phone call from the brother.' A windy sigh. 'Ethan, his name is.'

'Ethan's the attorney that Arlo mentioned?'

'Is he ever. Of the firm of Kester and Robbins, as he reminded me several times.'

'Lawyer Kester is somewhat assertive?'

'You might say that. Or you might just say he's a pompous asshole with a paranoid streak. Unfortunately I think he may have almost as much clout as he's threatening me with.'

'Let's make him prove it before we get worried. What does he say he can do to you?'

Cops take endless abuse all day long because they have to deal with people who are stressed out of their minds. Of course, I was much more understanding about this when it was the Kester brother attacking Ray than I had been when Arlo was shouting insults at me. Anyway, I knew that when Ray quit ranting about this rank injustice, we would decide together how to handle the uppity Kester. We're the police, after all. Unless somebody can prove malfeasance, we win most of our arguments.

'He says he'll get me fired for gross incompetence. How dare I send my officers out there scaring the dickens – that's what he said, "scaring the dickens" – out of his sister-in-law, telling her that her husband's been shot? I should have checked with him first. Like everybody in Hampsted County has to check in with him for permission to die, or even talk about dying.'

'That does sound a little overbearing.' I was listening with one ear while I Googled Kester & Robbins, reading off the screen that the firm specializes in corporate start-ups, tax law, and mergers. I read some of it to Ray. 'Looks like they are kind of big Cahunas for little old Rutherford. The Kester on the masthead must be his uncle. Ethan was just a couple of years ahead of me in high school. He'd still be a junior partner, I think.'

'Uh-huh,' Ray said. 'But a junior partner with the right family name, in a firm that's making a bundle off these green science guys that are all over us this year like ticks on a hound.'

When Ray and I were growing up in Southeast Minnesota, Rutherford was a quiet market town where prices for hog bellies and feeder calves were featured on the noon news. There's still plenty of farming going on in Hampsted County, but every year Rutherford – the town that we thought was stuck in its comfortable little rut forever – changes in front of our eyes. It's getting more like the Twin Cities and Chicago, becoming part of one vast urban sprawl in which biotech and new energy sources are beginning to upstage agriculture.

Maybe it's all good, but so many quick changes make people uneasy. Around Rutherford lately, a lot of conversations end with somebody saying, 'Where's it all going to end?'

'So what did you say to pushy Ethan?'

'I said, "You're only ten minutes away. If you think we've made a mistake, why don't you come over here and check it out?" I gave him the address and he made it in eight minutes.'

'And?'

'He was in a Cadillac El Dorado and the tires were smoking. I led him to the body; he made a couple of choking sounds, and went into the woods and began beating up on an oak tree. Oddest reaction I've ever seen – punching and kicking this big strong tree. Clint helped him bandage his hands afterwards – he wouldn't let me touch him.'

Ray sounded even gloomier over the next part of his story. 'When he settled down he started talking lawsuits again – saying this is no way to notify the family, lucky you didn't give that poor woman a heart attack. Says he's going to take this right to the top, it won't end here . . . and so on.'

'Well, you know, people look for somebody to blame.'

'Uh-huh. But Ethan seems to be a bottomless pit of anger and he wants to pull the whole police force in there with him.'

'That's very well stated, actually, Ray. And since it is a bottomless pit, let's leave Ethan to wallow in it while we get on with our jobs. Did Pokey say when he'll probably do the autopsy?'

'Well, for a change he didn't say dawn tomorrow. In fact, he said, "Hell, the body was frozen stiff and the crime scene hopelessly compromised by the time I got here, so no hurry. Wait till I see how many appointments I've got to move around and I'll let you know".'

'OK, Ray. Who's got the weekend duty this week?'

'Um . . . it's one of Kevin's guys . . . Josh Felder.'

'Is he the kind of nerdy one I've heard him talk about?'

'Yeah. The introvert with the great searching techniques.'

'Good. We don't have a whole lot for him to do, do we? Nobody he has to take to court?'

'I don't. I don't know what Kevin's got. Why?'

'Let's get him to look up everything he can find on the Kester family and related branches, huh? What they own, what they owe, any dirt he can dig up?'

'OK, good idea, yeah.'

'And then let's get all your People Crimes people together first thing Monday morning. Get LeeAnn to sit in and take notes, and we'll map out strategy. See where we stand, huh?'

'I guess.' He didn't disagree. He just said those two half-hearted words, and then didn't say goodbye.

'What?' I knew it was dumb to ask – but I can't stand phone calls that end on a dissatisfied note. And he knows that. Damn! I took a big tired breath and said, 'Say what you want in plain English right now or forget it, because I froze all day in that field and I just did "This Little Piggy" ten times with Ben, so I'm almost out of juice.'

'Well, if you're too tired I guess it can wait—'

'Ray, goddammit – state your problem!'

'OK, I know you said we don't have any money for overtime, but Rosie and Clint are worried about a locked outbuilding,

between the horse barn and the house on the Kesters' farm, that
they couldn't get into. When they asked Mrs Kester about it, she
said that's the smokehouse and the walk-in cooler. They use it
for all kinds of meat preparation, I guess. She says her husband
always kept it locked and she didn't know where he kept the
key.'

'That sounds like bullshit.'

'I know. But she was, you know, crying . . . so they let it go
and concentrated on getting somebody to come and stay with
her.' He stopped talking and breathed into the phone.

I can't stand agitated breathing either. I said, 'OK, what else?'

'Well, soon as they got back and heard Andy say he'd found
the pickup, but speculating with me about no signs of innards in
the snow there, they started saying we should get a warrant to
search that locked building. Because if we wait till Monday
whatever's in there could be gone.' He paused. 'If, you know,
there's anything in there that has anything to do with the body
in the field.'

*Like all the blood and guts that should have been where we
found the body. Damn!*

'I see what you mean but now it's Saturday night, and . . .
What are you thinking? Are Rosie and Clint still there with you?'

'We're all at the station, yeah. They didn't want to go home
till they heard what you had to say about it – they thought maybe
they should get back out there now and . . . look at that locked
building.'

'Just the two of them? Or are you thinking of mobilizing the
National Guard over this?'

'You think it's a bad idea.'

'I didn't say that, come on . . . You think they're onto something, huh?'

'I think they were the ones on the scene and they didn't get
such a strong feeling for no reason at all. I thought maybe,' he
cleared his throat, 'I might go back out there with them, carry
the warrant and take a little of the heat off.'

So there it was. Ray was just as tired as I was. I'd called him
away from his quite new bride on his day off but he was willing
to put his body where his mouth was, to back up his troops. I
looked at the rock and then at the hard place. After about thirty

seconds I told him, 'Keep your cell turned on. Saturday night, this might take a while.'

I'd had my neck stuck out all day, trying to handle this case without disrupting the chief's ski vacation, but now I felt it was time for a pivot. If Ethan Kester was mad now, wait till he heard we were demanding access in the middle of the night to a locked building on his family's farm. We were all going to need some cover then, of the kind only Frank McCafferty could provide.

He'd left me a number to call if I had to. He knew I was well aware how long it had been since they'd had a trip.

Sheila answered the phone. It was an hour earlier in the mountain chalet, so at least I wasn't waking anybody. In fact, to judge by the jolly noises nearby, the McCaffertys must have found a dozen or so friends to join them in after-ski revelry. The chief said he'd call me back on his cell so he could step outside to talk. I heard Sheila say, 'Here, take this blanket', and got a vision of his large bulk hunched in the cold starry silence of his cabin's front step, wrapped in some woolly comforter.

'We got a dead man just at the edge of the goose-hunting field on the north edge of town,' I said, and told him quickly, in short words, what we'd found and hadn't found, about the dead man's pickup, the weeping wife and the angry brother.

'OK,' he said before long. 'You want my approval on what you've done so far? No problem, I don't see what else you could have done. But now there's something else?'

I told him about the two conscientious detectives, the locked cooler and the body that seemed to be missing some innards.

He sighed. 'You're pretty sure it's homicide?'

'There wasn't enough blood under the body. It looks as if he must have been moved at least once. But the clean pickup with the keys in the ignition makes you think maybe he drove himself here. So there's a lot to figure out.'

'OK.' He sighed again and then said decisively, 'Screw the overtime, we'll find the money somewhere. The Kester family has lived on that farm for three generations that I know of – maybe more. Always been solid farmers, till Henry, the father of this victim, married into a family of lawyers. And now one of the sons is a lawyer, too, huh? Quite a powerful bunch. Let's be sure we leave no stone unturned, Jake. If we have to defend ourselves we want to be sure we did everything by the book. Tell those two detectives – who is it, by the way?'

'Rosie and Clint.'

'Tell them I said, "Good job". Hurry up now and try to find a judge who's not having too much weekend fun. Call me tomorrow at noon – sooner if you need to.'

Incredibly – it felt like the middle of the night to me – Judge Cartwright and her husband were just going out to dinner. She said I'd caught her at her front door with a key in her hand, but she kindly put the key down and listened to my reasons for wanting a search warrant. Halfway through my list she said, 'Stop, that's enough. What an interesting weekend you're having, Jake.'

I phoned her approval code to Ray, told him to pass on the chief's 'Good job' message to Rosie and Clint, and asked him to call me when they finished the search, regardless of the hour.

Part of me wished I'd been sleeping for an hour. But I was thirsty and the last-minute change in plans had made me jumpy, so I talked Trudy into sharing a beer at the kitchen table and ended up telling her about this surprise return to the farm.

'We might be close to wrapping up a murder case in one day,' I said. 'Wouldn't that make a good story?'

She gave me the kindly smile she saves for times when I say something dumb. That started me thinking about all the things that could go wrong for three detectives in the dark, on a farm where the dead owner's killer hadn't been caught yet. After that I wasn't sleepy any more.

'Let's have another beer,' I said, but Trudy reminded me she'd been baking holiday treats and care-taking our son since dawn.

'Gotta go to bed while I can still climb stairs,' she said, and went.

I read the evening paper and then a science journal I like. I fell asleep over some hot news about the God particle, and bumped my head on the reading light when the phone rang.

Ray sounded embarrassed. 'The walk-in cooler is full of sides of beef and pork, like Mrs Kester said it would be. The other half of the building is an old smokehouse, not used much anymore, she said, but it's still got all the tools and tables so they can fire up again if they decide to do their own hams.'

He gave a tired little chuckle. 'One reason Owen kept it locked is that he had a little weed growing under a couple of lights in a cupboard at one end. The night wasn't entirely wasted, Jake – at least when we found the pot Ethan Kester shut up about suing the department for a few minutes.'

'But it doesn't sound as if you found anything that's going to nail a murderer.'

'No. Rosie's really having a snit. She keeps saying, "I had such a strong feeling about that building".'

'I know how she feels. You do investigations for a few years, you start to think you have instincts. But not this time, huh?'

'No. It's funny, though. Usually Rosie's got a pretty good nose for stuff people are trying to hide.'

'Well . . . shit-oh-dear, huh? Do we have a door to pay for, too? Did you have to break it down?'

'Oh,' he snickered. 'No, when we walked in with the warrant Doris suddenly remembered Owen had a cabinet in his machine shop where he kept a lot of keys. We opened it up and there they were, hanging on a hook labeled "walk-in cooler".'

'Funny how that warrant works.'

'Yeah. Rosie said on the way back she thinks Doris knew right where it was the whole time. Probably knew about the cannabis too.'

'Well, sure she did. Hell, they were married – they no doubt shared the toke.'

'Yeah, that's what Clint keeps saying. "A toke in bed with that Doris might get pretty lively, I bet". He thinks we should keep our eye on the widow. Says, "That good-looking Kraut lady didn't just fall offa no turnip truck".'

'I have got to see this woman.'

'Well, I guess we'll both be seeing plenty of her before this is over, and after tonight I'm kind of looking forward to that part of the job. Great pair of knockers and she looks good with no make-up in the middle of the night.'

'I hope I don't have to verify that any time soon.'

'Me too. Can we quit work now? Because I'm already asleep.'

Sunday passed in an entirely different blur of work because, Trudy reminded me, in five days we were committed to hosting dinner for about two-dozen Swedes from Trudy's Hanson clan plus the half-dozen waifs and strays that make up my own extended family. 'I got most of the pastries done yesterday,' she said, 'but about the turkeys, now . . .'

'That's a plural? We're doing more than one?'

'Two if we can find two big ones,' she said. 'Otherwise three. My mother's bringing her usual specialties and cousins will bring all the veggies, I think. I need to pin that down, though. My sister does Waldorf salad and the aunts will furnish desserts and drinks. But I need to rely on you for the stuffing, Jake – we need to figure out the timing for that. And we have to figure out the table set-ups today.'

'You think I have a dressing recipe in my desk, just waiting for times like this?'

'No, but I do,' she said. 'And I'm going to guide your baby steps, poor, pitiful Jakey.'

'OK, then. Maxine wants to bring a pie.'

'Fine. We already have three or four, but the more the merrier, I guess. First thing we do today is go shopping. I make the list and you get to dress the boy.'

I had no idea what to put on the list so I couldn't argue, but she knew she was leaving me the hardest job. Lately dressing Ben Hines in three layers of clothing took roughly the same ergs of energy as running down a herd of baby buffalo and penning them up without ever putting a bruise on a single one. Benny knew almost as many moves as a wild animal his age, and he thought it was fun to watch me sweat. I pinned him between my knees and got the undershirt and hoodie top on, but the rules say you don't get to reverse them to do the bottoms, so that part is trickier.

'I certainly hope and expect,' I said as I strapped him into his car seat, 'that you will get rich and kindly when you grow up, and take devoted care of me in my dotage.' He bounced and drooled and threw a small plush toy on the floor to seal the bargain.

In the grocery store, while Trudy went into intense negotiations with the butcher about our turkeys, Ben and I took the rest of the list and shopped. He loves to ride in the basket, so that part was kind of fun when I remembered to allow for his adjustable arms, which magically extended so he could grab things he had no reason to want but would gladly throw down.

When we'd filled two carts and Trudy declared we had enough, we began a round of visits, to leave one turkey in her mother's refrigerator and drop off several food items she had promised her sister. At each stop the women discussed at length what each would cook, when they would bring it to our house, who else was bringing what and the hours at which all these items would be consumed. Fortunately Bonnie's husband was watching the Vikings fight for a rare win against the Redskins, so I didn't think about food logistics any more until Trudy poked me – twice, actually – and said she was ready to go. The game was tied six all and I hated to leave the excitement, even though I knew I had it on Tivo at home and could see it all again later.

I did, too, after we put a lot of food away, unwrapped Ben from his several layers, dressed him all over again for sleep, and ate a stew. Then we played musical sawhorses till we figured out how to make a second holiday table. We had big paper tablecloths with, surprise, painted turkeys on them, to disguise the fact that half the guests would be eating off the Sullivan brothers' workbenches. We had candleholders shaped like . . . wait for it . . . pumpkins!

When Trudy declared we had decked the halls enough, she took a magazine to bed and I finally got a look at my recorded ball game. It was a real sizzler of a contest, and I watched it with fascination until I fell asleep just before half-time. So I never did see that heartbreaking loss. I read about it the next morning, quickly, before Trudy reminded me, twice, that it was time to put the sports page down and triple-wrap Ben Hines again for the trip to town.

I love being a husband and father, but I would be the last to deny, if anybody ever asks me, that family life sometimes intrudes on time formerly devoted to all-out support for the home team.

FOUR

We didn't have a whole lot to work with, Monday morning. All the physical evidence from the shooting was in the hands of lab people, who as usual would say nothing till they finished doing what lab people do.

Josh Felder sat in on the first half hour of our meeting, to detail the research he had done for us over the weekend. He looked about fourteen, with round wire-rims and freckles – the only detective I'd ever seen who looked less like a cop than Winnie. He had brought us exactly what we asked for, though: the complete history of the Kester family in Hampsted County since the mid-1850s. Hardworking farmers with no unexpected adventures, they had prospered in Minnesota for four generations, never moving from their original homestead but adding some acres in each generation. When I saw my detectives sliding toward narcolepsy after thirty minutes of their history, I thanked Josh and declared a fresh-coffee break to revive us enough to read our own notes.

Clint declared that the search of the Kesters' farm on Saturday night had yielded two shotguns and a deer rifle, all in a locked cabinet in the house. Doris had produced the key to the cabinet with no fuss, and the weapons were in our own forensics lab in Rutherford.

'She even volunteered that there was one shotgun missing,' Clint said. 'Gave me the numbers on it and told us to ask Ethan if he has it.' He wiggled his ears and crossed his eyes. 'I am *so* looking forward to *that*.'

Late Sunday afternoon, Pokey had called Ray to say he'd put a hold on a lab for Monday morning. So Ray was at County Medical, watching the autopsy. The rest of us were sitting around his meeting table shuffling the meager notes we'd managed to scribble with cold hands on Saturday. But detectives live and breathe to process information, so with nothing much to read, the People Crimes crew were soon talking about first impressions.

'That's a helluva farm,' Clint said. 'You realize they had almost six hundred acres planted in corn this year? They're getting rich off ethanol and putting it right back into more land, plus blooded horses and a prize dairy herd in a neighboring farm. Smart, very smart. The ethanol craze is bound to end one of these days, but they'll still have all those beautiful animals and hundreds of paid-up acres of the most productive farmland in the country.'

'Which is inside the new city limits, you said,' Winnie said, looking at Rosie. 'How's that going to work?'

'Oh, the developers are going to want it enough to offer top dollar for it eventually, and when the offers go from high to obscene the farmers will sell,' Rosie said. 'But that's a long way down the road in the current financial climate.'

'Yeah,' Clint said, 'plenty of time to get rich off milk and corn first.'

'Isn't it fun to see Minnesota farmers in the winner's circle for a change?' Rosie said. 'But I have to tell you, I have seldom been more confused than during my first few minutes with the wife.'

'Oh?' I watched her flip pages around. 'What was confusing?'

'Well . . . she was baking bread when I got there,' Rosie said. 'And crying.'

'Crying? You mean bawling out loud?'

'No, weeping silently.' She tapped her notes with a pencil, thinking how to say it. 'Kind of eerie, actually – a tall, good-looking woman in a big white apron, with dough and flour spread out all over this butcher block table. She's kneading the daylights out of the loaf she's making and watering it with her tears.'

'So she already knew about the . . .'

'Well, see, that's what I thought. So I said, "Oh, so you already know?" And she said, "Well, of course I know, I've been out on the road with them since four o'clock this morning".

'I said, "What? Out on the road where?" And she said, "Where they got hit, County Road 230, by the back pasture gate". I just kind of stared at her, very confused, till she said, "Aren't you here to ask about the accident?"

'I said that's what we're trying to figure out, if it was an accident, and she said, "Of course it was an accident; nobody

runs over horses with a truck on purpose". So then of course I
had to say I didn't know anything about horses getting run over
by a truck and she said, "If you don't know about the horses
why are you here?"

'I felt like the whole investigation was sliding out of control
about then so I said, "Ma'am, do you know where your husband
is right now?" and she drew herself up like this . . .' Rosie did
the best a short Irish redhead can do to imitate a statuesque
German blonde, adding, in case we didn't get it, 'Kind of like a
Valkyrie, but with flour on her nose . . .'

'OK, Rosie,' I said, 'well-built blonde does power farm
wife – I think we all got that part.'

'I'm only trying to convey to you,' Rosie said, retreating behind
her stoic street cop's face – it means she'd like to throw a brick
at your head but is waiting for a better time – 'this woman is
not your average country hausfrau. And she doesn't seem to
match the dead man we found.'

'But she answers to Doris Kester? The horse lady?'

'Yes. And there's a barn full of elegant horseflesh at the
bottom of the yard, which I have no doubt she can handle with
ease. Turned out she was crying because two of their show
horses – "including the best quarter horse I ever owned!" she
said – somehow got out on the road and got hit. Jumped right
in front of a big tanker hauling milk and both of them had to
be put down. That's where her husband was, she said, fixing
the break in the fence.'

'Are you sure this bread-baking scene wasn't staged for your
benefit? It felt real to you?'

'Absolutely. She cut and kneaded six loaves of bread and a
panful of biscuits while she talked to me. Handles dough like
a baker.'

'OK, she's good at everything. What did you say to her?'

'I asked her if the pasture she's talking about borders the field
where the goose hunters were shooting. She said yes, up on the
north end it does. They own that cornfield too, but the hunters
rent it in the Fall. Then I said we'd found a man shot just inside
the goose-hunting field, and we're here to find out if it might be
her husband. She said, "No, no, soon as we heard the horses
were out on the road Owen sent two men out to inspect the fence

line, and they called his cell in just a few minutes and said they'd found the break".

'I said I was surprised they could find it in the dark and she said the break wasn't far from the gate at the bottom end of the pasture, so Owen told them to stay there and watch it so no more horses could get out. He went up to the barn to load the pickup full of fencing gear, to take out to them. "He's down there now, somewhere near the county road",' she said, "wherever they found the break, and he'll stay out there till they get the fence fixed. It must be one helluva break, it's taking forever. I expected him back an hour ago".'

Rosie blew hair up and said ruefully. 'Then I showed her the picture.'

'What did she do?'

'Dropped the knife she'd been using to cut off dough – kind of flung it away, so it clattered across the table and fell on the floor. And started yelling, making a God-awful amount of noise, this big voice coming out of a beautiful face, so surprising – yelling "Omigod!" and things like that and then names, and people came running – from the horse barn, the walk-in cooler and some older building on the other side of the cooler – they have a lot of hands on that farm. Couple of women in rubber aprons trotted in from a workroom that adjoins the kitchen, holding their hands up like this' – she illustrated, hands aloft like a TV surgeon after scrubbing.

'Why?'

'I looked out there later and saw they were making sausage. I guess they were greasy.'

'So, a busy place, what of it?'

'I don't know, I just – I felt like I was interrupting a peaceful flow of *useful work*, you see? Made me feel . . . rude. But after they'd all run around yelling for a while, I got a different feeling – that this was a real calamity for all of them, they were very distressed and –'

We all waited while she sat there, shrugging uneasily, trying think how to describe what she had felt. When I couldn't stand it any longer I said, 'Just say how it made you feel.'

'OK.' She took a deep breath, blew it out, and said quickly, 'I felt like they were very distressed and – alarmed, but at the same time not exactly . . . surprised. I saw a couple of them look at each other like, "You see?" Kind of the way my mother used to look at my father when we were kids and my brothers did something outrageous. She'd give him a look that said, "I told you to deal with this".'

She looked at us guiltily. 'I know that's not fair. Ugly picture of her dead husband, who wouldn't yell?'

'Well, right,' I said. 'But still, you've interviewed witnesses after crimes plenty of times before, so you must have felt that for a reason. Was it kind of a powder keg feeling – did it seem to you they'd been expecting something to go wrong?'

'Yes.' She searched her memory, head cocked a little like a pointer looking into a bush. '*Something* in the air . . . like distant thunder.' Inadvertently she shivered and rubbed her upper arms.

I said, 'How about you, Clint? You get any vibes?'

'Well, not from any of those people. Because on the way over there Rosie and I agreed that it would be best use of our time if Rosie talked to the wife while I kind of moseyed around the yard and outbuildings looking for . . . you know, *whatever.*'

He looked so sheepish when he said it that I remembered how he had tried not to go on this errand.

I gave him my coldest eye and said, 'So you managed to weasel out of the death announcement after all.'

'Well, now . . . OK, call it that if you want to. But it was lucky I was outside when the ruckus started. Because that's when I met Maynard.'

'Who's Maynard?'

'One of the hands . . . not a cowboy, they don't herd those beauties they got in that dairy . . . probably wrap 'em in bubble wrap and haul 'em in padded vans. Maynard's just a journeyman stall-mucker and hay-hauler, I guess, but his major talent is gossip. Maynard's got his ear to the ground – he's curious about everything, especially the boss's wife. And he loves to talk – my kind of a guy,' Clint said, beaming proudly.

'So you got lots of skinny from him?'

'Boy, did I. Including a run-down on the big farming operation and a description of the major family fights.'

'This rich industrious family fights? When do they find time?'

'Morning, noon and night according to Maynard. Ethan and

Owen argue constantly about the best way to run the farm. Ethan's got shares in the corporation, they all do. Including Doris after she practically staged a revolution, said she was working just as hard here as Owen and if she didn't get her own shares she was going to quit and go work in town. Maynard says there's nobody like her with the newborn calves, and the horses are entirely her doing, so they had to give in.'

'So it's all about money?'

'Not exactly. There's a third brother named Matt. He's the maverick who recently returned after years away on the rodeo circuit. That seems to be mostly about jealousy – Ethan didn't want to let him back into the corporation because the folks always treat him like a star, he says, at least the mother does, and he doesn't pull his weight. But Owen says, "He's our brother, he belongs here. I'm the one doing all the hard work so butt out", and Ethan says, "I'm doing the legal work that makes it pay so I've got every right to an opinion".

'He told me something else – maybe this accounts for the feeling Rosie got. He said the farm has had a strange run of bad luck lately: the horses getting out are just the latest in a string of bad things happening.'

'Like what?'

'Um . . . a whole load of milk spoiled before the hauler could pick it up – somehow the power failed on the cooling station where they hold it. Let's see, what else? Oh, yeah, a good horse pulled up lame in the pasture, they never could find out what happened to it. And then in the last rainstorm a tree fell on the house at River Farm, so now they're all fighting over whether to repair it or tear it down and build a new one like Matt wants.'

'So does your gossip see some sinister plot behind all this bad luck?'

'No, but he says the old hands are shaking their heads and saying these things never used to happen when Henry was running the place. Henry's the old man – he's retired now.'

'You and Maynard must have really hit it off.'

'Well, he likes to talk and I like to listen, so it's a match made in heaven. And listen to this – there's a new fight that's getting really hot this year, because the family got an offer from some Canadian company for a piece of land they call the River Farm – the one I've just mentioned – over near Red Wing.'

'Another farm?'

'Mostly hay land, Maynard says – he hauls a lot of hay from there to the dairy farm.'

'OK,' I said. 'What's the issue?'

'The company making the offer is a sand-mining firm. Apparently River Farm has huge deposits of silica sand.'

'Ah. One of those money-versus-ecology fights. Nasty.'

'You lost me about two sentences back,' Andy said. 'What the hell is silica sand?'

'Andy,' Clint said, 'come on, you know what silica sand is.'

'If I did would I ask and give you a chance to sneer at me?'

'It's those perfectly round quartz crystals we have in the Jordan formation,' I said. 'And the, what's that other name? Wonowoc. Big deposits underground. Good for making glass.'

'Only now,' Clint said, 'the big demand is for fracking.'

'Oh, fracking, I heard about that.' Andy scratched and stretched. 'But that's over in the Dakotas, isn't it?'

Andy doesn't follow the news very closely because he thinks most of what's happening in the twenty-first century is utter nonsense. Every time he turns on his TV set, he says, he sees something sillier than the time before. 'One day last year I came across this program called *Dancing With the Stars* – you ever see that? Jesus. There was a guy on there, used to be in the US House of Representatives, now he's on that show dancing the tango. Making a horse's ass of himself – a Republican, can you beat that?'

'Andy,' I said, 'about the fracking?'

'Yeah, OK. They mix that sand with water, right, and pump it into the ground?'

'Along with certain chemicals nobody wants to talk about,' I said. 'It breaks up the rock and lets the gas and oil percolate up where they can pump it.'

'So we can have our own oil wells,' Clint said, 'and tell Iran to take a flying leap.'

'Which is probably a good thing,' Rosie said, 'but the big question is, what's all that slurry we're pumping underground doing to the aquifers?'

'Not to mention how much people in the tourism industry hate those sand mines being dug near the Mississippi,' Clint said. 'Messing up the bluffs – hate it! But Maynard said to me, "Lotta farmers in this part of the country spent their lives struggling to pay the mortgage and taxes. Easy money's hard to resist after years of hard labor".'

'Easy money's hard to resist no matter what you been doing,' Andy said. 'Who's winning?'

'So far, in the Kester family it's a draw. The parents say hold off a while, as a lot of counties have a moratorium on sand mining right now – they want to see how much the bidding goes up when that ends. They figure sooner or later the moratorium can't last because the need for new sources of oil is so great and the profits so high, no government can hold out against exploiting it for long.'

'Maynard told you all this?'

'Yes. I told you, he's a talker; he knows a good story when he hears one.'

'Or makes one up?'

'Most of what he told me has the ring of truth about it, it seemed to me. Ethan wants to sell now because he's afraid Minnesota and Wisconsin have so much sand that pretty soon the price will go down. Doris and Matt both say they want whatever Owen wants, and Owen's been saying, "over my dead body will anybody turn my beautiful River Farm into a sand pit".' Clint cocked one cynical eyebrow. 'Looks like he got his wish.'

'My, my,' I said. 'You do give me interesting items to talk over with Ethan. Anything else happen outside while Rosie was inside doing what she was assigned to do?'

Clint scowled over the cheap shot but answered anyway. 'I don't know where it fits in all this but there is something odd about that boy who ran into the house when the yelling started. The one Maynard says pokes his nose into everyone's business but never talks.'

'Wait, now. Whose boy?'

'I don't know, but he lives there. He talks funny; I couldn't make out what he said. Once it sort of sounded like "Mama" but he looked too big to be saying that.'

'That's Alan,' Rosie said. 'He's her son.'

'What?' Clint stared at her. 'You sure? Who told you that?'

'The sausage ladies. I know – it's hard to believe.'

'Boy, is it ever. A wimpy little weenie who won't look anybody in the eye? He belongs to that tall, beautiful dame?'

I said, 'So he's another member of the corporation?'

'Not exactly,' Rosie said. 'He's Alan Kester, the bread lady's strangely silent boy. The help out there say he's autistic.'

'What's that got to do with the case?' Andy shook his notes impatiently as if they might have crumbs.

'Probably nothing. I'm just reciting facts as they come along, OK? They say – the employees there say – that their orders are to leave Alan alone and let Doris handle him. Which they say they're glad to do because if he gets puzzled or agitated Alan can get pretty hostile.'

'OK,' I said. 'We got a lot on our plates here, so let's not argue. We still haven't settled the main question: was Owen Kester's death accidental or a homicide?'

'I thought we were going to answer that when we went back to look in the cooler Saturday night,' Clint said. He was carefully not meeting Rosie's eye. She was glaring at him like a hungry hawk, waiting for a chance to sink her talons in him if he said one word about her mistaken hunch. 'But since we didn't find anything but a little weed on that excursion . . .'

Rosie pounced. 'You make it sound like I just wanted a little joyride. You think I do that for fun, stumble around strange outbuildings in the frozen dark while family lawyers hurl threats?'

'No.' He faced her squarely with his good-boy-scout-freckled face, sick of dodging her anger. 'I wanted to go back out there as much as you did and it's not my fault we didn't find anything, so why don't you quit trying to make me the bad guy?'

'Yeah, Rosie,' I said, 'I stuck my neck out on that maneuver too, so ease up on the defensiveness, will you? Nobody's blaming you; we're all in this mess together.'

'Anyway,' Clint said, 'maybe when Ray gets back here he'll tell us the autopsy just settled the question.'

'Wouldn't that be fine?' I said. 'Meantime, Ethan's coming in for an interview in a few minutes, and according to Ray he's all primed to rip me a new one.'

'And Doris is scheduled for some time this afternoon,' Rosie

said, 'if she shows. I tried to get a firm time but she says she's
got a hundred jobs to do on the farm now; the whole staff's
waiting for orders and there's nobody but her to keep the place
running so "you guys are just going to have to take a number".'
Rosie held her hands out palms up. 'I'm just telling you what
she said.'

'Rosie, you know we don't stand in line for anybody in a
homicide investigation.'

'I know, Jake, but the woman is understandably somewhat
frantic and I'm trying to give her a little space.'

'Yeah. Well . . . I want you to sit in with me on the Doris
interview, Rosie. Clint, you better be my second on Ethan, since
Ray's not here and you know him better than the rest of us do.
And Winnie, you monitor both conversations outside.'

'OK. I suppose we're looking for inconsistencies, right? But
I'm not sure I know enough yet to spot one.'

'Well . . . evasions, accusations – Ethan seems to be into
blame. Why's he so angry? See if his answers agree with Doris's
– did she seem at all shifty to you, Rosie?'

'Not a bit. Everything right upfront. Confidence up the ying
yang – you'll see.'

'Guess I will. Decide if she strikes you the same way, Winnie.
What other questions does anybody have before I see these two
powerhouses?'

Clint said, 'Maynard says the third brother's quite the ladies'
man. Anybody else hear anything about that?'

'No,' I said. 'I'll ask Ethan about him if I get a word in
edgewise, but let's not get too scattershot with our questions
now – we don't want to lose focus—'

'Oh, shit,' Rosie said, looking at the ceiling light.

'What?'

'What you just said about scattershot – I just thought of something.' She pushed her curls around and they got wilder than
ever. 'But I suppose since I didn't think of it earlier it's too late
now, isn't it?'

'For what?' I said.

The phone on the conference table rang. LeeAnn answered it
and said, 'I'll be right out.' She hung up and turned to me.
'Ethan's waiting at the front desk.'

I stood up and began gathering my few notes together, asking Rosie, 'What is it too late for?'

She said, 'That walk-in cooler? I noticed some odd marks in the meat that was hanging there.'

'What?' I put all my papers in a fresh manila folder and clipped a ballpoint to the front. 'It's a typical home-butchering operation, isn't it? They kill an animal and hang up the sides on hooks?'

'Uh . . . that's how it looked to me,' Clint said.

'So why wouldn't we expect some of the cutting to be less than professional?'

'Well . . . sure . . . although it looks like they have a couple of hands that are pretty good meat-cutters. But I'm talking about little dimply marks in some of the carcasses. Did you see that, Clint?'

'Some small holes – looked like maybe the animal ran up against a barbed wire fence, or . . .'

'Or if you think about it,' Rosie said, 'couldn't they have been scattershot? Overspray made by little pellets like the ones we watched Pokey picking out of the snow?'

I was already turning to go out the door. I had asked LeeAnn to put Ethan in an interview room and I knew he would not take kindly to a long wait. But when I turned back, those two faces, Rosie's and Clint's, were looking at me with identical expressions. Clint was back on Rosie's team, his eyes alight. Hers were too; they looked like a pair of barn owls that have just heard a mouse rustle.

'You're right, by God, now that you say it . . .' Clint said, 'and we might still be able to dig out one or two . . . and if they match . . .'

'Jesus, you two.' I walked back to the table. 'You don't make things easy, you know that?'

Rosie said, 'If I hadn't been so tired Saturday night . . .'

'All right,' I said. 'Shut up and listen, because we're all out of time. Rosie, call Judge Cartwright, get her to reopen the search warrant. Clint, while she's doing that, get a lab crew together, tell them what you suspect and that you need them to come along with you right away – bring the Luminol or whatever they're using to raise blood spatter now . . .'

'Jake,' Clint said, 'there's going to be blood traces everywhere in that cooler.'

'Let me finish. Take somebody along who's qualified to lift a DNA sample . . . dig down in that drain where you thought the remains of Owen might have been flushed – isn't that what you thought? Because I need you to bring back some good stuff, or we're all going to get certified as lunatics. The three of us,' I said, turning to the rest of my crew, who were watching us wall-eyed, 'Andy and Winnie and I, we'll handle these interviews. Right?'

'Of course,' Winnie said, pleased with this part of the play.

Clint grinned at me. 'Hope you're wearing your big-boy pants today,' he said. 'Ethan's a tough nut.'

'Say one more word,' I said, 'and I'll go to the farm myself and leave you here to do this interview.'

He knew I was bluffing. I'd been making do with hearsay evidence long enough. Today nobody was going to cheat me out of a first-hand look at the Kester family.

FIVE

Even allowing for the absence of deathly pallor, I didn't see much resemblance between the brothers when I met Ethan in the interview room. He looked a lot younger than Owen, for one thing. He was sleeker and showed less wear, and had smooth hands. It was only after he took off his hat and coat that I discovered his hairline, forehead and nose were almost identical to his brother's. With his hat off he looked older, too – nearer Owen's age.

He was better groomed and dressed than his brother but less attractive, with the sallow skin and liverish look of a man who never got much exercise. I could imagine him hunched over his desk, scowling at a computer screen in a dim room. The reality of his brother's death had begun to eat at him, too – almost literally: he looked leaner than his picture on his firm's Facebook page. His mouth was clamped tight and turned down at the corners – plainly, Ethan Kester was not a happy man.

I'd asked LeeAnn to set him up in an interview room because I wanted everything we said on tape. We had not been friends in school: he was a couple of years older and I was far below him in the social scale, a grubby kid working my way through. I was only vaguely aware of him then and I was pretty sure he wouldn't remember me at all. If, as Ray said, he was focused on blaming the police force for his troubles, I wanted his attempts at intimidation documented.

He started talking as soon as I came in, not waiting for any questions. 'I told your Detective Bailey in no uncertain terms,' he said, 'and I want to repeat to you first thing: I'm not satisfied with your department's handling of this investigation.'

'Yes, you've made that very plain. Now I want to be equally frank with you,' I said. 'You can keep on getting whatever satisfaction you're getting out of blaming us for your misfortune, or you can cooperate with the investigation. Then with any luck, we might have some of the answers you need quite soon. It's up to you.'

He blinked, stared in disbelief for a few seconds and began to swell up like an alarmed puffer fish. Nobody, his face said, talked like that to Attorney Kester. 'Now see here,' he said.

'No.' I shook my head. 'You're the one who needs to see. Nobody on the Rutherford police force caused your brother's death. It's a terrible calamity and we all feel sympathy for your sorrow, but blaming us is just a waste of time. You can calm down and answer some questions, and get the help you need, or you can keep on making threats and get yourself nudged a little higher on the list of suspects.'

It was a gamble, and I almost lost. He stood up and put his hat back on, muttering, 'We will see about this,' and reached for his coat. But halfway through shrugging into it, he turned back and said, 'What do you mean, higher on the list of suspects? You're not suggesting I killed my own brother, are you?'

'We always look at family first.' I said it as blandly as if I was discussing the weather, but I knew it was a shocker. It had the added weight of being perfectly true. Go look at the stats some time. We're all in more danger from our nearest and dearest than from anybody else.

'My God,' he said. 'I feel like I've wandered into a nest of lunatics. First you invade my farm in the middle of the night and now you accuse me of being a killer.'

He had a number on speed dial, and he called it now, standing over me with his hat on crooked, one arm in his overcoat and one out. It was answered quietly, halfway through the first ring.

'Uncle Jonas?' His voice trembled a little, which I suppose made him angrier. 'This is Ethan. I'm at the police station, talking to a detective named, um,' he looked at my name tag, 'Jake Hines. Yes. Yes, you got the name right. But listen, he doesn't seem to realize . . . He looks as if he probably didn't grow up around here, so I don't think he understands what we . . . who I am. Will you speak to him?'

I used to get this reaction a lot when I was a rookie cop. I'd be writing up a ticket and the voice of the speedster would say, 'You're not from around here, are you?' My face looks like it was assembled by a committee at the United Nations, and in those days, Minnesota's population was about ninety-eight per cent white, mostly descended from northern Europeans. Most of the people I dealt with thought a guy who looked like me should be trimming their lawn.

I still don't know whose child I am, but I do know I'm a true native son. I was raised by the State of Minnesota since my first day on earth, when I was found in a dumpster at the back of a motel in Red Wing. Minnesota is a somewhat impersonal parent, but it's been fair to me and I try to return the favor.

The voice that came over the phone had the sandpapery quality of seasoned old age. 'Jake Hines, hello,' he said. 'This is Jonas Robbins. I haven't had the pleasure of speaking with you in some time.'

'Jonas?' I said. 'I didn't know . . . I'm afraid I didn't make the connection with your name and . . . Was Owen Kester your nephew?'

'My grand-nephew, actually,' he said. 'Anna Carrie's boy.' As if I should know who Anna Carrie was. Even distaff relatives of the Kesters seemed to think everybody knew who they were. But I was never aware of this family connection so I hadn't associated his law firm with the angry brother who confronted me now.

I got acquainted with Jonas when I was a new detective and he was getting ready to defend a bad apple named Updike. It was maybe ten years ago, an assault case – his firm must have been a little less focused on corporate clients then. We had the DNA evidence and two neighbors' testimony that Jonas' client routinely beat up his girlfriend and then talked her out of signing a complaint. This time she'd stood firm and the case was going to trial, because even though every word of her complaint was true, Updike was counting on his buddies to come up with enough damaging slurs on the woman's character to get him off. The chief was determined to put him away, saying, 'He's going to kill her one of these times if we don't stop him.'

Jonas came to us during the discovery phase as he was preparing his defense. 'Show him everything,' the chief said. 'Convince him we got the goods on that numbskull, so we can all save the trouble of going to trial.'

Robbins was wary, sure he was going to get snowed. I was guarded, on the lookout for put-downs. Less favorable conditions for beginning a friendship would be hard to find, but he was an intelligent man and a good listener. As he saw the weight of the evidence we had, his questions became more and more incisive. I began to enjoy the conversation, and realized it was because this man was really interested in what I had to say and didn't give a shit about the color of my skin. It made me wonder if maybe *he* was from out of town.

Minnesota was already transitioning out of heartland all-whiteness then, but there were still many citizens around who found my face – about the shade of good spice cake and with an odd collection of features – puzzling as hell. It was tough enough being a uniformed officer, but when I made detective and began working in street clothes, I soon learned I had to have my shield in plain sight when I knocked on a door.

Talking to Jonas today made me realize that my town has been moving at a blistering pace – culturally speaking – in the last twenty years: it's as diverse as the Twin Cities now, school enrollments nearing twenty per cent non-white, scatterings of Hmong and Somali and Vietnamese, and almost enough Muslims around to start our own Sunni/Shia conflict.

And Jonas Robbins is still the smart, good-natured gent he always was. I'd forgotten how much I liked him, back when I was a newbie investigator and he shook my hand and said, 'His father's an old friend and I wanted to help. But facts are facts, aren't they? You've saved me a lot of time and work. Thank you.'

A couple of days later the chief said, 'Robbins is dropping the Updike case. Good job.' So I knew the lawyer had put in a good word with the chief too. You remember guys like that.

Today I told him, 'Ethan's understandably upset about his brother's death. We're hoping to have more information for him soon.'

'I appreciate your patience,' Jonas said. 'May I speak to him again, please?'

The old man must have told Ethan to cool his jets, because he folded up his phone after a minute and said, 'My uncle said that I'm talking to one of the good guys. He wants me to help you as much as I can.' He looked around him, sniffing, as if he might be inspecting the interview room for vermin. Finally he brought himself to say, 'So please accept my apology.'

'Accepted.' He had eased out of the coat and crookedly-placed hat and dropped them on the floor.

No use letting the moment go to waste, I decided. 'You ready for questions now?'

He blinked once, swallowed and said, 'Sure.'

'Tell me where you were Saturday morning from four a.m. till noon.'

'Dear me,' he said. 'You mean you don't know yet when he died?' Relapsing at once into lawyerly tactics, he put the onus back on the questioner. My hackles went back up.

He was right, though – Pokey hadn't given us an estimated time of death yet. Even when he did it would be just that, an estimate. We knew Owen had been out on the road with the dead horses in the predawn hours, but we hadn't established yet when he was last seen alive. Possibly five or six hours had elapsed between his last live sighting and the electric moment in late morning when his body was found in the snow. And so far, it was anybody's guess how much of that time it had lain out in freezing weather. So no, we were not even close to having a time of death.

When I asked Ethan the question, I was ready to accept rough estimates – most people don't remember times very precisely unless they know they're going to be asked. But if he was going to throw up roadblocks I was going to kick them down. So now, by God, I wanted detailed information about every minute of his morning.

'Well, at four a.m.,' he said, giving it plenty of irony, 'I'm pretty confident I was still sleeping soundly.'

'They didn't call you from the farm, then? About the accident on the road.' When he stared, looking surprised, I said, 'The horses?'

'Good heavens, no. Why would they?'

'I don't know. You said you were very active in the organization, responsible for its recent rise in profits, so I thought they might ask your advice about the dead animals.'

He sat back in his chair then and looked me over carefully. 'Now that sounds somewhat . . . hostile,' he said. 'Have I annoyed you in some way?' He knew he had.

'Nope. Just trying to understand how your organization works. If they didn't call you about the horses, when did you wake up?'

'Seven minutes past five.' I raised my eyebrows over the

precision of his answer and he added: 'Coffee's set to start perking at five and the alarm goes off seven minutes later.'

'I see, regular habits – that makes it easier. What's next?'

'I get a cup and bring it back to bed to drink while I glance at the paper. Then I get up and shower . . . do you really want all this?'

'Please.'

'Dress, eat a bowl of cereal, and I'm on my way to my office by a few minutes after six.'

'Even on Saturday?'

'Every day but Sunday. Yes.'

'Do lawyers usually go to work that early?'

'Some do. I'm the junior partner in my family's law firm, so I do most of the dog work – billing and routine correspondence, case law from Lexus, other research on the Internet. Then there's legal work for the farm. I try to get that out of the way early so it doesn't interfere with the firm's regular work.'

'Anybody see you leave home? Are you married?'

'Yes, I'm married and no, my wife does not wake up to watch me get dressed and wave goodbye.' He snickered to indicate how ludicrous he found the concept of morning companionship.

'She's a sound sleeper then?'

'I believe so but we don't share a bedroom, if that's what you're trying to find out.'

Now that, I briefly thought of saying, *sounds more than a little hostile.* But then I'd be tetchy too if my wife had quit sharing my bedroom. In fact, I'd be too pissed off to think about much else for quite a while, I realized, and wanted to ask Ethan Kester how long ago she had moved out and how the marriage was going since then. But it didn't seem to bear on the crime at hand so I shook off that distraction and pressed on, anxious to get out of his bleak morning bedroom and get on with his day.

'Anybody see you arrive at your office?'

'No. Well, maybe the janitorial service in the building. Sometimes we run into each other, sometimes we don't. I'm trying to remember if I saw any of them Saturday morning. I don't think so.' He thought. 'I log in on my computer first thing – I guess you could check that.'

'Uh-huh.' We looked at each other across our mutual

awareness that anybody could boot up his computer if he wanted them to. Did he have a little helper? 'But nobody else comes in early?'

'My secretary gets there about eight.' He paused a couple of beats. 'Usually.' He seemed to reconsider. 'Actually, my Saturday secretary sometimes comes in a little earlier.'

I was just going to make a note: Secretary, 8 a.m., till he added that carefully considered, 'Usually.' I looked up then, in time to see him lick his lips, and add the third estimate of his secretary's arrival time. By the time he'd said 'my Saturday secretary', I had quit writing and was watching him carefully.

'Your Saturday secretary?' I asked him. 'You have different ones for different days?'

'Only on Saturday. The regular one, Angela, works five days a week, and until recently I got along without help on Saturday. But lately my work load's been heavier, so we found a student from the college to come in for one day.' He looked into the corner of the interview room for a few seconds before he added: 'And sometimes she comes earlier so she can get away earlier. For a, you know, a game or something.'

I said, 'How much earlier?'

'Well, last Saturday I believe it was actually around seven.' He still seemed uncommonly interested in the corner of the interview room, which was dingy and undecorated and only three feet away.

I said, 'Give me her name and address.'

'Patty . . . um, Patricia. Is it Johnson or Carlson?' He said he didn't know, offhand, where she lived – had trouble saying the word 'offhand'. But, let's see, he guessed he knew her email address. After some confusion over where to put the dots he said he'd send it to me.

By now I wanted that Saturday secretary right here in the interview room with us, and the hell with her email address. But I didn't want Ethan to get back up on his high horse, and I thought that whether they were working or romping she was a witness to his whereabouts, so I just asked him to send it as soon as he got back to his office, and went on with what I really wanted to know: did he stay in his office till he got the news about his brother?

'Sure did,' he said, 'because I was working on a land deal for a difficult client who's always in a hurry. It was complicated, a three-way swap involving land and money and they both kept moving the goalposts so I—'

'I don't need all the details,' I said. Like all of us, Ethan thought his own work was fascinating.

'OK, well, I was still working on that when Doris called from the farm. Crying, saying that Owen was dead.'

'What time was that?' I was looking for wiggle room, holes in the story.

'I don't remember exactly but I'll get it for you. It was whenever I logged off my computer. I got in my car then and drove straight to the farm.

'I learned as much as I could from Doris and her employees – it was just chaos out there, nobody really knew anything. So I came back to the office, thinking I'd call the Chief of Police and find out who was handling the investigation and . . . I found a message from your detective . . . Bailey, is that his name? Yes. I called him, he told me where he was working and I went there. The rest of the morning I guess you know.'

'Yes.' So far, his story looked solid as a brick wall. 'Now tell me about your relationship with the victim.'

'The victim.' He made a face. 'Do you have any idea how shocking it is to hear your own brother referred to that way?'

'I'm sorry. I know none of this is easy. I'll just call him Owen from now on, OK? Was he older or younger than you?'

'Older. I'm the lucky second son. I was free to go to law school because the folks always knew, since we were boys, that Owen would stay and run the farm.'

'Somebody had to?'

'Well, the family's had the place since great-grandfather's time. It was always taken for granted – I mean, nobody's ever talked about selling the home place.'

'Isn't there another brother?'

'Yes. Matt is five years younger than me. But he wasn't inter-ested in farming – he liked to sing and ride horses.' He shrugged, and Matt pretty much vanished off-screen.

'So Owen stayed on the farm and you went to law school. But you seem to have remained very interested in the farm.'

'Yes. I guess in a way I never left home either. Owen and I have both worked there since we were toddlers. Our dad insisted we do our chores, no matter what was going on in school – and I came home to work all vacations through college and law school. Now . . . I don't do chores any more, of course' – he settled the crease in his pants, looking briefly pleased with himself – 'but as soon as I passed the Bar I took over the legal and financial work.'

'Are your parents still involved?'

'Oh, you bet. It's a family corporation now. They're on the board of directors and take part in all major decisions.'

'That would be Anna Carrie and, let's see . . .?'

'Henry. They kept very close tabs on the place for the first couple of years after they moved to town. But lately they're enjoying retirement more. They go south for a couple of months every winter, miss a few meetings. They stay in touch by phone, though. And God forbid,' an ironic smile and eye roll here, 'we forget to send the monthly statements and check. Also, we can count on them to question any big expenditures they haven't agreed to.'

'Like buying more land?'

'Oh, we'd never do that without their approval. We grew slowly at first – a couple of nearby pastures that people didn't need when they sold off herds. Then a whole adjoining farm, the one we call Halfway, about ten years ago. That's when we began to buy pure-bred Holsteins – Owen's idea and it's finally paying off. And when I saw how lucrative the ethanol market was becoming, I pushed to buy River Farm three years ago, so we could grow our hay down there and put more of the Home Farm acreage into corn.' He crossed his legs and sighed. 'Growth isn't easy, of course. We've been land-rich and cash-poor, like most farmers, for a lot of years.'

'But Doris has quite a successful riding stable too, doesn't she?'

He made a small, dismissive sound: 'Hmmp.' I watched him consider how to make his case without sounding mean-spirited. 'Depends how you define success. She enjoys a wonderful reputation for producing winners – horses and riders both. But horse sales and riding lessons . . .' He sighed. 'More flash than

cash, a lot of the time.' An ironic smile next, to show forbear-
ance. It seemed to me he had these little set pieces composed
and stored up for making his points. 'County fairs and
gymkhanas must be the most expensive form of advertising
ever devised by the mind of man.'

'So the farm doesn't make enough money to satisfy you?'

'I didn't say that. It's always made a fair living, and I have
my own practice. But it's only in the last few years, since we
expanded the corn crop – at my insistence, I'd like to point out
– that we're showing a good return on investment.' A small,
self-deprecatory chuckle. 'In fact, we did so well last year I was
finally able to charge for my legal work.'

The lawyer who was proud of doing no chores on the farm
wanted to be sure I understood how central he was to the success
of the place.

'But now there's an issue, isn't there, about whether to sell
the farm by the river to sand miners?'

'Oh . . .' he cleared his throat, 'we have had an offer, yes.
Nothing's decided yet.'

'But you're quite interested? It's a lot of money?'

'Dear me, how gossip does travel.' He sniffed again – he had
a knack for accusative sniffing. 'These offers do tend to be quite
sizeable, because we're talking about a unique resource that exists
in only a few places and is essential to certain processes. Glass
manufacture is one . . .'

'And fracking?'

'That's another use for it, the one that's got everybody all
excited right now. It's very lucrative and quite controversial. And
of course Minnesota folks will seize any excuse for a fight, as
you must have noticed.' He had a little humorless laugh that
seemed designed to reduce any opposition to a joke. 'Fortunately
controversy is very good for the law business.'

'How did Owen feel about the sale? Was he for it?'

'Not so far. But the folks like the idea. After all, it's not the
Home Farm the buyers are after – just the River Farm, that piece
of land by the river that we bought three years ago for a hay
field.'

'So you figured you could talk Owen into selling when the
time came? There wasn't any argument going on?'

'We always had a lot going on and it wasn't in the cards that we could run a family business together and never argue. There are pros and cons about the River Farm sale and we haven't figured them all out yet. But luckily my firm's doing fine and so is the farming operation as a whole, so there's no hurry about making a decision.'

'Whose idea was it to rent the cornfield to bird hunters?' I asked.

'They came to us. But we all agreed on that deal right from the start – there simply isn't any downside. After the corn's harvested, you know, usually we sell right away but sometimes it's better to hold out for a better price. Renting the field – it doesn't make any big fortune, but it's money coming in. Makes it easier to wait.'

'And Owen agreed – it was OK with him?'

'Once he was sure . . . he made me go back to the hunt company several times till he was satisfied about their safety measures.'

'Then how could he possibly have wandered into the line of fire and gotten shot?'

'Don't you think I've asked myself that question over and over?' When his anxiety peaked his face resembled a death mask: the skin grew sallower and his eyes seemed to sink in his head. 'Doris says he wasn't even supposed to be in that end of the field. The break in the fence where the horses got out was down at the other end of the pasture, near the gate.'

The call-waiting light showed on my cell phone. I said, 'Excuse me,' and walked out of the interview room to answer.

It was Ray. 'Pokey finished the autopsy about an hour ago,' he said. 'But I stopped here at the crime lab because I thought you'd want to know as soon as possible . . . that was number seven-and-a-half birdshot Pokey took out of the body. Very small lead pellets suitable for upland bird hunting. The ammo used for waterfowl is number four steel shot – well, you know that, don't you?'

'Boy, do I. They made sure that's what everybody was using, checked it more than once.' Waterfowl ammo is larger, for long-distance shooting, and these days it has to be steel because a lot of environmentalists started to claim that lead shot was poisoning the dabbling ducks that feed off the bottom of rivers. There was a public argument that went on for some time, and some hunters still mutter from time to time that 'the tree huggers never made their case'. But the law got passed anyway, and steel shot is the only legal ammo now for hunting waterfowl.

'Arlo's got all his guides ready to confirm that they scrupulously make sure their hunters use only steel shot,' Ray said. 'This is very good news for the Hiawatha Valley Hunt Club.'

'I got that part,' I said, thinking about Ethan Kester's conflicted face across the table.

'Not such welcome news for us and the Kester family, I guess,' Ray said, and asked the question I had asked myself earlier. 'Because if the bird hunters didn't shoot Owen Kester, who did?'

SIX

Ethan said he had to hurry back to his office. 'Letters to sign, a contract to check on.' He always seemed to be at pains to appear busier than anybody else. 'After that I'll be with my parents.' He gave us their number. 'I'm sure you can understand they're simply devastated. If you can give them a day or two, I'll really appreciate . . .' Even when he said compassionate things, his pomposity somehow leached all the sympathy out of the room. 'They want to help, of course.'

'Good. Tell them to call me tomorrow,' Ray said, handing him a card. He was back in charge of his department now, hot to go on the investigation. He glanced down at the note I'd just passed him and added: 'You have another brother? Where can I reach him?'

'Oh . . . Matt.' Matt's name called up a shrug that suggested he was easy to forget. 'Yes, I suppose you do need to talk to him.' Ethan sighed. 'He called the folks late Saturday when he came to town on his regular supply run. He hadn't heard about Owen and when they told him he got very upset. Owen was his buddy, he depended on his support.

'He lost control and started to cry, Mom said, when he heard Owen was dead. He said he couldn't talk any more right then, but he promised he'd come back in town Sunday. But Sunday he never showed.' He opened and closed his mouth a couple of times. 'So typical,' he said, in a strained, choked-sounding voice. 'Matt's always been . . . kind of juvenile. You can't count on him to remember his promises, and in a crisis he's just . . . useless. Owen and I are the strivers, I guess you'd say. Matt's the playboy.'

'I need to talk to him. What's his number?'

Ethan gave him a number but added: 'He's hard to reach, though . . . he's outside most of the time and he often forgets to carry his cell phone. But I'll find him,' he said hastily, seeing Ray's expression. 'I'll have him call you.'

'He needs to come in here. I can send somebody out to the farm to talk to the employees who were working Saturday morning. But family members, we need to interview each of you here, at the station. I know everybody's upset,' he treated Ethan to a Grade-A example of the Bailey frown, which has been known to raise blisters, 'but accidental death has been ruled out now. The bird hunters didn't shoot your brother; the shot that was in him doesn't match. This is a homicide investigation, and we need to get on with it.'

'Well, I still think, in some way we don't understand yet, this is going to turn out to be an accident. Who'd want to kill Owen? But nobody's trying to dodge you, detective,' Ethan said stiffly. 'Ask around. The Kesters are one of the founding families of this county. We have no need to play tricks.'

'Good,' Ray said, clamping the muscles of his jaw tight. 'Then I'll expect him to call soon.'

As soon as Ethan was gone we huddled around the conference table. I told Ray why Rosie and Clint had gone back to the farm, and that Doris had just called to say she could come in now, and was this a good time?

'Yes, yes, let's get her in here today,' Ray said. 'And listen, can we leave the interview line-up the way you had it? Because I already talked to this woman. I'll monitor outside with Andy for a while, and if I don't hear anything unexpected I'll go on and write up the autopsy.'

'If you're acquainted,' Andy said, 'tell us what you know about her.'

'Rosie and I both thought this lady was perfectly straightforward. So if you see any fancy footwork that I missed, make a note. Jake, you'll be going for the timeline, right?'

'Yeah. We need to be sure they're all telling the same story. And Winnie' – she was sitting beside me, trying not to show how pleased she was that Ray had not bumped her out of the interview – 'we need to get some sense of the marriage, of how things were between them. Little early for that, of course, but . . .' I stopped when I saw them all nodding, wearing the look cops get when a colleague restates the obvious. Such as: at first, the newly deceased will be universally praised, remembered for his many virtues. In time, his faults will resurface.

Doris Kester walked into the station a few minutes after three looking calm and capable – no sign of the hysteria Rosie had reported on Saturday. Her beauty didn't seem to need or get much assistance – a shine of lipstick, hair in a bun. She wore clean Levis and a turtleneck sweater, and made both garments look like the luckiest cotton in town.

We got her settled in an interview room without much preamble and began to review the terrible events that had torn up her life on Saturday morning. The dying horses that had caused so much distress in the predawn darkness concerned her less now – she basically waved them away, saying, 'Accidents to animals happen on farms, no matter how careful you are. But Owen . . . I keep asking myself, "How could this happen?" I've been over it and over it, and it just doesn't make any sense – Owen shouldn't even have been in that end of the pasture, and why would he wander in front of men shooting guns? He wasn't a careless man.'

She was still trying to explain her husband's death as an accidental shooting by goose hunters. Without knowing how much of that assumption might be a ruse, I had to get her to abandon it now.

'I know you've had a terrible shock and I wish I didn't have to ask you to go over it all again, but there's some new information I need to share with you . . .' I explained the lab findings to her.

She wasn't a shooter but had lived all her life with men who were. She understood about the ammo and saw at once that the goose hunters were no longer suspects.

'But then who' – as she processed the information, her voice got a little higher, raspy and short of breath – 'who did shoot him?'

'That's what we need to find out,' I said. 'Who did shoot him and why?' I watched her do some more fast thinking. 'You got any ideas?'

'Well, God no. Why would anybody? I mean . . . Owen was . . . a quiet farmer who kept to himself.' She blinked several times, fighting for control. She turned sideways in her chair, said something silently to herself, turned back and took a deep breath. 'This is . . . hard to believe.'

'I know. But we need to keep this investigation moving forward and right now you're the only one who can help us.'

'I am? I don't know how I can help. I've just been out there in the country, doing what I always do.'

'Let's start with that,' I said. 'It wasn't a normal morning, was it? The horses getting out on the road, how often does that happen?'

'Never! Owen keeps our fences right up to snuff! Kept.' She shuffled her feet and looked embarrassed. 'I keep doing that. He's not gone for me yet.'

'Perfectly natural,' I said.

'Is it? I can't tell. Nothing feels natural to me right now.'

'I bet. Have you figured out what happened?'

She stared. 'Isn't that your job?'

'To the fence, I mean.'

'Oh. We've been calling it a break in the fence but now Elmer says the wire was cut.'

'Elmer's one of the men your husband sent to find the break?'

'Yes. Now they tell me Owen never got back to them with the tools and wire, so they went ahead and jury-rigged a mend with the tools they had on them, then rode back to the barn and went to work. By the time they got all the horses fed and watered your detectives were there with the picture, and we all got kind of crazy.'

'But Elmer can show us where the break was?'

'Sure.'

'Were you surprised when Elmer told you the wire had been cut?'

'Well, in a way, because who would do such a thing? We all know each other out there. But on the other hand, I asked Owen that morning, out on the road, "How could the horses get out?" and he said, "I don't know but I'm sure as hell gonna find out". Real disgusted, because he always kept his fences solid and tight, and he ragged on everybody about closing gates. Another thing: the horses weren't torn up – they had broken bones from the truck, but not the cuts they'd get from barbed wire. And we both knew a horse that broke through one of Owen's fences would be cut up bad.'

'Why would somebody cut your fence? Got any feuds going with neighbors?'

'Absolutely not. We both grew up here. We have lifelong

friendships in our neighborhood. And I run a riding school. I know the value of good will, and I work at keeping it.'

'So who do you think cut your fence?'

'I have absolutely no idea.'

Confronted with that dead end, I decided to back off and approach the morning from a little more distance. 'Tell me,' I said, 'a little more about your life. You grew up in the country? Your parents were farmers?'

'Still are. Their place is farther north, on the other side of the river. Smaller . . . and quieter. The Kleinschmidts are not as . . . hell-bent on progress as the Kesters.' She showed a glint of amusement. 'My dad has the same three-hundred-and-sixty acres he's always had and he and my brothers do all the work themselves.'

She had married Owen Kester, she said, at the end of her first year at university, 'which turned out to be my last year, because by the time we were married I was pregnant'. She told this part of her story matter-of-factly, with no embarrassment over the early pregnancy. Owen finished his degree less than two years after the wedding, going full-time to class while she toughed it out in student housing with a baby. For his graduation, Owen got the present he'd been promised: a job on the family farm.

'Most of my friends thought I'd feel cheated, quitting school for a shotgun wedding. But they were wrong. Owen and I had been dating since our first year of high school and we were ready to settle down and raise a family. We felt lucky to be farmers on our own place. Naturally we weren't glad when his dad had a heart attack four years after Owen graduated, but to be honest it fit right in with our long-term plans. We'd been living in a double-wide next to the house, but as soon as Henry got out of the hospital, Ethan and Owen helped their parents move to town. Ethan went back to his dorm at the U and on to law school, and we moved into the main house.

'But by then it was clear that our son Alan had some problems.' She hunched her shoulders and brooded, briefly, then took a deep breath and explained. 'He'd hit all his marks as a baby, learned to walk all right, a little late but they said that wasn't unusual for a first-born. They don't have, you know, examples to follow. He'd been babbling like they do when they're getting ready to talk, but shortly after his second birthday he just . . . quit.' She shook her head, still struck dumb by the suddenness of his retreat. 'Like he just folded up his little tent and walked away from camp.'

I thought about my nightly romp with Benny, how joyous he got when we played. Any questions I thought of were too painful to ask. I waited, and presently she said, 'The next two years, we went for all the tests.' More silence, until she was able to say, 'I finally settled for a diagnosis of autism. Not that the name helps much because the symptoms vary so widely. But so-called experts place kids "somewhere on the spectrum" and tell you to accept it. Learn to make do, they say, with very small successes. Which I've done.

'Alan pretty much lives on his own island and life on the farm flows around him.' Her voice had grown gravelly, as if her throat hurt. 'He talks to me, a little. Not to anybody else. He watches and listens, though.' A flash of a smile. 'Some people would be surprised to learn how much he knows about them.'

'You have other children?'

'Two. Not an easy decision, but Owen said, "Why let one misfortune rule our lives?" So we went ahead with Heidi and when we saw what a joy she was we rolled the dice again and got Jeff, a good little farmer like his dad. They're five and eight now and normal in every respect. I was about ready to take a deep breath and relax a little, if that might ever describe life on a farm that's going flat out like a runaway train. But now my husband gets . . . murdered?'

Her face was suddenly all craggy and furrowed – a preview of how she would look in old age. 'Is that what we have to call it now? On his own f-f-farm?' She broke down. Tears flew out of her and she cried out, 'How the hell am I supposed to accept *that*?'

'You're not. It's too soon for that.' Winnie surprised me, leaning forward suddenly on my left, talking softly across the little table to the top of the sobbing woman's head. She nudged the box of tissues closer to Doris's side. 'Mrs Kester, my grandmother died last year.'

She did? Why didn't I know that?

'She was the one who always held the family together, even

in the refugee camps, and here during the first years when nobody wanted us around. So now . . . I find that I can't afford to let her go. I need to tell her things the way I always have. So I just go ahead and talk to her every day.'

I was astonished, hearing spiritual confidences spill out of the normally stoic Amy Nguyen in this bleak little room. *Didn't she go through the same training course we all took? What the hell's come over her?* But then I saw that it seemed to be working for Doris Kester.

'You do?' She pulled a handful of tissues out of the box, mopped her face and smiled crookedly down at Winnie. 'Does she ever answer?'

'Not in so many words, but I feel her goodwill and encouragement there.' She gave the small, stoic shrug of the survivor, one she must surely have learned from the unsinkable boat lady. 'She never knew much English anyway.' The next shrug melded rue and a wince. 'And my Vietnamese was so spotty . . .' She made a small, rocking motion with her right hand. 'If I could get her back I would learn more.'

'Yes,' Doris said. 'We think of things we'd do better, don't we? I've already got quite a list.'

Their four hands hovered over the tabletop now, the tips of their fingers all but touching.

I hated to break up the party but we had to move along. 'Mrs Kester, can I ask you . . .'

She turned on me impatiently and cried out, 'Oh, for God's sake, will you call me Doris? I'm not my mother-in-law!' Then, realizing she had answered politeness with rudeness, she clapped her hand over her mouth and said behind it, 'I'm sorry, I'm sorry.' She took her hand down and put it in her lap, sat up straight like a good kid in school and said, very quietly, 'I'm a little crazy right now. Please don't take offense.'

'I won't.' I waited a couple of beats and said, 'OK to go ahead now?'

'Yes.'

'Who called you about the horses on the road?'

'A sheriff's deputy named . . . I forget. I can get it for you.'

'We'll get it. Why was he there?'

'He happened to be patrolling nearby when the truck driver

called nine-one-one. The deputy's daughter is one of my students. He recognized my horses.'

'Tell me how that went. Is there a phone in your bedroom?'

'Yes. It's on Owen's side and he answered it and I heard him say . . .' So now she'd told me what I wanted to know, whether they were sleeping together. It didn't guarantee amity, but at least I knew separate bedrooms were not a fixed feature of Kester marriages. My attention cut back in as Doris said, '. . . so we threw on some clothes and went out in the Jeep.'

'Who else was out there?'

'When we got there, just the truck driver and the deputy, but Owen had called Charlie Blaise, our foreman, and told him to roust some of the hands. Pretty soon Charlie came in the pickup with Elmer. Owen said, "Charlie, you and Elmer trade vehicles with me. You take the Jeep and go look for the break in the fence. I'll take the pickup back to the barn and load up supplies to fix it. Soon as you find the break you call me and I'll come where you are – you just stay there and make sure no other horses get out". He left in the pickup and that's the last time I saw' – her face started that terrible collapse into gray creases again – 'saw him alive. Highway Patrol got there, and the vet . . . let's see.' She blew a stray hair off her face and thought herself back into the moment. 'I traded insurance card numbers with the truck driver.

'Owen called as he drove into the yard, said Charlie had just called him and they'd found the break, so he said he was going to find Maynard and put him to work in the barn, to start the morning feed and watering and get the stalls clean.' She blew her nose. 'And then he said that he'd take the fencing stuff out to the other two hands and they'd . . . fix the fence?' The last was not a question but came out like one because she was weeping again.

I waited for some time before I asked the top of her head, 'About what time was that?'

'Um . . . five-thirty . . . maybe quarter to six?' She had her hands over her face and the tears were coming out through her fingers.

Get her to think, so she'll stop crying. 'Doris,' I said urgently, 'can you stop right there and hold that picture in your mind?'

She took her hands down and looked at me, a little alarmed, like, *What now?*

I turned to a fresh sheet of paper in my notebook. 'I need to figure out where everybody was on your farm that morning, and you're the only one, now, who can help me do that. So can we do that now?'

'I guess – sure.' Sniffle. 'Where do you want to start?'

'Right there at the beginning. It must have been about, what? Four o'clock when you got out to the wreck?'

'Few minutes after.'

'Who was with your children while you were out there?'

'Oh . . . I have a cousin who's divorced. Her husband pretty much just abandoned her after they'd raised a family together . . . long story short, she needed a place to live and I needed help, so she moved into the double-wide and works as my nanny.'

'OK. Now . . . you were near the gate on the county road . . .'

That was how it started and we went on that way, through the arrival of the vet, the highway patrol, the disposal unit that came to haul the dead horses away. She gave me the name of her vet, detailed for me the identities and functions of the many hands that spilled out of the house and other buildings as the sun came up and the commotion built. I drew one diagram after another, with icons for farm buildings and fences, and stick figures for people which I put wherever she told me to, with names and functions noted. Before long we had a kind of graphic novelette showing the Kester farm organization as it moved through that morning, 'that crazy morning', she kept saying.

The craziest part, I thought, was that when Rosie found her in her kitchen, near noon, she was forming dough into loaves of bread.

'How in hell,' I asked her, 'did you find time to start a batch of bread? I should think it would be the last thing . . .' Thanks to my wife, the skilful cook who often greases my lucky chin with home-made goodies, I know a little something about baking: bread-making takes time.

'I didn't,' she said. 'Aggie, my morning cook, mixes a batch when she starts work, so it's ready for me to make up and bake before lunch. With all that was going on, I never thought to tell her to skip it. By the time I got up to the house it had been rising so long it was about to spill out of the pan. I had to deal with it right then or throw it out, it's a firm rule on our place – and family has to set the best example.' She showed us her severe face. 'If it's humanly possible, we never let anything go to waste.'

I bookmarked that place in the video – it summed up her world-view rather neatly, I thought. Crying over dead horses was permissible for a short time, but no excuse for letting good bread dough go to waste.

I had begun to agree with Rosie and Ray – this woman was a straight arrow. Like all investigators I have a sensitive bullshit meter, but it wasn't ringing any bells – she seemed fiercely loyal to her husband, proud of his farming methods, and until this calamity caught up with her, more content with her life than most people, though she admitted it wasn't always easy.

'And the farm's doing very well lately, Ethan said.'

'Yes. It keeps us hopping – there's a big crew to pay every month, and we're still paying down the mortgage on River Farm. We moved the entire dairy operation to the neighboring farm we bought ten years ago, and remodeled its farmhouse into dormitory housing for the crews. Not cheap, but housing cuts down on turnover. And Dairy Farm grows enough grain to feed all the animals. So Home Farm's planted entirely in corn now, the best cash crop you can have these days.'

Thanks to the demand for corn created by ethanol, she said, and the 'greatly improved' milk production they were getting from their blooded dairy herd, the operation had been very profitable the last three years. 'So I was looking forward to taking my best horses to some shows next spring. If Star Bet showed as well as I expected him to, I intended to sell him for top dollar and raise my training rates on the school.'

'Is that what Owen wanted too?' Winnie asked her.

Doris's cheeks did a jittery dance, threatening to turn back into those terrible hills and valleys. But she pulled herself back from the brink and said, 'Owen just wanted what he'd always wanted – to keep on farming.'

'He liked the life?'

'Loved it – the life, the work, the seasons . . . the crops and the animals . . . he wasn't like so many farmers now, looking to cash out while the good times last. Good years and bad, Owen

said, farmers have the best life. "I don't want to sell out", he
always said, "what would I change this life for?"'

My bullshit bell was dinging a little now – their life on this
high-speed farm sounded a little too perfect. 'You and Owen didn't
find that working together put extra stress on the marriage?'

She shrugged it right off. 'All farm couples work together. We
knew that going in.'

'Well, but . . . I understood there were some issues about your
wanting your own shares in the corporation.'

'Oh, that.' She smiled grimly. 'The help's been talking, huh?
The whole family was in on that fight and I guess it did get
pretty noisy in spots.'

'But it's settled to your satisfaction?'

'Sure. Owen's folks are old school: the man has to be the
boss, period. My folks were the same way so when I came here
as a bride I just went along with whatever the men decided.
But when we bought Halfway for a dairy farm and Ethan started
talking about having a corporation for tax purposes, I decided
it was time to look out for myself. Everybody was shocked at
first, but I made my points and now . . . she won't say so, but
even my mother-in-law likes having her own shares.'

'And your husband was OK with it?'

'Not at first but he came around. Owen was my best friend,
since we were kids. We argued about things when we disagreed
– all couples do. But when he saw how much having my own
money and my own voting stock mattered to me, he wanted it
too.'

She wasn't embarrassed when I asked her about the small
pot-growing operation. It was Owen's little peccadillo, she said,
and they enjoyed it together. 'It was just for the two of us – for
a little evening whoopee once in a while. We hardly ever go to
bars – we're too tired at night to drive into town.'

'All the Kesters have profited from the recent prosperity?'

'Yes.'

'All satisfied with what they were getting?'

'Oh, for the last few years, it's been smiles all around. Why
not? Owen and I did all the work and everybody shared in the
rewards. Even Ethan was happy enough with what his shares
earned, until this sand mining business came along. Now he

keeps saying, "How can you turn your back on three million dollars?"'

'He really had a bona fide offer for that much?'

'To start the bidding. Maybe double before we're done.'

'But you weren't tempted?'

'No. I've got everything I need here, and I love the wildlife on the Mississippi. I don't want to see sand mines in the flyway.'

'How about Matt? Does he want to sell?'

'Oh, well, Matt . . .' She made the same gestures Ethan had made: a shrug and a little hand wave. 'Matt's easy. He wants his beers in the evening, some dancing and flirting on Saturday nights. Now and then a trip to Vegas, that's about all it takes.' She chuckled.

'He's not ambitious like his brothers?'

'Amazing, huh?' She smiled and I saw, briefly, what a blazing beauty she must be when she had things going her way. 'He's far from perfect, but he does like to laugh.' She chuckled. 'I think he'd take the money in a heartbeat if Owen was for it too. But he knew Owen got him back into the family business three years ago – Henry was dead set against taking him back. Said, "I don't care if he begs". And Ethan declared Matt never did his share of the work, always show-boating around at the fairs and rodeos in the summer, and he left as soon as he saw something he liked better. "Why take him back and let him screw us again?"'

'My, my. What did he *do*?'

'I don't know the details. It was before I married Owen. His mother claims it was just teenage irresponsibility. Henry and Ethan seem to think it was more serious than that but they don't want to talk about it.'

'How's it working out, having him back?'

'Well, the River Farm isn't very demanding – I mean, two cuttings of hay, three in a good year – how hard can it be? If anything breaks we have to send somebody to fix it; he's hope-less at making repairs. A tree fell on the corner of his house and you'd think the whole thing blew away . . . Owen had to go down and patch the roof.

'But he offered to help me in the riding school, and he's . . . well, not the greatest teacher I ever saw. He's a bit of a showboat, you know – he'd rather show than explain, so he can't work with beginners; he just intimidates them with dazzling displays of skill. But he is good with horses and the older kids idolize him – especially the girls. The big rodeo star? Whee.

'He even tries to help Owen sometimes . . .' She started to smile about that but then bit her lip, which had begun to tremble again. 'Tried, I mean. I keep sliding back into the present tense.' She glanced at her watch for the third time in ten minutes. 'Speaking of which, can we wind this up pretty soon? I should really get back.'

'Yes.' I shook her hand. It was firm and dry. 'You've been very helpful, and given us a good time frame for the investigation. Thank you.'

'You're welcome.' Standing with her purse strap over her shoulder and her keys in her hand, she said, 'You understand, we're all just living day to day right now.'

'Yes.'

'But before long . . . I expect the family's going to have second thoughts. Ethan and his folks will say I'm not strong and smart enough to manage the farm by myself, and try to take it back from me.'

'Well, I—'

'Then Ethan can sell River Farm to the sand miners and his folks will probably sell Home Farm and the dairy to the first developer that offers a decent price. They'll all take the money and run.' She licked her lips. 'I'll get my share too, of course, but that's not what I want. I can manage the farm all right – but in the long run, I'm not sure I'm strong and smart enough to fight the family on their own turf and win. All I know right now is that I'm going to try. I want my kids to have the good life Owen built for them there.'

'Isn't the city going to grow around you pretty soon?'

'Five years ago people thought so. Now it looks as if it's going to be quite a while before that happens. Long enough for me to raise my kids and get out with a nice nest egg.'

I nodded. Against all the rules in my training manual, I had begun to wish I could help her. She kept her clear blue eyes on me while she told me how I might.

'It would help a lot if you'd find out who did this.'

'Believe me,' I said, 'we will use all our resources to do that and we expect to succeed.'

'Good.' She took a deep breath. 'When you find him, put him away someplace quick, will you? Because if I see him I'll kill him with my bare hands.'

There was nothing I could say to that. I tipped a minimal nod to Winnie, who put a small hand under Doris Kester's elbow and escorted her through the front lobby. Just as the door closed behind them I saw Winnie say something softly to Doris, who turned to wait while Winnie darted back in.

'What?' I said.

'We never told her about the team we sent out to the farm. They'll probably still be there.'

'So?'

'So how would you feel if you found somebody going through your house again—'

'They're not in her house.'

'You know what I mean. She might think we tricked her and quit talking to us.'

'Well . . . officially, she's still a suspect, but . . .'

'She's the best asset we've developed so far. I think she's been straight with us and we should be straight with her.'

I sighed. 'OK. Tell her who's at her farm so she doesn't get surprised. No details though!'

'Right.' She went back out and escorted Doris onto the landing and down the grand staircase. They stood inside the tall front doors, heads together, talking quietly for a few minutes before they shook hands and parted.

I was as anxious to see her out of the building, by then, as she was to be gone. A lot of talk and thumping of gear bags was coming from the direction of the back elevator, and I knew what it meant – Rosie and Clint were back.

SEVEN

'We had to wade through deep shit to get back in that walk-in cooler,' Clint said. We were all around Ray's conference table, leaning toward them, listening. 'Doris was gone and the foreman – what's his name? Charlie – he claimed she took all the keys with her. He said, "Sorry, Detectives, I don't think I can help you".'

Clint's gingery freckles folded into a crafty smirk. 'Rosie said, "That's OK, I don't need your help. I've got a search warrant and a set of picks and if that doesn't work I've got a Glock and a crowbar".'

'They're all so defensive out there,' Rosie said, huffing. 'I mean, OK, they breed great horses. They sell a lot of corn. And I suppose they're used to their privacy, but really, does that mean they don't have to follow any rules but their own? I just got *sick* of it.'

'But you did get in,' Ray said, watching the hands move on the wall clock.

'Charlie remembered he had an extra set of keys in that dormitory over by the dairy, and he liked that better than the Glock and the crowbar. Actually I bet they have two or three sets hidden under rocks out there. They all have unpredictable schedules and none of the work can wait, animals have to be tended all the time—'

'Rosie—'

She looked at his impatient face and said quickly, 'Gloria sprayed a patch of the floor around that storm drain with the Luminol and it bloomed like a rose.'

'Ah.'

'That's what we all said. For about two seconds. Then the DNA techie started screeching, 'That's enough! Don't spray any more till I get my swabs!' But she needn't have worried. Once we started looking we found plenty to scrape. She took smears and scrapings from the seams in the cement, the back wall, around all the bolts in the built-in table . . . pulled a couple of strands of some kind of fibers out of that drain, too, that never came off a pig. She's there now, getting ready to cook it. I can't prove it isn't all pig and calf blood yet . . .' she shared a triumphant grin with Clint, '. . . but I bet we're going to find some of Owen's DNA mixed in.'

'But that's not the best news,' Clint said. 'The little dimples in the beef hides? We dug 'em out and sure enough, they were shotgun pellets. Found two more in the edge of the shelf behind the carcasses.'

'So now if the size matches what Pokey took out of the body, we have a homicide scene,' Rosie said. 'And better times will be along soon.'

'Not soon enough,' I said. 'You see the morning paper? The chief's going to lose his new tan when he sees all the protests.'

'Good picture of Owen, though,' Rosie said. 'And the story . . . all the boards and commissions he served on . . . Family's been busy all weekend, huh? Feeding reporters all these sidebars about his awards, making sure he gets his due.'

'And the reporter did a helluva job with the outraged quotes from alarmed citizens, didn't she?' Ray looked pretty outraged himself. 'Which is why your next date is with the information officer, Rosie. Tell her to feed a story to the media right away, about detectives returning to the farm today to gather more evidence. Nothing about DNA or the BBs, it's too soon to talk about that. And don't specify which buildings. But all the help around there knew where you were looking, right? So word's going to circulate fast at the farm.'

'Won't it, though?' Rosie chortled. 'Stir 'em up a little.'

'Which is good unless it gets somebody hurt,' I said. 'You're hoping he'll panic and make a mistake.'

'Or she,' Ray said. 'Don't we all keep saying, "Nobody's ruled in or out yet"?'

'Including the parents and that younger brother,' Andy said. 'We haven't ruled any of *them* in or out because we can't get them in here to talk to us. How much longer are we going to put up with *that*?'

'Tell you what,' Ray said, looking nettled, 'why don't you make Matt Kester your personal project? Ethan called me a few minutes ago and said his parents will be in first thing tomorrow. But soon as we're done here, start calling Matt and leaving messages on both his phones. Tell him if you don't get an answer in the next two hours you're going to call the sheriff of Goodhue County and ask him to send a deputy out to bring Matt Kester in as a person of interest.'

'Good!' Andy said. 'Happy to do that.' He began copying numbers out of LeeAnn's notes.

'Andy,' I said, watching his lips move as he copied the numbers, 'you walked all around that pickup the day we found Owen's body, didn't you?'

'Sure did.'

'Did you see any evidence that Owen walked himself into those trees? Or any sign he was dragged or carried?'

'Damn good question,' Andy said. He finished copying, sat back and looked at me thoughtfully. 'Blair was with me for a lot of that walk – the photographer? He got plenty of pictures but I don't think you're going to learn much from them.'

'Too few tracks?'

'Too many. The two-track that follows the fence line is in steady use by several farm vehicles. Seven or eight sets of boot tracks lead from the road into the trees where the body was, but all so trampled by each other – nothing there we can use.'

'Blair got pictures of all that?'

'Yes. But there was no blood trail or anything like that. No sign of dragging. Two sets of what could be a dog or coyote, some rabbits and numerous smaller animals had run through the area as well. And an unshod horse had walked through there – maybe two, there's quite a bit of manure close by. But remember, it's one end of a pasture and they have at least a dozen horses walking free out there with winter coats – there's a feeding station up near the barn.'

'So,' I said, 'one way or the other we think he got there in his own pickup. But the hard part to figure out is the time, isn't it? Somebody had to shoot Owen in the walk-in cooler, if that turns out to be the place, and get him carried to the field before the hunters set up out there. Not much time.'

'I know,' Ray said. 'Doris says Owen got the call from his two men that they found the break in the fence line a couple of hours before sunup, more or less. She thought he was loading up with fencing materials, to take to his crew. But there was no fencing gear in the pickup, you said.'

'That's right. Looks like he ran into his murderer before he ever got started loading up.'

'There wasn't a whole lot of time,' I said, 'for somebody to shoot him and get him planted by the fence before the hunters arrived.'

Ray pondered a minute, tapping a tango rhythm with his pencil eraser. 'You know what? I'm going to set up a spreadsheet and start entering all the time estimates people give us.'

'Color code it,' Rosie said. 'Put the ones we can prove in red.'

'There you go. Blue for the ones we're not sure about, then change them to red when we can verify them.'

'And if you spot a stinking lie,' Clint said, finding a way to amuse himself as usual, 'you can color it purple.'

'Be serious,' Ray said, frowning. 'We need to zero in on those crucial hours just before and after sunup Saturday – what time did you get to the range to set up, Jake?'

'I remember groaning as we drove over there about the short night, but I'm not sure how short. Let's see – we parked in the Walmart parking lot and the shuttle car met us there . . . Oh, I remember now, the sun came up as we were crawling into that blind.'

Ray said, 'OK, sunup last Saturday – we can get that time from the weather channel, right?'

'I got it,' Clint said, Googling busily on one of his many small screens. 'Seven-fourteen.'

'Good! There's our first anchor time. Now, Clint, you find that truck driver, get his times – they must keep records – and we'll have two solid times to build the rest of the story on. Times are critical, people! Pin them down in all your interviews!' He rubbed his hands together. What else?' He peered at his notes. 'Anybody want to say anything about the interviews so far?'

Winnie said, 'That Ethan?'

We all turned to look at her. Ray said, 'Yeah, what?'

Besides being the newest detective, Winnie was usually polite and quiet, reacting to what other people said. But now she volunteered, 'Ethan doesn't seem to think Doris has a right to an opinion, does he? He just talked about what *he* might decide, what he and *his parents* might want. Remember what he said about selling to the sand miners?' She read it out of her notebook, '"My firm's doing fine, so there's no hurry about making a decision".'

She looked around at us. 'Owen's death makes it easier for Ethan to be the decider, doesn't it?'

'I've been thinking that too,' Ray said. 'But I got off to such a bad start with him, I been trying not to show bias.'

'Aw, go ahead and show a little,' Andy said. 'I'll be right behind you. Almost every word he says makes me mad.'

'Me too,' I said, 'but that doesn't make him a murderer.'

'No, just a pain in the ass,' Clint said. 'But then, like Maynard said, all the Kester men have big egos.'

Ray looked up from his notes. 'Who's Maynard?'

'Oh, that's right – you were at the autopsy when I told that story. Maynard's my new buddy at the farm.'

'Somebody's trusted factotum?'

'Better. A sneaky little gofer with a big mouth.'

'Oh, excellent. What did he blab?'

'He says the Kester boys have fighting in their DNA. Got it from their dad, Maynard says – every time Dad comes to visit, he starts an argument. Dad and the two older boys all fight like pit bulls. No wonder, Maynard says, Doris likes having Matt around, nudge, nudge, wink wink. Maynard is a world-class winker.'

'Matt's not a fighter?'

'Doesn't need to be, Maynard says. Ladies and horses just putty in his hands. Maynard calls Matt "The Horse Whisperer", and he says in his opinion "it ain't only the horses he's whispering to". I said, "You mean he's getting it on with the students?" And Maynard said, "You bet – and I wouldn't be surprised if he's getting a little from his sister-in-law too. That lady's so hot we all keep waiting for the barn to catch fire . . ." '

'Why are you listening to dirty gossip like that?' Winnie demanded. 'Doris is a serious lady who deserves your respect.'

'Wow,' Clint said, open-mouthed, 'now who's showing bias?'

'I'm just saying—'

'Winnie,' I said, 'dirty gossip is about half of what you get when you canvass a neighborhood, isn't it? And we can't stop doing that. Be realistic.'

'Anyway,' Ray said, 'everything I've heard indicates Doris was never out of sight of at least three or four people after four a.m. Saturday morning, when the sheriff called her out to see her horses, till almost noon when Rosie found her making bread in the kitchen. If that's true, the only way she could kill her husband or dispose of his body was with a couple of helpers. So keep your eyes peeled for any of the help that seem especially close to her, huh?'

He looked at his watch. 'Damn, almost four-thirty already. Tomorrow, the two of you, Rosie and Winnie, go out to that farm and get a final head count. Identify exactly who was working there Saturday morning. Then take each one of them off by himself, in a room or just sitting on a stump, I don't care, but turn your recorders on. Go over the time between when the horses got out and when Rosie and Clint got there.

'Make charts like the ones Jake made' – he held one up – 'of where they claim to have been and who with, and doing what, every hour. Bring them back and we'll make a . . . kind of a graphic movie' – amusement and hesitation chased each other across his face, but in the end he couldn't resist – 'kind of a cross between *Red River* and *Rashomon*.'

'Oh, I like it,' Rosie said. 'Maybe we can get Jude Law to play Matt? I'll have my people call his people.'

'Nah,' Clint said, delighted by the distraction, 'I think Jude's a little past his sell-by date for this part. How about—'

But LeeAnn, who had just answered the ringing phone, put it on hold and said, 'Mr and Mrs Henry Kester are in the lobby to see Ray Bailey.'

'Geez,' Andy said, 'be careful what you wish for, huh?' He asked Ray, who was frowning at the clock, 'Do I have to set up an interview room or can we just bring them in here?'

'It's going to run past five o'clock,' Ray said. 'But I suppose . . .' He looked at me.

'Oh, hell,' I said, 'we better grab them while we can get them.'

'Yeah, bring them in here,' Ray said. 'We can use my recorder. Andy, you can stay for this? Good. The rest of you,' he shouted above the scraping of chairs as they all got up, 'remember where we left off and come back here in the morning. Jake, you want to stick around for this, or—'

But then the phone rang again. LeeAnn answered and told me, 'The chief is back and wants to see you.'

'Go ahead and start without me,' I said. 'I'll go see what he wants and come back as soon as I can.'

I went up along the crowded hall, edging past LeeAnn's desk, which had started as a small island a couple of years ago and was growing into an archipelago as we all piled work and messages on her. Noise and foot traffic boiled around Kevin Evjan's office, patient Property Crimes detectives slogging through reports on auto thefts and burglaries.

In the chief's outer office, Lulu's desk didn't even slow me down, since his secretary wasn't due back till tomorrow. The chief wasn't scheduled to be here either, but here he sat with his big, sunburned face lighting up the room.

'The king of the slopes is back,' I said. 'Was it good?'

'My thighs are just raw meat but yes, it was great snow and everybody had a blast.'

'But you couldn't wait till tomorrow for your homicide fix?'

'I just stopped to pick up my mail,' he said. 'But I thought I'd see if you had anything new.' He had phoned in twice. We have plenty of crime in Rutherford but the homicide rate is low. And this case, involving a large and prominent family, had him quite concerned. 'That Kester farm . . . is the whole thing inside the city limits now? Or just that field where the shooting was?'

'The whole place is just inside the new city limits, the – ahem – proposed new development we were supposed to feel so good about a couple of years back. The one that was going to bring us those whopping new property taxes as soon as the farmers saw the light and sold out to the developers.'

'It's going to happen eventually. Soon as the banks quit jacking the economy around and go back to lending money for a living.'

'Good. Meantime, if the city council starts having heart attacks about the cost of this investigation I hope you'll rub their noses in all those hopes and dreams.'

'OK. Soon as you're done talking politics can you tell me how far this expensive sleuthing has taken us?'

I told him how the ammo had ruled out the bird hunters, and that the second trip back to the farm had yielded DNA scrapings and some overspray pellets.

'Aw, shit,' he said. 'You mean it's one of them?'

'Well . . . not necessarily but you have to wonder . . .'

'If a total stranger came along and got into a locked cooler to do the job? Not very much, I don't. Oh, Jesus, this is really going to get ugly now.'

'I didn't realize . . . are these people friends of yours, Frank?'

'Friends? No. They're farmers, they still think like farmers no matter what we do to the town boundaries.'

'Which means?'

'They don't mingle much with townies. I knew a couple of Kleinschmidts in school but the Kesters were all older or younger than me, and the rest of the family's always been a level or two above my pay grade. No, it's just . . . Hell, these families go back to pioneer times in this county. They've got connections all over the county . . . Wait till you see how many cousins they've got. We're going to have plenty of eyes on this one, Jake. Be careful.'

'I have been. We'll treat it like any other case, though, right?'

'Well, of course. By the book. Absolutely. Where are we on it?'

'Autopsy reports tomorrow but I don't expect any surprises. The man was shot at close range with a high-powered weapon, so there can't be many surprises about cause of death. We'd very much like to find the weapon, of course, but . . . And we've got a ton of interviews to do. We could sure use some help.' I gave him my sincere look.

'I know. Damn shame we're short-handed right now. Maybe Kevin could lend a hand?'

'Don't start, Frank.' Kevin and Ray barely manage to get along under the same roof. Having them on the same case is my worst nightmare.

'OK.' He got up, stifling a groan over his creaking joints. 'I promised Sheila I wouldn't get stuck down here. My kids are suffering buyer's remorse about all the homework they didn't get done on ski vacation. They're saying, "Now we have to study over Thanksgiving break!" like that was child abuse. Plus a ski trip for five produces a pile of dirty underwear you would not believe. See you tomorrow.' He stomped out carrying an armload of mail. In McCafferty's world, massive workloads are always just around the corner.

I heard a woman's voice as I approached the space around Ray's conference table. It's not really a room, just a wide spot in the hall that developed when we jury-rigged new work spaces to expand the detective crews. It's like a water hole in the desert: everybody's drawn to it.

'We thought we should come on in today and explain that Matty can't get here till tomorrow. River Farm keeps him *so* busy.' The voice was sunny and pleasant, delivered with a little extra sweetener, like somebody addressing the Ladies' Aid Society at a church supper.

'Matty's been our manager out there ever since we bought that place. Which is, my goodness, three years ago this month, isn't it, Dad?' Mrs Kester was seated at the oblong conference table, a smallish lady with a soft face. She wore a blue print dress that sagged at the neck, gray hair in a timid perm and what I would guess were her second-best oxfords. 'This week's Thanksgiving, isn't it? And that's when Matty came back, three years ago, just before Thanksgiving. It was quite a sacrifice for him to quit the rodeo circuit – he was winning all the time – but he did it for us, because we needed him to manage River Farm.'

'Managing, is that what you call what he does?' The answering rumble came from the powerful-looking man seated beside her, across from Ray. He had strong arms and a beautiful thatch of thick white hair that made his head look even bigger than it was. 'Yeah, I think it was around Thanksgiving. Why don't you tell it like it was? He came back needing a job so we put him to work. He hasn't broken anything yet that couldn't be fixed, so yes, I guess we're still calling him the manager.'

'Now, now,' she said, nudging his elbow. 'Always so critical.' She treated Ray to a little head-shake and a rueful smile. 'I think I should have had girls,' she said. 'Maybe there'd be less fighting.'

'Anyway,' her husband said, 'probably these fellas don't need to know our whole family history, do you think?'

'No, but they do need to understand that you and Ethan always talk as if Matty isn't worth anything. Just because he isn't as good at farming and tinkering as you are. He can ride rings around the two of you and sing and play the guitar – can you do that? I always have to stand up for Matty,' she told the detectives in front of her, 'and then they both say he's a mama's boy. But Owen, that sweet boy' – she dabbed her eyes with an embroidered hankie – 'didn't mind looking after Matty a little. My Owen. He was always willing to do things to please me.'

'All this psychology stuff gives me a pain,' Henry Kester said. 'Listen,' he looked into Ray's eyes and then into Andy's, making sure he had their attention, 'all three boys worked on the farm growing up. I made sure everybody did his share. Then Owen stayed home while the other two went off and did their thing, as they say. For the last few years, now that the money's rolling in, everybody's back on board. Nothing complicated about it – the other two finally saw which side their bread was buttered on. But what's that got to do with the problem?'

'What problem?' She blinked at him.

'What happened to Owen?' he demanded. He slapped the table. 'Pay attention, for God's sake!'

'That's what we want to ask you,' Ray said quickly. 'Who had any reason to want Owen out of the way?'

'Why, nobody,' Mrs Kester said. 'My goodness, what a question. Owen's always been our dearest boy . . . the easiest one of the three to raise. Ever-ready, we used to call him. Always ready to lend a hand . . . even after he started going out with the pushy Kleinschmidt girl, he was still my main helper.'

'Mr Kester?'

'I have no idea,' Henry said, shaking his head. 'He didn't do any of the things that usually get the young guys in trouble. Didn't go in bars much, or get into fights or gamble. Didn't chase girls, even – he was always with Doris, from when they were kids. It really beats me. You're sure it wasn't an accident?'

'Of course he's not sure,' Mrs Kester said. 'Somebody made a mistake somewhere, I keep telling you that. There wasn't a mean bone in Owen's body – who'd want to hurt him? I mean, think about it. Even after she tricked him into marrying her, letting herself get pregnant like that, he never said one word of complaint against Doris.' She looked around the table, soliciting our support. 'Barrel racing, really.' She rolled her eyes up. '*Showing off.*'

'His body was moved,' Ray said, over her head to Henry, 'from where it was shot to where we found it.'

'Now how in the world,' Henry Kester said, 'could you possibly know that?'

Ray and I looked at each other, alarmed by how much he didn't know. Ethan had identified Owen's body Saturday morning in the field, so his parents had been spared the trip to the morgue. But what did this family talk about when they were all together? The parents didn't seem to have the current information.

Ray took a deep breath, trying to think how to say it. 'There wasn't any . . . He has a big gunshot wound in the middle of his belly with a bigger exit wound in back, but there was hardly any blood in the snow under him.' It all came out in a rush and then he sat back, looking as if he felt personally responsible for this outrage.

But he wasn't ready to talk about the second trip to the walk-in cooler just yet, apparently. Just as well, since Henry Kester, who had wanted to know how we knew, now looked as if he might not survive hearing the details. He must have been coping by not thinking about what had been done to his son's body. Now he shrank in front of us, became older and quieter.

'This time of the year,' his wife was going on, staying afloat by not listening to a word we said, 'there's hunters all over this county, and some of them don't know the first thing about safety rules. I always say they should have to pass a test to get their license renewed. Oh, yes, you always shush me when I say that,' she accused her husband, who had his hand off the table, shushing her, 'but now look what's happened to Owen.'

'Anna Carrie,' Henry said, 'will you please, for once . . .'

Becoming agitated, twitchy and red-faced, his wife began to collapse toward her husband's side, complaining. 'I knew I shouldn't come out today, I can feel one of my headaches coming on . . . I don't feel the least bit good, Henry. You best take me home.'

The big man looked at Ray, shrugged helplessly, and said, 'I better do it. She gets spells.' He got up, supporting his wife, and added: 'OK if I come back later? I need to hear, uh, the rest.'

'Sure,' Ray said. 'Any time tomorrow. Um . . .' They looked so frail, tottering there, as if many years had passed since they came to this table fifteen minutes ago. Ray tipped his head briefly toward Andy and said, 'We'll show you the way out.'

Andy stepped to Mrs Kester's other side, and her elbow dropped into his hand with practiced ease. She might regret having no girls, but she had adapted very well to having more than one man around to fuss over her. Her face was buried in the hankie now. Together, the two big men led and half-carried her out through the lobby and into the elevator.

It was just past five o'clock. In spite of all that had happened I was only going to be a little bit late picking up Ben. I said, 'Let's re-cap this in the morning, OK?' Ray nodded, looking fagged. Hardly able to believe my luck, I sprinted down the front stairs and into the parking lot. I hummed a vague, abstracted tune as I pulled my red pickup into traffic. What day was this? I felt as scattered as grass seed on a lawn.

Our babysitter, Maxine Daly, was my foster mother for the best nine years of my childhood. I'd never have left her house willingly, but HHS took me away when they discovered that Maxine's husband sometimes swiped my aid allotment to support his need for binge drinking.

My social worker found us sitting hungry and cold on the couch one day, wrapped in a blanket while Maxine read to me and her blind daughter Patty. Years of good eating have erased the habitual hunger pangs that dogged me through high school, but I can still recite some of the poems she taught us. 'Oh Tiber, father Tiber, to whom the Romans pray . . .'

Maxine's wardrobe is the best she can pick off the rack at Goodwill, and her hairdo usually looks as if it might have been left in the yard overnight. Children trust her instinctively and are never wrong. Next to my wife, she's my favorite woman in the world to spend time with. She has a hard life but she's fun to be around.

I lost her when I was eleven, and found her again by a lucky accident – I was a cop by then, looking for someone else. Trudy was polite but somewhat puzzled by my delight at finding this down-at-heels woman. Now that she knows her, and especially as she sees how our son thrives under Maxine's care, she agrees we must never lose her again.

Ben was awake, sitting in a high chair gumming a graham cracker. He did his usual bouncing and crowing when he saw me, then sat on my lap and grew very long arms to grab at everything within gorilla reach.

'How does he do that?' I asked Maxine, as I moved a salt shaker farther away and handed him a spoon.

'They just have adjustable arms till they learn to talk,' she said. 'After that they holler for what they want.' Ben, who had been reaching desperately for the spoon until I handed it to him, promptly threw it on the floor and grabbed my ear.

'I've been thinking about families,' I said.

'Oh, dear.'

'What?'

'Whenever you get anxious about something,' she said, 'you start obsessing about families. What's going on?'

'You read the paper lately?'

'About Owen Kester? I saw the headline, I didn't have time . . . That's a shame, isn't it? Guess he shouldn't have rented out his field, huh?'

'So you haven't read the later stories. We're pretty sure now it wasn't an accident.'

'Somebody killed Owen Kester on purpose? Shee, no wonder you're tense.'

'You know him?' I was surprised. Maxine doesn't get out much.

'Not personally but that family . . . he married a Kleinschmidt, didn't he? The girl who did so well at barrel racing? And his mother was a Robbins. She and her sisters sit on the boards of charities that fund my kids' benefits.'

I was amazed. If the Kesters had penetrated Maxine's awareness they really had reach. I remembered Frank saying, 'Wait till you see how many cousins they have.'

'So,' Maxine said, 'now you're afraid you might have to arrest a Kester? Hoo. No wonder you're upset.'

'Why does everybody say that? They're not that rich.'

'Maybe not really rich . . . but they've been around so long and they're so flaming respectable.'

'Underneath it all they fight like anybody else, though.' Ben strained longingly toward the spoon on the floor. I picked it up and handed it to him. He waved it triumphantly and threw it down again. 'What I started to say about families? They take these little mean digs at each other, but you have a feeling they're showing off, in a way, while they ambush each other.'

'Oh, you bet. Just try agreeing someday. Say, "You're right, he's a wretch". They'll turn on you like a nest of snakes.'

'I guess Ben will never have anybody he knows well enough to do that with,' I said. 'I mean, I don't even know where I got my name. All I have is you, and we don't fight like that, do we?'

'Praise be. But don't worry. He'll get all the family wrangling he could ever want from Trudy's side.'

I said, surprised, 'How do you know about that?'

'She told me, one day just before Ben was born, about the many fathers who followed Mr Hanson into her life. She was wondering how old the baby ought to be before she told him about them.'

'It wasn't Ella's fault she had so many husbands,' I said. 'They were all rotten to the core.'

We both laughed, but then I said, 'I used to think Trudy's mom was a terrible piece of work. But she's a terrific granny to Ben. Nothing's too much trouble.'

'You see? You're starting to feel defensive about her.'

'And if I commit to that I won't have time to defend myself! Which I must do because before long this kid will start pointing his adjustable arms at me and saying, "What's up with you? Why don't you look like anybody else?"'

'No, he won't,' Maxine said. 'He'll say, "How come we look just alike but you're darker than me?"'

'Oh, no, no, no. Didn't I tell you? I have a firm contract with my spouse – all offspring, no matter what gender, have got to look like her. Come on, Tonto,' I got up and hoisted him onto my shoulder, 'we gotta mount up and get home to that beautiful dame you resemble so much.'

I still had hopes. He was born a towhead, and so far his hair hadn't darkened much. There was a little something strange going on around the nose, but what did an eight-month-old nose know about shape? He was going to revise it soon.

EIGHT

'Hey, remember those three guns we brought back from the farm? I've got the lab results here,' Ray said Tuesday morning, waving them.

'And?'

'Nothing. They're all completely clean and the ammo that was in the cabinet with them is number six birdshot, which doesn't match the hunters' ammo or what Pokey found in the body.'

'OK,' I said. 'Could we handle easy answers if we ever got them, I wonder? What about the DNA and pellets from the walk-in cooler?'

'We just found that stuff yesterday,' Rosie said. 'Did you expect me to process it on the way back to the station?' Something about this case must be getting to Rosie, I thought. Lately she'd abandoned her customary feistiness and become downright contrary.

'No, Rosie, I believe we agreed you would put a rush on it. Did you do that? Did they say how soon they could show results?'

'Not exactly. They said how far behind they are. They said they'd do the best they could.'

'I'll ask the chief to have a word,' I said. 'He's very nervous about this case.'

'What is so special about these farmers?'

'Frank says they have many cousins and shit will soon rain down on us.'

'What's new about that? Anyway,' she turned to Ray, 'you want us doing interviews at the farm today, is that what you said?'

'Yes. You and Winnie. Start with Doris. Get her to give you the names of everybody who was working there Saturday morning. Not just the ones involved in the accident, Jake got those – but everybody working anywhere on the three properties. Call me when you've got all the names and we'll decide whether you need more help or you and Winnie can do the whole crew.

'In the meantime, Clint, you go after the driver of the truck that hit the horses. When you finish talking to him will you go across the hall, please, and get the name of the sheriff's deputy who called Doris Saturday morning? Then find him, talk to him and get a timeline from him for everything he saw and heard.

'And Andy, I want you to go out to that farm and talk to the two men who mended the fence. Get them to show you the place, ask them how they managed without tools – listen to anything else they want to tell you. Keep in touch, folks!' he said as everybody got up and began to assemble gear. 'Results to me as fast as you get them!'

Something had his ticker turned up high this morning; he was being Ray Bailey, Organizer of Most Persons. As I got up to leave he said, 'You got a minute, Jake?'

'Sure,' I said, and then something in his face made me say, 'in my office?'

He followed me in and closed the door, sat down and got right to it. 'I ran into Bo Dooley in the grocery store last night. He had Nelly with him and he was picking out potatoes. Looking at them the way he does, you know, like they better all be perfect or he might shoot up the store.'

'Bo's always been wrapped pretty tight,' I said. 'But I thought he relaxed a little after his divorce went through.'

'He did. But now I guess he's got a new problem. He's passed all the tests for the DEA, but their funding's been cut for this area so no jobs are going to open up in the . . . well, maybe never.' Ray looked at me kind of sideways. 'You think we might ask the chief to hire him back? I sure could use the help right now.'

'I know you could. We were behind with those two assault cases before this killing happened.'

'And Bo would hit the ground running. Not like taking on a new guy.'

'I think it's against all the rules, but . . . tell you the truth I was sorry to see him leave. I've wished several times I'd talked him out of it.'

'Well, you were afraid it was going to be awkward if he and Rosie moved in together. He saw that and he didn't want to mess up her career so he took that job with victims' services. That's what started the fight with Rosie, remember? After he messed her up in court that day.'

'I forgot about that,' I laughed. 'Bo was always going to fit like a sore thumb in a baseball glove at victims' services. But when he heard DEA was going to open an office here, we all thought it would be the perfect job for him.'

'And it would have been. He'd had years of drug interdiction experience, so he looked like a shoo-in to be the local agent. But now that money's so tight they're closing offices rather than opening new ones.'

'OK, I'll ask the chief what he thinks. Right after I ask him to speed up the DNA test. Anything else I should bedevil him about on his first day back?'

'See if he knows any dirt about the Kesters, will you?' He did the ironic wobble with his eyebrows. 'We still haven't recapped the parents' interview, by the way.'

'What's to recap? The Bickersons get bad news and react in their time-tested way by disputing every point.'

'Yeah. Do all marriages end up like that, you think?'

'God, I hope not. Though lately Trudy does seem to get pretty critical when I fart and scratch my crotch.' We enjoyed that thigh-slapper for about ten seconds, till a phone call summoned all available street cops to a domestic disturbance that turned out to be an all-out family fight so horrendous, we had to pull all the detectives back from the farm to record the details of abuse and neglect. By the time I got to the chief's office I was ready to beg on my knees for more help.

'I don't know,' McCafferty said. 'Dooley's resignation is all but final. Though come to think of it we might not have finished the paperwork before we went on vacation . . . hang on a sec.' He walked out to Lulu's desk, they did some muttering and shuffling, and he came back with an impressive sheaf of paper. 'Well, talk about just in time. Lulu's fit to be tied; a lot of work goes into one of these things.'

'Sorry about that.'

'Yeah, well . . . Is this for real, now? He won't change his mind again?'

'He's a family man with no savings, Frank. I think he'd just about kiss your foot for his job back.'

'God forbid. Well, he hasn't collected any retirement checks yet so I think I can just blow recall on the whole thing.'

'Excellent. Can I start him right away?'

'Just about. Get him in here to talk to me first, though, will you? Bo's a helluva cop but I want to look him in the eye and be sure where his head is at before we put in any more time on his case.'

'Right away,' I said. I felt like I'd just grabbed the balloon that might loft me back to normalcy. Ray and I had worked most of our Saturdays since September, and were still woefully late closing cases. Bo's a tiger for work, just what we needed. I went out and called him, got no answer. So I called Rosie's cell to ask her if she knew where he was.

She was thrilled. 'You mean it? He might get his old job back?'

'It's OK with you?'

'God, yes. We've been afraid he was going to have to go out of town.'

'Is that why you've been in such a bad mood lately?'

'Did it show?'

'Well, a few tooth marks on my ankle. Nothing serious.'

'Hey, I'm sorry. But if Trudy was talking about moving to Chicago how cheerful would you be?'

'Don't even think about it.' I shuddered. 'Listen, help me get Bo back on staff before anybody thinks of an objection. Where is he?'

'I'll find him. Trust me – he'll be in there soon.'

'Good. How's it going out there?' I could hear children wailing.

'Awful. Worse than the first report said. At one point the two married folks who started the fight took exception to something Ray said, and decided to help each other kill him. It took five of us to pull them off. Ray lost most of the buttons off his shirt.'

'Wow. Is he all right?'

'Oh, sure. You know Ray – skip the drama and get on with it. And we're almost done with our part now. The rest is up to social services.'

'Rotten shame we had to call you off the farm. How far did you get?'

'Nobody wants to stop and talk; they're all spooked out there. And I never got to talk to Doris. She was in her office next to the kitchen, with the door closed, giving somebody a royal dressing down.'

'Oh? Who's getting the grief?'

'That field hand Clint likes so much. Maynard.'

'What, he ran his mouth once too often?'

'No, it's something more serious – she's been checking up on his work because she's noticed he's skipping a lot of the chores assigned to him. One of those women on the kitchen crew – the ones I called the sausage ladies before? Well, there's one named Aggie who's a talker like Maynard. She sidled up to me and whispered that it sounds like he's getting fired. Said it's about time – he's a sneak and a liar and he's always trying to stick other people with his jobs, so the other hands all hope he's gone.'

'Huh. Clint'll be sorry to lose his favorite source of skinny.'

'Oh, Clint won't have much trouble finding another one. It's a regular rumor mill on that farm right now. Everybody's all stirred up.'

'I hope we can get you back out there pretty soon so you can collect some of that.'

'Good plan but it won't be me today. We got at least two abusers here to book. Ray wants me to take one and Andy the other.'

'OK. My light's blinking. *Find Bo*.' I pushed my call-waiting button.

LeeAnn said, 'Matt Kester is here, Jake.'

Damn! Nobody here but me!

'I set him up in interview room two, is that all right? The video recorder's all set to go.'

'Good girl. Be right there.'

It's better to have at least two investigators working an interrogation. The observer will notice details that may elude the number one examiner, who may get focused on covering all the questions. But now that we finally had Matt Kester in the building, I wasn't going to let him walk away without a chat. The video equipment would have to be the second pair of eyes.

I stopped at LeeAnn's desk before I went in and said, 'If Ray gets back while we're still talking will you call me?' I set my cell to vibrate before I unlocked the room.

Matt looked like Kester Lite. Smaller and slimmer than his brothers, he had the same hairline but lighter hair. His eyebrows were bleached by the sun the same way Owen's had been, and he was tanned and fit-looking, with a dimple like his mother's. That little dent in his cheek probably accounted for some of her special fondness for him, I thought – her other two sons were virtual copies of their father.

He was wearing a blue button-down shirt with clean Levis, and a belt buckle the size of a salad plate. It featured a lot of silver and turquoise and said he had won first prize in calf-roping at the Frontier Days rodeo in Cheyenne, Wyoming. That kind of artifact has been known to raise a snicker from Minnesota working stiffs like me, but secretly we would all like to look the way Matt Kester does in tight pants and western boots.

He kept his pale hazel eyes on me as I sat down. I dug out a card and laid it in front of him. Without glancing at it he gave me a mocking smile and said, 'I'm not a mad dog, you know. You don't have to lock me in a cage.'

'What? Oh . . . the door. Sorry about that; it locks automatically when you close it. But this is the best place we have to talk in private.' Which wasn't true, exactly – he'd have been more comfortable in my office – but I wanted the conversation on videotape. And since we'd had to chase him for four days to get him in here, I wasn't quite as concerned about his comfort as I might have been earlier.

I put out my hand and said, 'Jake Hines.' He shook it without getting up. His hand was smallish but surprisingly strong. The sleeves of his shirt, rolled up two precise turns, showed muscular forearms, taut wrists, and a heavy steel watch with several extra dials on its face. It looked as if it might be the last timepiece working after the building collapsed.

He wasn't quite ready to let go of the locked door issue. 'Seriously, this is kind of offensive, Sergeant – is that a camera light up there? I thought Ethan said you just wanted to visit.'

'Captain.' My pay grade's not an issue till somebody makes it one. It was plain enough on the card he refused to look at. 'The videotape protects you as well as us, Matt – there's no argument later about what we said.'

'Ah.' He glanced at the card finally. 'Oh, so you're the head

Sherlock, hmmm? Well. Good, then.' He gave me a friendly smile, and the air in the room cleared up a little. 'You going to help us figure out which hunter shot my brother?'

Was he really still that far behind the information curve? I said, 'Didn't Ethan tell you? We've eliminated the goose hunters from the list of suspects.'

'No, I – I guess I've only talked to my mom. She still seems to be sure it was an accident. She said it must have been the hunters – who else was out there shooting that day?'

'I don't know yet but the evidence plainly shows the shot could not have come from the goose hunters.' I began to explain about the ammo again, wondering, as I did so, why didn't Ethan tell him this? Or his father? Are none of the men in this family talking to each other?

I was just getting into the details about mandated steel shot for waterfowl when my phone buzzed and I excused myself to take the call.

Ray said, 'I'm here. OK to come in?'

'Yes, please.'

He must have been right outside the door – he came in as I closed my phone. He was not the very model of the clean-cut police investigator – in fact, he looked as if he might have run through a wire fence and into a chipper before he found the station. His shirt had lost most of its buttons, and stray patches of his skin were missing too.

I introduced him blandly, as though I saw nothing amiss, and he surprised the hell out of me by treating Matt to a big, friendly smile. Ray Bailey is not a schmoozer and I have gone many days without seeing a smile that warm on his face.

He said, 'Pleasure to meet you. You've got quite a reputation as a rodeo rider, haven't you? I looked you up and you're all over the place, a list of awards as long as . . .' He indicated most of his arm and turned to me. 'Did you know that this man was ranked near the top in earnings every year, the last three years he competed?' He turned back to Matt, who was looking pretty pleased now too, and said, 'I'm curious. Isn't farming kind of quiet after all that applause?'

'Oh, you know' – Matt stretched and smiled, flashing a gold tooth – 'I was starting to think I probably had enough pretty belt buckles, tell you the truth.' He turned a little sideways, casually, but moving just enough so Ray could see the one he had on.

Ray asked him, 'You got bored with winning? Is that why you came back?'

'Well, and there was a spot for me here – they bought another farm.' He had a little half-laugh like Ethan's. 'I felt needed at last! River Farm desperately needs a new house, but it's beautiful hay land and there's a little barn for my horses. And of course, having been raised by Henry Kester, I knew all about how to put up hay.'

'Your father said you boys did plenty of work growing up.'

'Better believe it.'

'He was a hard taskmaster?'

'Oh, yes, indeed.' Time seemed to have boiled off any bitterness and left only irony.

'Is that enough to keep you busy, just putting up hay?'

'Well, that and the riding school. It was plain that Doris needed help with that. I couldn't believe it, she was taking all night to teach those kids how to side-pass through a gate.' His mocking put-down laugh was like Ethan's, too, but gentler: it only put people down about half as far.

'So there it was, you see, two big jobs I already knew how to do. I was shovel-ready, as they say.' This time the laugh was for him. Or the two big jobs? Hard to tell. 'And I thought, hey, from now on I can stay on the horse – I don't have to keep jumping off with a piggin' string in my teeth.'

He didn't seem to realize he was admitting to burnout. His face still held the self-satisfied half-smile of the coolest Kester. But I was beginning to notice some body language – a line under his jaw that looked like an imperfectly healed injury, a little stiffness in his left knee when he crossed that leg over the other one. I decided maybe Jude Law would not be too old for the part.

It seemed to me that Ray had probably buttered him up enough for us to get on with the business at hand, so I said, 'I guess Matt has really been out of touch. I was just explaining to him about the size and composition of shot that eliminated the hunters as suspects.'

I went over the information again while Matt watched me, looking bemused. Surprisingly the same information that Doris had understood right away seemed puzzling to him. Even after I explained, for the second time, the law about steel shot for waterfowl, he couldn't seem to accept the information. He liked his mother's explanation and he didn't like mine.

'I don't understand you,' he said. 'You sound as if you think it might not have been an accident.'

'It's early in the investigation,' I said. I wanted to move him along, to tell him about the certainty that the body had been moved, but he was so adamant I thought I'd better take it in easy stages. 'The bird hunters didn't shoot your brother. Homicide's a strong possibility.'

'Well, that's the craziest thing I've heard in quite a while,' he said. 'I mean, come on. Who would want to kill a sweet guy like Owen?'

'Well, see, Matt,' Ray said, leaning forward, sounding confidential, 'that's what we wanted to ask you.' He was friendly but earnest. 'You seem to have been closer to Owen than anybody but Doris, so you're the best one in the family to help us figure this out. What's he been involved in that might make somebody want him out of the way?' His thin fingers held his ballpoint poised delicately above his notebook as if he really expected the answer to come tumbling out of Matt's mouth so he could write it down.

I had never seen Ray's gullible shtick before and I found it surprisingly effective. His normally gloomy face had taken on very appealing lines. If he turned that look on me, I thought, I'd probably tell him every bit of what little I know.

But Matt was shaking his head. 'Owen wasn't *involved* in anything,' he said. 'Owen was a *farmer*, to the marrow of his bones.' The little mocking laugh again, and then an imitation. '"*Why's that heifer walking like that? How many days till the hay's ready to cut?*" That was Owen, every day of his life.'

I said, 'Doris mentioned that he also said, "Over my dead body will anybody dig sand pits on my beautiful River Farm". Did you agree with him about that?'

'That River Farm's a beautiful place? Sure. I mean, it lacks a few basic essentials like a decent house, but it's good hay land with a nice view of the Mississippi, so I agreed it was a good buy.'

'And you weren't anxious to sell it to the sand miners?'

'Oh, I didn't get into that fight. That's Ethan's baby. He's hot to sell while the price is high.'

'But you didn't care about the money?'

'Oh, come on, everybody cares about money. But Owen was my buddy, so I said, "Whatever you say", and after that I just stayed out of it. Ethan and Owen would argue while the world burned down around them. It was better not to get caught in the middle between those two.'

'All right then, you've explained that very well,' Ray said, still with that strange Boy Scout smile on his face.

I found myself reciting, *trustworthy, loyal, helpful* . . .

'So what I think we should do next,' Ray said, with the ballpoint twitching above the lined paper, eager to be used, 'is go back to the beginning, and cover the same ground we've been asking everybody else to go over. Starting with this: tell me where you were every hour Saturday morning from four a.m. until noon.' He sat back, looking pleased with himself for saying that right, and then leaned forward again with an apparent afterthought. 'Oh, and who you were with that can verify that.'

Gullible Ray Bailey didn't seem to play as well with Matt Kester as he did with me. Till now, I would have described the youngest Kester's personality as 'mostly sunny'. But the longer Ray talked, the cloudier Matt's expression got. And when he heard the word 'verify', his personal weather forecast appeared to change from 'partial overcast' to 'lightning and thunder with a strong chance of hail'.

'Mom said Ethan told her you were trying to blame this terrible tragedy on the family,' Matt said, his eyes flicking suspiciously back and forth between the two of us, 'but I didn't believe it. I said, "Oh, that's just Ethan being paranoid again, I'll go in and straighten it out". But now, by God, it looks like she was right, you *are* trying to pin this on us.'

'Nobody's trying to pin—'

'So let me tell you something right now that you had better keep in mind,' he said, getting up, looking more like Ethan every minute. 'This family has been farming in Hampsted County for almost a hundred and fifty years, adding land as we went along and getting a little better off with each generation. And we didn't get where we are by being anybody's pushover, you know what I'm saying? We survived by sticking together and watching out for each other. So you better be careful who you accuse of premeditated murder, Mr Chief of Detectives,' he said, pointing at my chest. His anger had somehow slid off Ray and fastened on me. 'Because four generations of Kesters didn't maintain this good life here all this time just to let some upstart who doesn't even know what his real name is or where he was born—'

'All right,' Ray said, 'that's enough now.' He was on his feet, reaching out for Matt, who stood facing me with his fists clenched. Matt's face was white with rage, and Ray, I noticed, had the cover off his Taser.

'It's all right,' I said, keeping my voice pleasant. 'He's just looking for a way to change the subject. Everybody needs to chill now, OK?' The two of them stood over me, breathing hard. I went on sitting because hardly anybody throws a punch at a seated man in front of witnesses. After they both took a few more breaths I said, 'We're in the middle of a very busy day here, so it's fine with us if you want to end this conversation now and go home, Mr Kester. Eventually you will have to answer these questions, and you're going to like it even less if you're doing it in court.'

'We'll see about *that*, too,' Matt Kester said. He reached back, picked a beautiful white Stetson off the console behind him, and set it on his head at a jaunty angle. It looked exactly right with his belt buckle.

I couldn't help but admire the figure he cut as he walked out on us. I was in a good mood anyway, because Matt Kester, without answering any questions directly, had just told us a whole lot of useful stuff.

NINE

Ray wasn't discouraged by Matt's rejection of his Good Cop act. He said it just confirmed what he'd suspected. 'Underneath all the flash he's still a Kester, isn't he?'

'Yup,' I said. 'And you're still Ray Bailey, whose life is just one fight after another, isn't it? I'm glad to see you're not bleeding, much.

'No. Skinned in a couple of places. Nothing serious.'

'Rosie said the folks at your domestic disturbance tried to kill you.'

'My own detectives saved my life.' He kind of chortled, an unusually cheerful sound, coming from him. 'What do you think of that?'

'It's a touching folk tale. Those people did kind of destroy your shirt, though, didn't they?'

He waved away his missing buttons. 'The uniforms had it under control when we got there, but when the fighters saw fresh meat walk in . . . they just had to show all over again how tough they were. That case is going to take a while to sort out – it's an extended family and there are several badly traumatized kids.'

'But no fatalities, right?'

'I hope not. We sent a couple of kids to the hospital for check-ups. The dad's a big guy and he just went berserk.'

'Rosie said you made two arrests?'

'Yeah, there's a family friend . . . looks like he got a little too friendly with Mom. I think that's what started the fight.' Ray's expression took on the swampy gloom I have come to think of as the Full Bailey. 'No matter how hard we work we can never fix stupid, can we?'

'No. Listen, may I go back and ask a question about Matt before I forget?'

'Sure.'

'Why did you come on with all that admiration at the

beginning and try to snow him? I've never seen you behave that way before.'

'Oh . . . well.' He looked at the ceiling light. He was actually blushing! 'My wife . . . Cathy talked me into joining a Toastmasters Club. She said sometimes she thought I was too . . . reserved, I think is the word she used, for my own good.

'So I went to a meeting this week and they talked a lot about what they called *cordiality*. But the way they described cordiality, it sounded a lot more like plain old fawning and flattery, to me. And they went on and on about how it greases the wheels, gets people to loosen up and talk about themselves and then you're friends and great work gets done. I decided to try some of the things they suggested.' He managed to smile and look morose at the same time. 'Sorry about that. I shoulda known I'd screw it up.'

'Oh, you didn't. You really had him going till you got the part about verifying. Then I think he just needed a way to get out of the room, and he looked around and there I was with my face that doesn't fit the Kester world view. After that I thought you handled it very well indeed.'

'Uh-huh. Is that another little dose of Toastmasters?' He rubbed his cheeks, started over. 'Let's talk about the good news. The chief approved a rehire for Bo?'

'He wants to talk to him first but yes – if Bo convinces him he's back to stay we can have him.'

'He'll do it. Then I think I'll put him to work – Bo, I mean – on this new pile of family garbage so the rest of the crew can get back out to the farm.'

'Did Andy find the fence menders yet?'

'He said he was just starting to talk to them . . . he'll get back to it as soon as he's done chaining up Dad so he can safely take him to booking. Dad still wants to fight.'

'But Clint can get back to finding the truck driver?'

'Yeah, he's already on his way. Man, but there's so much else to do out there – we still haven't found the weapon that killed Owen, we don't know for sure how his body got to the field and we don't know where half the farm's crew were Saturday morning.'

'Also, we haven't looked in any of the buildings at that farm where the dairy is, have we?'

'No, and that barn over there's got a hayloft the size of a football field: you could hide an armory in it. Every time I think about this case I line up another two days' work.'

'So I better not mention that I'd like to talk to you about Matt's interview.' He steepled his hands in prayerful desperation. 'Never mind, I'll make notes.' I left him punching in a phone number with one hand while he buttoned a fresh shirt with the other. Back in my office, I got about three words typed on a fresh screen before my phone rang.

'Got a cancellation,' Pokey said without saying hello. 'Gave me time to finish autopsy report. You want lunch? My turn to buy.'

I so seldom hear that offer from him that I accepted at once. I thought maybe he'd found something unusual in the body of the victim and wanted to celebrate, but when he handed me the fat envelope he said, 'No hurry about digging through that, I guess. It's just what it looked like: healthy young guy got offed at point-blank range with powerful weapon.' He took his time over the menu, finally maxing out his grease and salt content with a Reuben sandwich and fries.

'You know,' I said, 'if I ate the way you do my arteries would clog up and kill me in about a year. How do you manage to graze like a goat and still look as if you ran marathons?'

He turned his palms up. 'Generations of dirt-poor Ukrainians,' he said. 'I'm descended from blockheads who learned how to thrive in any conditions.'

'I don't think that's logical but who am I to argue with success?'

'Longer I do autopsies,' he said, tapping the envelope he had just put on the table, 'more I think it's . . . what's that thing they say in poker? Yeah, luck of the draw. Most of life is luck of the draw.' He gave me the smile that makes him look like a devious fox. 'So don't worry, be happy.'

'Maybe you're right. Owen Kester, for example,' I nodded toward the envelope, 'lived a good, clean life, didn't do drugs any stronger than a little pot and got plenty of exercise. Now he's died young because somebody, what? Didn't like his attitude, I guess.'

'Mmm. Boy, nothing like hot sauerkraut, huh?' He stuck his tongue around his greasy sandwich to nab some cheese melting off the edge. 'Tell the truth, though, the guy who shot Owen

Kester probably helped him dodge another bullet down the road.'

'Whaddya mean?'

'Pretty sure I saw precursor signs of Alzheimer's in his brain. Didn't put it in my report. Would take a specialist to be sure.'

'No kidding? You can tell in advance?'

'Years in advance. Funny little folds of protein . . . I ain't no expert, so don't quote me. You might want to tell his family, though . . . if they want to be sure, they could hire a diagnostician while the victims' still in the morgue.'

'You mean,' I said, thinking about Benny, 'any one of us might be carrying the beginnings of our doom around for years and not know it?'

'Of course. Where the hell you been? Everybody carrying a lot of crap around. Just depends what triggers it. But hey, cheer up,' he punched my arm, 'you're a cop, chances are some stupid lummox gonna off you before disease can get you.'

'Oh, hey, thanks – you're a great source of comfort.'

'No trouble. Victims' brain don't matter to him now,' he said, still nudging around the edges of his testing idea, 'but in case his brothers ever gonna need 'em, you know, better treatments coming soon.'

'I'll think about it.' I remembered Anna Carrie's strange behavior in Ray's office, and her husband saying, 'She gets spells . . .' But if the brothers couldn't even accept the idea that Owen's death wasn't accidental, how hard was it going to be to convince them to test for an allele that might eat their brains?

I decided to put off trying.

'That's a real shocker, Pokey. I thought Owen Kester looked exceptionally healthy. I mean, for a guy who just bled out.'

'Now there we have expert cop's opinion worth quoting.' Pokey's smile lit up the whole booth. 'Probably oughta embroider that one on pillow.'

Bo hustled into Frank's office soon after lunch, and satisfied the chief's concerns about his intentions. He took his drubbing like a soldier when he got to Lulu's desk too. When she had made it crystal clear how little she enjoyed self-duplicating tasks, he appeared in my workspace, only slightly paler than usual. I waved away his attempt to express gratitude.

'We need you more than you need us,' I said. 'You'll soon see how much. Let's go talk to Ray.'

The two of them had had an uneasy relationship when Ray first took the helm at the newly created People Crimes. Part of the problem was Bo's somewhat anomalous position as our specialist in drug interdiction – he was in Ray's department but often working independently, and I added to the problem by giving him some orders I forgot to clear with Ray. That problem was disappearing fast in our rear-view mirror, because thanks to the explosive growth of both Rutherford and the Midwest drug trade, most of Bo's former workload had been taken over by the feds.

And right now we had to deal with this epidemic of disruptive and violent behavior that had broken out in Rutherford like a bad rash. Ray's only question for Bo today was, 'How soon can you start?' I left them prioritizing his tasks for the following morning.

I finished three pages of notes about the Matt Kester interview and added them to the case file. Ray poked his nose in my office shortly after, to say that Winnie was the first detective to finish up at the domestic carnage and he had sent her back to the farm to try again to get a list of employees from Doris.

He also reported that Clint had found the driver of the milk truck that had hit Doris's horses. 'Get this, his name is Rhodes. So of course his nickname is Dusty. I mean, why not Bumpy?' When Ray gets tired his sense of humor, never the sharpest in the building, begins to slide back to about sixth-grade level. 'Anyway, he's meeting him in Dusty's favorite after-work bar, which is that raunchy Blue Moon joint in the North End.'

'You sure Clint didn't pick it? Let's hope he comes back with all his buttons. Are Andy and Rosie . . .?'

'Still booking their prisoners.' He laughed. 'Our guys got stuck at the end of a long queue. Property crimes guys grabbed a trio of knuckleheads today. Get this: they were loading a houseful of furniture into a truck with an expired license and a broken tail light. Kevin's boys stopped to cite the driver and everybody ran away.'

'So it turned into a chase?'

'Yup. The furniture, the truck – even the two-wheeler – it was all stolen goods.'

'What's come over our peaceful village? Never mind, there seems to be a lull right now. I'm going to sidle out of here while it lasts and pick up Benny. On time for once!'

My son was sitting in a high chair, pounding on the tray and whimpering. As soon as he saw me he put up his arms, but when I picked him up he went on whining.

'I think he's teething,' Maxine said. 'I've been expecting it. He's red and swollen here in front, see?' She tried to hold his lip down so I could see, but he jerked away and yelled louder. 'Trudy's got a teething ring in the refrigerator at home – take it out and let him chew on it.'

He complained without interruption all the way home, drooling and punishing his car seat. For some time we had been mercifully free of the weeping rides homeward that he had subjected me to in his infancy, and I'd forgotten how hard it is to listen to. I'm sure we'll be glad about his fine big voice when he's older – maybe he'll win oratory prizes in high school and make me proud. But all I could think about that afternoon was that kids should come with volume control.

I pretty much tore the refrigerator apart looking for anything that might possibly be a teething ring – was it metal? Would it be in the freezer? – I'd never seen one and had no idea what I was looking for. Finally, in the butter cooler, I found an unopened blue box labeled 'teething ring'.

'Egad, Watson,' I said, 'a clue.' I pulled it out and read the cover as if it was Holy Writ. It said it was cold, harmless plastic and I should let him chew on it.

I tore the device out of its wrapper and stuck it in his mouth. Looking startled, he growled around it, spat it out a couple of times and then settled down to serious chewing. By the time his bottle was warmed up, he had a hard time deciding which pleasure he wanted more.

Then Trudy walked in and said, 'Why's all the food out of the refrigerator?'

I may have overreacted. Not to put too fine a point on it, I blew my cork.

'Would it be too much,' I asked her, 'to let me know when one of these epochal changes is coming at me? How in the flaming fuck am I supposed to know what a teething ring looks like? I never even—'

'It looks like whatever comes out of a box labeled "teething ring", usually,' she said. 'And I told you where it was when I said Maxine thought Benny looked about ready to pop a tooth.'

'You did?'

'Twice.'

'I never heard you say that.'

'I'm not surprised. You've been so obsessed lately about your precious injury-and-arrest-prone Vikings, that getting your attention is often like pulling, pardon the expression, teeth.'

She stomped upstairs, where she made a little more noise than usual changing clothes. Like mother, like son, I thought – I mean, ordinarily it isn't necessary to slam all the dresser drawers five times to get out a sweatshirt.

I held my son close while he finished his supper. Trudy came back downstairs in soft clothes and felt slippers. When she was close enough to hear I told Benny, 'You know, son, some days your father misses perfectly good opportunities to keep his trap shut.'

Trudy snorted and switched around a while, then came and touched the baby's cheek and said, 'And sometimes your mother has a bad lab day and comes home looking for a fight.' She leaned a hip into my arm. 'Is any of that beer still cold? Let's each have one and cool down.'

'Excellent idea. And if you stay close to us while you drink it, I will seize the opportunity to tell you how good you look today.' She leaned some more. 'And feel,' I said, shifting Benny a little so I could nuzzle her neck.

Benny mostly gnawed on his new plastic soothing device for the rest of the evening and made do with only occasional bouts of wailing. 'Maybe we should get another one of these things,' Trudy said, rinsing the drool-covered plastic before putting it back in the freezer for a quick chill, 'to take to Maxine's house.'

'Oh, indeed,' I said. 'Let's buy half a dozen and we'll carry them around with us in a cooler.'

By his bedtime, Trudy decreed Benny was eligible for a low-dose aspirin and I gladly fetched it.

'Just think,' she sighed as he finally quit twitching and drifted off to sleep, 'this tooth is only the first of twenty.'

'All the same to you I'm going to try not to think about that,' I said. And neither one of us did, very much, because we went to bed early and fell asleep as we pulled the covers up.

People Crimes detectives clustered around Ray's table Wednesday morning, antsy and anxious to finish debriefing and get on with the day's work.

Partly, they didn't want to talk about yesterday's domestic disturbance – it was brutal and sordid and they all felt bad about the children involved. The social workers who were getting handed most of the follow-up work grumbled that it was very hard to place kids anywhere during Thanksgiving week, and they thought better policing could have prevented much of this. My cops reported giving them level stares and saying, 'Easy for you to say.'

'Oh, hell,' I said. 'Tomorrow's Thanksgiving, isn't it? I don't have time for that this week.'

Andy, who had spent a couple of hours getting a bellowing Dad into a jail cell at the cost of several patches of his own skin, said, 'I do. I want to give thanks for good ear plugs and sturdy belly chains.'

Winnie described her late-afternoon visit to the farm. 'Doris was schooling a horse when I got there and she said, "I can't stop in the middle of this but if you can wait a few minutes I'll give you your list". So I watched.'

Winnie's normally stoical face lit up. 'She was teaching a young gelding to change leads in a straight line.'

'How do you know? You mean you ride horses too?'

'Well, not lately, but . . . when I was in grade school one of those charities decided to offer riding lessons to underprivileged kids and I qualified. My grandmother had grave doubts about letting me go out in the country and muck around with huge dangerous beasts, but I talked her into it and I really loved it.

'I have to say, though, I never thought of horseback riding as an art form before. But that Doris is so skilled – she sat on that horse like an elegant statue while he trotted around the arena several times, getting more and more – I think they call it collected. Then he cantered across the central space on the right lead and I swear I never saw her do anything, but in the middle of the ring he twitched his ears, and as if she'd thrown a switch he was leading with his left front foot. And you know what? After that smooth-as-silk move they were both sweating.'

Ray, who didn't understand or approve of Winnie's fascination with Doris, watched her carefully for a few seconds before he said, 'But then you got the list?'

She gave him her Yellow Peril look. 'Yes. Here.' She slapped a list down in front of him, and read it out for the rest of us. 'One full-time housekeeper and two part-time kitchen helpers, one foreman and three field hands on Home Farm, a manager and two full-time assistants on the dairy place, and one manager, that's Matt, on River Farm – he gets along with no help except during haying, when they hire transient workers or send somebody from the other two places.'

'So eleven and Doris makes an even dozen. And we've talked to three of them.'

'If you count Maynard, but he's evidently been fired.'

'All the more reason to talk to him some more if you can find him.'

'And there are two new employees now,' Winnie said, 'but I don't think we need to interview guards, do you?'

'If they just got there? No. What are they guarding?'

'Oh . . . Doris started thinking about the "new vulnerabilities" – I think that's how she said it. She's worried that all the stories in the paper about crimes at the farm will attract other bad people – that people will start thinking she's just a sitting duck out there. Henry's worried about it too, so they've hired two people from a security service to walk around the place at night. Watching for prowlers is how she says it. I suppose she likes that better than calling them murderers.'

'Call it whatever she likes, I'm glad she's started to go proactive. I've been worrying about it too. Now, back to our twelve current employees. Can you and Rosie do them today?'

They both nodded happily – Winnie and Rosie love working together. I once asked Rosie why and she said, 'We get the job done with no fuss. People see two small women, look right past the shields and think, "Harmless". They let their guard down and tell us stuff.'

People would be well-advised to put their guards back up.

Rosie has a black belt in Tai Kwon Do: she can break a board with her foot. Winnie does kick-boxing and runs marathons and has a wall full of swimming medals. It's good they get along and don't compete with each other.

'There's another curious thing that keeps happening to me on that farm,' Winnie said. 'That son of Doris's, the one who doesn't talk?'

'Yeah, what about him?'

'Maybe it's just because of my grandmother,' she said. 'We didn't have very many words in common, so we learned to communicate a lot with body language. And after I noticed that boy Alan following me around . . . he wasn't getting in my way or anything, just kind of shadowing . . . I sort of started talking to him with my eyes, and he caught right on to that.'

'How do you know?'

'He showed me . . . a couple of things.'

'What things?'

'He saw me looking in the horse stalls, you know . . . I was wondering how the hay gets delivered to the horses, they all had full racks . . . and he climbed up on one and pushed open a trapdoor, so I could see there's a chute that comes down from the haymow. I think he knows how that whole place works.'

'Well, good,' Ray said. 'Did he show you the haymow, too?'

'No, but I think I can get him to.'

'OK,' Ray said, not very interested. He's told me lately he thinks Winnie's approach to detective work is a little too 'woo-woo', that 'she seems to rely on instinct too much'.

'Also on being incredibly fast and strong,' I said, 'think how she ran into that river last spring to rescue Rosie.'

'Yeah, that was something, all right. I'd like her to be a little more . . . systematic, though.'

'Give her time,' I said. 'The system itself will teach her that.'

Now he said, a little impatient, 'Who's next?'

Clint said, 'I found my milk hauler. His name is Dusty Rhodes, can you beat that?' Clint's smile indicated he liked Dusty almost as much as Maynard. 'He plays bass guitar in a country band. He's had five wives and he's not exactly sure how many children he can legitimately claim. Says he knows every roadhouse and honky-tonk between here and the Florida panhandle. His information's a little stale on the saloons, though, because this last wife looks like a keeper so he's trying to hang onto this day job and stay home nights.'

Ray said, with exaggerated patience, 'Did you get around to talking about the accident at all?'

'Sure. He feels really bad about it, because he likes animals. And the people on that farm, he said, were very likeable too. They understood the horses were just crossing the road in the dark, so when he came around that sharp curve by the gate he had no time to stop. He drives that route regularly and knows the road, but that morning he had no good choices.'

'The time – did you get a timeline for all this?'

'Absolutely. That was the easy part, because Dusty's company requires them to stay in touch electronically and report any glitches as soon as they happen. He just brought up his email and showed me. He sent word about hitting the horses at four-eleven a.m. and reported he was on his way again at five-twenty-five a.m.'

'And that's all going to be in your field notes?'

'You got it.'

'OK. About the sheriff's deputy—'

'I got a date with him, I'm going there next. Steve Hanrahan, did I tell you that?' He looked at his watch. 'I should be back by ten o'clock so whatever you want after that, I can do it.'

'Good. Now, Andy?'

'Back to the farm. I found Charlie and Elmer yesterday – they're willing to talk.' He showed us his you-can't-make-this-up smile. 'They're more than happy to have me come back today. They want to hear all about the fight we were called away to.'

'Fine. Keep them entertained and pick their brains.' Ray looked around the table. 'Do we all see a connection between the horse accident and Owen's death?'

'Sure,' Andy said, 'the fence was cut. Somebody wanted all hands out on the road.' All the detectives nodded.

'I agree,' Ray said. 'I thought at first we should look for a robbery at one of the farms and consider Owen's death an unintended consequence. But I asked Doris to have her most trusted hands looking for missing items and they haven't reported anything.' He frowned. 'If this was a plan, though, it's hard to see – you'd think having everybody up running around would make it impossible to plan anything. Well,' he slapped his notebook shut and stood up, 'let's roll.'

When they had all charged out, Ray said he was going to read through the case history he'd compiled so far, make lists for the next few days' work and see if he could spot a clever plan in there somewhere.

I was due at a planning meeting with the chief and the city council, an event I approach with about the same enthusiasm I give to a root canal. What's the use planning for a department where anything can happen and usually does? But I was there to back up the chief in defense of our budget, about which the city fathers have a favorite verb: cut. So I went along and blew away an hour explaining why police cars need gas and why law enforcement weapons work best with frequent testing and plenty of ammo. Before it was over, I had begun to long for a teething ring.

Back at my desk, I encountered the usual blinking phone, fought down an impulse to ignore it for a while and then was glad I answered, because Ray's voice on the tape sounded anxious. 'I've got two things happening at once. Can you help me?'

I trotted right over, glad of a chance to do something useful with the rest of my morning.

'Rosie called from the farm,' he said. 'Said all hell's breaking loose out there. Doris and Matt are having a fight.'

'Doris and— I thought they were the two who got along.'

'I think they did till now. But yesterday when she fired that hand that Clint likes so much – what's his name? Maynard – apparently he went running to Matt and Matt hired him back. I guess Matt thought he could keep him hidden at River Farm, but Doris sent one of the other hands, Elmer, over there for a load of hay and this morning she heard Elmer laughing, telling one of her kitchen helpers, "Guess who showed up to help me load that hay!" Now she's got Matt on the phone telling him – Rosie says you can hear her all over the farm – "I'm not going to have this!" Doris says Maynard is going to go, that's all there is to it, and if Matt interferes with her again he's going to go too.'

'Wow.'

'Yeah, wow is right. Rosie said, "What do you want us to do?

Nobody wants to talk to us right now; they're all afraid of saying something that will get them fired."

'And just then LeeAnn sticks her head in and says Henry Kester just called her, said he was on his way in here, and hung up. Remember how he had to take his wife home all of a sudden but he said he'd be back? Well, today he's coming back.

'And right after *that* Clint called and said the fight is spreading to the help now. He thinks I better send a couple more cops out there because they might need some help. But you know Henry Kester is not going to take kindly to waiting. So could you talk to him? I know he's not easy, but I'd like to go out to that farm, see for myself what's shaking.'

'Of course,' I said. 'Go ahead. Don't worry about Henry,' I told his gloomier-than-usual face. 'I've been yelled at before.'

But Henry Kester, when he walked slowly off the elevator, did not seem at all aggressive. Grief had hollowed him out. He looked like a dry husk that any wind might topple.

I explained that Ray had been called away. I made up an errand since I didn't want to tell him my chief investigative officer was hurrying to a fight at his farm.

He just asked quietly, 'You going to tell me what happened to my boy?'

'I'll tell you what we know,' I said. 'It's not enough yet.'

'Fair enough,' he said, and sat down in my visitor's chair. He was too big for it, overlapped it, shrugged his jacket and shuffled his feet till he got settled.

I thought it would be too cruel to put him on one of the tiny seats in an interview room, so I decided I could live without the video and turned on my desk recorder. 'I have to record this conversation, OK?'

He flapped a hand at it indifferently and said, 'Fine.'

I explained to him the curious coincidence by which I happened to be at the goose-hunting field on the day Owen's body was found there. Then I took him carefully through the autopsy that showed us the birdshot in his son's body was not the steel shot that waterfowl hunters were allowed to use, and reviewed as gently as I could what we'd told him before – the evidence that indicated the body had been moved.

He stayed with me through all of it, squinting and wincing

here and there but not turning away – determined to learn as much of the truth as he could.

My next news was the toughest, about Rosie remembering the odd dimpling of hides in the walk-in cooler, how they went back and found trace remnants of blood and tissue in the floor drain that were being tested as we spoke. 'We haven't got the DNA report back yet, but we think maybe at least some of it is Owen's blood.'

'He got killed right there in his own cooler?'

'We think so. We haven't proved it.'

'And even if you prove it . . . that won't tell you who killed him, will it?'

'Not unless the killer did some of the bleeding. Or a lot of sweating, which is possible, but then – a lot of people use that workroom, right? So it's going to be pretty hard to prove anything from sweat.'

'What else then?'

'Don't know yet.'

Perversely that answer perked him up a little. He gave me an ironic half-smile and said, 'I do like an honest answer.'

'Me too,' I said. 'You ready to answer a few of my questions?'

'Sure.'

'Why would anybody cut your fence?'

'Boy, that really beats me. We're all friends around here.'

'You haven't had previous incidents of mischief?'

'No, no. Well, some accidents lately, but . . . accidents happen on farms.'

'Got any grudge fights going?'

'No. And the kids don't, I asked Doris. I mean – we've got good neighbors, nobody's mad at anybody.'

'OK. Try this one: could Owen have enemies you don't know about?'

He lifted his hands, turned them palms up, shook his head. 'Up until the last couple years, I would have told you nobody in the world could possibly want to see anything bad happen to Owen. I mean, he was the one that kind of smoothed things over for all of us. Anna Carrie's right about that part: he was the easiest one to raise and he's always been the one that's willing to help.'

'But something's changed in the last couple of years?'

'Them damn sand miners. You know about this silica sand craze that's happening?'

'I heard a few things. It's for fracking?'

'It is now. Always been just a little getting dug up for glass, little two-bit sand-and-gravel yards around, no problem. Then they found that big deposit of oil and gas in North Dakota. Just what we need, everybody said, so we can quit importing so much.

'But the catch is, the oil's so far below the surface and trapped in the rock. Don't ask me how they know that but they say they do, and so far everything they said they knew has proved out. So they have to drill this deep hole, then go sideways a lot more, and pump down a slurry of sand and water and a couple chemicals. It fractures the rock and the oil bubbles up.'

'Sounds simple but I don't suppose it is.'

'Good thing it ain't up to me to figure it out is what I said. But what they say is, "Don't worry, we know what we're doing".'

'Does that reassure you?'

His eyebrows did a little dance. 'Every time they say it I think about General Custer galloping into the Indian camp yelling, "We got 'em now, boys!"'

I was beginning to wonder how I was going to explain to Ray that I had started to like Henry Kester.

'But that's all out in the Dakotas. Where we come in is where the sand gets dug up. Because it turns out half of Wisconsin, and parts of Minnesota including our nice little hayfield, sits on top of tons of that silica sand they like so much to put in the slurry, and there's two or three companies competing to bid on our land.

'And to begin with, I was all for it. I mean, it's so much money . . . you would not believe. Millions of dollars. For sand!' He laughed, a shocking sound coming out of his tragic face.

'I've worried about money every day of my life. I mean, farmers – it's what we do: work our butts off and worry about money. If it don't rain enough, or it rains too much, or frost comes early – the whole crop depends on the weather, and who knows what that's going to do? To think about never having to worry about money again – I said I can't imagine it but I'm willing to try.

'But then Owen started saying, "Think what you're talking

about doing – turning our beautiful River Farm into a sand pit". But Ethan said, "Come on, you can't turn your back on that much money".

'"Sure I can", Owen said. "Money don't last. You know we wouldn't keep it. We'd just buy more land and more stock and have bigger worries. But once the flyway and River Farm are gone, they're gone forever".

'Then Ethan said, "But maybe once an opportunity's lost it's lost forever too. And that's just an ignorant primitive thing to say, that money don't last. Money can be turned into beautiful invest-ments that can do a world of good". And Owen just sneered and said, "Oh, yeah, we've just seen how beautiful investments can be. Wall Street can make those disappear in a blink".'

I said, 'So the family fight went on and on.'

'You bet. They're both smart, those two, and they've been arguing all their lives; they've had lots of practice. Sometimes I think it's their favorite thing to do.' He peered at me sadly over his wall of sorrow. 'In the end Owen said, "Over my dead body will anybody turn my beautiful River Farm into a sand pit". I think of that about ten times a day now. That he said that, and now he's dead.' He looked at his hands, unable to meet my eyes.

'Then the county passed a moratorium against sand mining for the next eighteen months while they study the issues, and that stifled the argument for a while.

'But we all know moratoriums don't last long. There'll be lots of testifying on both sides but in the end . . . so many people want this to happen for so many reasons, you know . . . they'll be talking about patriotism pretty soon and how this can keep us out of trouble in the Middle East . . . all that stuff. But really, it's the money calling. So some counties will go for it, and then the others will say, "Well, why should we lose out if it's going to happen anyway?" And in end the whole country will go for it; no president can hold out against the pressure that's going to build up to get at that oil . . . it's just too . . . *attractive.*'

It was such an unlikely word to come out of his mouth, I watched him and wondered who'd put it there.

'I don't care about the damn money anymore; it won't bring Owen back so how can I enjoy it? All I want now is for you to figure out this terrible crime and prove that Ethan didn't do it.'

'Is that what you're afraid of? That Ethan did it?'

'What? No. God, no.'

'But you said—'

'I know he didn't do it. But I can't *prove* it. And every day we walk around each other now, with this terrible thing between us that we can't even mention. Because anybody with half an eye can see that Ethan had the most to gain. Owen was the one standing in the way of the money. And he was stubborn as a post, he would never change.'

'But you don't believe Ethan would kill him.'

'Never. I raised them both, I know them as well as I know myself. My son's ambitious, like all the Kesters that came before him, but he would never kill his brother. Never. But you fellas in here with the labs and all, you're the only ones that can prove it.'

Ah, such faith in science. I wanted to say, 'Oh, why aren't they all like you?' But then on second thought, no, let's not make any more Kesters.

'We're going try, Mr Kester,' I told him. 'We'll use everything we've got, believe me.' I thought of telling him how highly skilled our lab people are, but I was afraid he might start talking about Custer again.

'One more thing before you leave,' I said.

'Sure.' He was in no hurry. Kind of enjoying the talk, I thought. But I knew about the fight that was waiting for him at his farm, and I thought before he got bogged down in the next big mess, maybe there'd be time for me to fill in one more piece of family lore.

'What did Matt do to you? Before?'

'Oh . . . well.' He shook his head, shuffled his feet.

'Nobody ever wants to talk about it,' I said. 'But you can't seem to let it go, either. What was it?'

He turned sideways in his chair and told it to the wall. 'He stole from us.'

'Stole what?'

'Money and a new pickup, with a nearly new horse trailer on behind, and my best roping horse. And what was worse, he made a fool of me in public so everybody knew.'

I waited. After he'd wrestled with his little chair a while longer, he told me the story. 'It was June, first cutting of hay. Fourteen years ago. Or fifteen? The weather was perfect for once. Matt wanted to go to the rodeo at the Preston fair. I said no, we got hay to put up. He begged me, "Please, just let me go Saturday, there's a couple of events I know I can win if you let me take ol' Brownie". Said he'd be home Saturday night or Sunday morning for sure and go right to work. I finally gave in but I said, "You be careful with Brownie, he's the best I got".

'Hot Sunday, the other two boys and me sweating all day in the field and Matt never showed. Evening, I called the Fairgrounds in Preston, got the events manager on the phone. He looked up the records, said no Matt Kester registered for any events here this weekend.

'I called the sheriff, put a tracer on the truck. They found him in Kansas City. He had planned the whole thing, charged a full tank of gas and wrote a couple of checks for cash on his way out of town.

'Sheriff said, "You want me to bring him back?" I said, "No, leave him be". I figured that he'd been planning to teach me this lesson for some time and I was probably lucky it didn't cost me more. But I told the boys, "This is it – he don't get to hurt us twice".

'But Anna Carrie, she just couldn't stop grieving over losing her boy. Had to find him – got help from her sisters, old school chums, I don't know what-all. After she got an address she sent him money sometimes, didn't think I knew but of course I did, it was all over her face every time. You want to make a killing at poker some time, get Anna Carrie into the game.

'Both boys got married, we jogged along adding this, adding that. Got into blooded cows and added a whole adjacent farm to put the dairy on – that was a stretch. Ethan said we should have a corporation, declare shares – we had our biggest fight then, when Doris insisted on her shares. I was just as shocked as Anna Carrie at first but in the end I saw she was right. As Charlie Blaise says, she works harder than anybody and she's good at all the jobs – what more do you want? Helluva lot better than Ethan's wife with her nose in the air – she won't even come out to the farm. We have to go to her house on her schedule if we want to see Ethan's boys.

'Anyhow, we got the dairy going along good and then three years ago Ethan started talking about this tidy little farm near the Mississippi he thought we should buy, grow the hay down there and plant more corn up here. It made sense and as soon as Owen saw that River Farm he just fell in love with the place. So I said, "I guess we can swing it". Ethan drew up the contract – everything's going according to plan – and then one day there's Matt with his hand out, smiling, and Anna Carrie's saying, "Look who's here".

'She really snuck a whizzer on me that time. Ethan didn't like it at first but she worked on him till he said, "Oh, well, how much harm can he do to a few hayfields?" And Owen said, "It makes Mom happy and where's the harm?" One of those rare times they agreed about something and I didn't even get to enjoy it. I said, "I'm just gonna say it once but mark my words: if you let him stay around you better watch your back". But my wife tut-tutted me till I quit talking about it.

'But now, see where we are? We're stuck with him and we don't have Owen to run interference for us anymore.' He sat still for a long time, shaking his head. When he met my eyes at last he said, 'Find out who killed Owen, will you?'

He made his sad way out of the station. I thought of telling him he should call Doris before he went home, but then I thought, Hell, she's probably calling him every ten minutes, he'll get the news soon enough.

I ducked out to a drug store on my lunch hour, bought a couple of teething rings and took them to Maxine's house so her ears could have a rest from Ben's noise. But he wasn't yelling when I got there – he was having a snooze on a bed-pad on the floor while two small boys I'd never seen before built a Lego castle around him.

One of the charms of Maxine's house is that you're likely to come upon small bodies anywhere – sometimes awake and sometimes not, so you have to watch where you step. The kids concentrate on the toys and take a constantly shifting slate of playmates in stride.

If you sit still a minute they'll use you for a spare seat, a backrest, bookshelves – today they had made my sleeping son into the mountain in front of their castle. Several action figures were pulling guard duty on the mountain, propped on his terry sleepers, gently rising and falling as he breathed.

I said, 'How'd you get him quieted down?'

Maxine stuck the teething rings in the refrigerator, still in their boxes, and said, 'I think his tooth came through this morning. He was very fretful and then he got quiet and looked tired. So I rocked him a while and he fell asleep. I've got chili on the stove, you want some?'

'If you've got enough.'

'Sure. The boys and I have had ours.'

'New kids?'

'Three days a week while their mother takes some classes. My pre-schoolers will be here in an hour or so, and Eddy gets home on the bus about four.' Eddy is her foster son, another one of Maxine's rescues after a family disaster. 'I don't see Nelly much since Bo quit his job.'

'You'll be getting her back, I guess. We just re-hired him after his new job went south.' Nelly is the amazingly poised, charming daughter Bo somehow managed to raise while his tragically addicted wife disappeared into her cocaine habit. A striking feature of Bo Dooley's striving life is that luck has a hard time finding him. I'm hoping we can avoid any conflicts on the job so he can stay close to Rosie, who even if she seems to me to be about as cuddly as a piranha, is totally devoted to Bo.

Maxine sipped coffee while she watched me crunch crackers into chili and said, as casual as if it was regular news, 'I've been doing some Internet searches.'

'Oh? Since when do you go roaming in cyberspace?' She has an ancient computer I gave her when we upgraded at home. I thought she wanted it mostly to trade emails with her daughter.

'I don't even know what that means. But I think I may have located the placement service that assigned you to your first foster mother. I sent a couple of queries.'

'You did? Maxine, you fox, I've never known you to – you always claim to be so baffled by technology.'

'Oh . . . well.' She looked inscrutable for a few seconds and then laughed. 'I am! But on Google it's so simple . . . you just type in the words you're thinking, and something's going to come up. Maybe not what you're looking for, but sometimes better stuff that you never thought of.'

'That's an interesting search plan. I must try that.'

'Yes, well, I know I'm a . . . what's that Eddy says? A dork. But I'm willing to try most new things, if they don't have claws.'

'You're not a dork. Don't let anybody tell you that.'

She smiled. 'OK. Is mincemeat pie good for Thanksgiving?'

'Perfect.' I kissed her cheek. She smelled like talcum and onions. 'I gotta go.'

Ray hailed me from the door of his office before I even got into mine. He was talking on the phone but waved me in and kept me there with one pointing finger while he said, 'Yeah. Yeah. Can I call you back? Good.'

He hung up and said, 'I think we just got a fresh body.'

TEN

Of the dozen questions needing immediate answers, I picked the most obvious, 'Where?'

'That's what's giving him fits. It's in his car.'

'Whose car?'

'Ethan's. Parked behind his office in his marked space. When he came down just now to go to lunch there was a man sitting in the passenger's seat. He opened the door and the man fell out on the asphalt and a shotgun fell out on top of him. It must have been leaning on him, Ethan says. He said he's sure he's dead because he's very cold and not breathing but he called nine-one-one and asked them to send an ambulance, and what did I advise him to do next?'

Bewildered by the way his pronouns were stacking up, I put my hand up like a traffic cop and said, 'What did you say?'

'Told Ethan he did fine and now he should tell me his address so I could send somebody to help him. Turns out his office is two blocks from Pokey's so I called him . . .'

'Pokey?'

'Yes. Isn't that who I said? Told Pokey what Ethan said and asked him to see if he could beat the ambulance over there. Because you know how long we'll all be at this if an ambulance takes that dead guy to the hospital? Midnight, at least.'

Ray paused, a little winded. I said, 'OK, what's the problem?'

'Right now there's nobody here but me and I hate to call anybody off the farm because they all got God knows enough to do where they are. So could you anchor this end while I run over there? Are you free this afternoon?'

'If I've got anything I'll cancel it. Go ahead.'

Ray charged down the stairs and out the door. I told LeeAnn I was taking all the calls for People Crimes, unlocked my office, and got a notebook ready to take a lot of notes. I thought I'd be flooded with anxious calls from the detectives on the farm, but either they were staying afloat on their own or they were too overwhelmed to talk. While I waited to find out which, I got all my emails answered. I was down to leafing through yesterday's phone messages when Kevin Evjan poked his head in my door. He frowned at my empty room, said, 'God, nothing's happening over here, either', and slumped into my visitors' chair.

The genes of the sergeant who runs Property Crimes section are split evenly between his Irish mother and Norwegian father. Somehow, he got all the best of both. The result is a tall, confident Nordic type, much handsomer than anybody has a right to be. As a result of all that good fortune, underneath his surface charm he's even happier than he usually lets on. A bachelor, he scores easily and often with the ladies of his choice, so he radiates optimism. Ray, of course, can't stand him.

I picked him to run Property Crimes because I guessed, rightly, that his high self-esteem would support him during the endless slog of stolen autos, sports gear and electronics that his section must record. We describe so much and find so little! You look at the lists and say, 'Why are people so damn rotten?' Alternate that with 'Bugger all' and you've nailed the attitude for a Property Crimes detective. Kevin just smiles and keeps up his stats.

I said, 'Heard you found some bad guys carting off a houseful of stuff.'

'My keen-eyed detectives noticed that their truck license was expired and one tire looked a little flat, and said, "Gosh, fellas, what kind of a moving company is that?" '

'So they stopped to chat.'

'Yes. To write a ticket actually, but then everybody ran away, so they got to play Chase-the-Thief instead. I have to say, these idiots came along just in time. That cold snap we had at the first of the month sent a lot of homeless guys scurrying for the bus station, I think. Burglaries are down, vandalism's all but vanished. In terms of job security, this month has been a disaster.'

'A disaster with no overtime, I love it. Been thinking maybe I should transfer a couple of your guys to People Crimes for a few days – *they've* got plenty to do.'

'Would you? Could you? Come to think of it, how about me? Give me a chance to broaden my horizons.'

'And work for Ray Bailey?'

'Why not? I'm flexible. I mean, I wouldn't have to actually

take ord—' He paused with his mouth open, closed it before anything flew in and said, 'No, I guess that wouldn't work.' He recrossed his legs and said, 'OK, which one of my guys are you after? Since that's obviously your devious plan.'

'You came to see me, remember? And now you're conducting this dialogue with yourself and doing just fine on your own.' I picked up a handful of pens and dumped them in their mug. 'I'm just here to observe.'

'I mean, you won't keep him over there forever, will you? Because as soon as things get back to normal . . . what particular skills are you looking for?'

'They've got a lot of interviews to do.'

'Ben Kellogg then. He's a whiz at interviews, nails them with his eyes and just burrows in.'

'Kevin, he's hard of hearing and about two months from retirement, come on.'

'Oh, well, picky picky. How about Jimmy Vee? I know his expertise is mostly automotive but—'

'Jaime Valenzuela knows the insides of every car made in the world in the last twenty years. And his accent makes him perfect for interviewing any recently arrived tourist from south of the border who accidentally got in the wrong car by mistake after he popped the lock with the Slim Jim tool he just happened to be carrying. Jimmy Vee is not ideal for the jobs I have right now. Who else you got?'

'Jake, what are you looking for, your dream date?'

'Well . . . we need to search some records now too. You got anybody good at that?'

'Oh. Then you should take Josh Felder – he's a real nerd.'

'Is he free? Can you spare him?'

'This week I can spare anybody. But if we get another rash of break-ins like we got over the Easter holidays, I'll be yelling to reclaim him, don't forget.'

'I won't. Can he start tomorrow?'

He stared. 'Jake, tomorrow is Thanksgiving.'

'Oh, that's right. Damn, I keep forgetting. Rats! We've got about a hundred people coming to eat. Do you realize how many loaves of stale bread I have to break up? I don't have time to give thanks!'

'Really, Jake.' Kevin Evjan shook his head sadly. 'Where would this country be if everybody had your attitude?'

'Free of this silly habit of basing an entire national holiday on turkey gravy, for one thing. Can Josh start Friday morning?'

'You bet. Can you remember all the words to the Thanksgiving hymn? Come on, all together now . . .' He went out air-conducting his own orchestra, singing in his pleasing baritone, 'We gather together to ask the Lord's blessing . . .'

Kevin knows all the coolest ways to rub your nose in it.

Ray phoned in from time to time, told me Pokey was there, had determined the man on the asphalt was in fact plenty dead, and turned the ambulance around as it drove into the lot. He had commandeered a couple of uniforms to string crime scene tape and help him keep people away, and called the lab for a couple of techies to come do the prelims.

'Lab people are slow today,' Ray said, 'so I took a bunch of pictures in case we have to move him before they— Oh, here's a couple of them now.'

When he phoned again, an hour-and-a-half later, the lab crew had come and gone. Pokey had finished his preliminary exams and ridden away with the body to the morgue, and Ray said, 'I'm coming back to the station now. I want Ethan to follow me in – I offered him a ride because we had to impound his car, of course. But his uncle insists on bringing him to the station and coming back for him later. These people like to show their independence, don't they?'

'Oh, yes. It's who they are.'

'Right. So will you get an interview room ready? Ethan's pretty unnerved and while he's still feeling that way I want to ask him some questions and get his answers on a disk. Because this is a freaky odd thing that's happened here and he's the only key we have to whatever the hell it is.'

LeeAnn helped me, got the video recorders loaded and the camera set. We set up the monitor so she could observe from outside if nobody else got back in time.

Ray came hurrying in, wearing surgical gloves, and dropped a lot of records and gear – hurriedly, carelessly – in his office. Then, very carefully, he laid a shotgun on his conference table. I watched him silently, since he seemed too concentrated to interrupt. He hooked his camera up to the computer on the meeting-room table, scrolled until he found a picture he liked and fiddled with it till he got the clarity he wanted. When the dead face of a fortyish white man showed clearly on his monitor he said, 'Jake, you know this man?'

'No. Is that the victim you just sent to the morgue?'

'Yes.'

While we gathered up legal pads, pens and a box of tissues, he told me about his visit to the law offices. He had found Ethan miserably prowling the parking lot between Pokey's Jeep and his own car, where Pokey was kneeling over the victim.

He kept saying "I don't know what to *do*". Wringing his hands as if indecision was the worst calamity he could imagine.'

'Well, it might be, for a Kester,' I said.

'Maybe so. He said, "It didn't seem right to leave him lying out like that, uncovered, but they say you're not supposed to touch anything till the coroner . . . God, I hope I did the right things".

'I told him, "Go back in your office, I got this". And he did, right away – he was glad to get away. And of course it was a lot easier out there with him out of the way.'

The victim had certainly not been shot by the weapon that fell out of the car with him – in fact, on a preliminary examination there was no sign of any gunshot at all, that Pokey could see. He had no other wounds, either – he hadn't been bleeding.

'Petechiae in his eyes and mouth indicated that he might have suffocated – Pokey'll tell me more about that later,' Ray said. 'Otherwise . . . could be anything that . . . kills people without leaving any marks.' Big shrug. 'I don't know.'

'The gun, though . . . wait a minute.' He pulled up the Kester case file and scrolled through. When he found the right place in the file he pointed at the gun on the table, and said, 'Read me the numbers.'

I squinted under the light, and found the number stamped above the trigger guard. '629741V.'

'Bingo.' His eyes were shining.

'What?'

'This is the shotgun Doris Kester said was missing from the gun cabinet in the farmhouse.'

'No shit? Oh, Ray.'

'Yes.'

'You know what this means? If this gun fired the shot Pokey took out of Owen's body . . .'

'Yeah. Ethan's in the weeds.'

'Except why was it in a car with a dead man who didn't get shot with it?'

'Maybe he intended to shoot somebody.'

'Hell, maybe he *did* shoot somebody. Ray, did you bag his hands?'

'Of course.' He looked offended, rightly so in a way, but am I going to be the top dick who forgot to ask? Never. Nobody's ever going to complain if we test and find nothing. If we forget to test, even if the victim never fired a shot in his life, we can well and truly get screwed to the wall.

'Pokey didn't waste any time, man, he just made the calls.' The many phone calls necessary to get a crime scene organized, Ray meant. 'Wednesday afternoon, we were afraid everybody might be trying to get away early, so we wanted to get that body put away.'

'Good call. Some of those morgue guys can get testy if you call them back in on a holiday.'

'True that. And Pokey's good at getting everybody mobilized, you know, so before long the meat wagon was rolling out of there and I went into Ethan's law office to see if he was ready to talk.

'Nice big suite of offices, busy secretaries scurrying around, and these two old gents – they're both his uncles, did you know that? – in there, worried, in front of their walls of books. Ethan was stretched out in a big leather chair in one of their offices, very white, moaning and shaking. He'd been hurling in one of the lavatories. They were trying to find out what was wrong with him.

'I leaned over him and said, "Pull yourself together. We got work to do". And for once, he didn't object. He seemed almost anxious to talk.'

LeeAnn said, 'Ray, your man's here. Shall I—'

'Put him in the interview room, please. Get him a glass and some water? Tell him we'll be right there.' He met my eyes. 'Do you love this? Ethan Kester *wants* to talk to me?'

'Let's go help him with that.'

Ethan was perched on the little seat, drinking the last of a big glass of water. He set the glass down and carefully poured more out of the pitcher LeeAnn had left for him. He licked his lips and said, 'I don't know why I'm so thirsty.' He had stopped shaking, but all his arrogance was gone.

Ray said, 'Here we go now – I want Jake to hear the story from the beginning. You drove your car to work this morning at . . . what time?'

'Few minutes after six. Like always.'

'And parked it in your spot behind the building there, where I found you, is that right?'

'Just as I always do. Yes.'

'And you never went near it again until near one o'clock when you were going to lunch?'

'Well . . . that's right, but—' He was starting to look queasy again, like there might be more to come up.

'Take it easy, now,' I said. 'Think about it. Was it sitting in the lot all morning or wasn't it?'

'Well, no, that's what I remembered on the way down here. But I don't want you to think Nicole had anything to do with . . .'

'Who's Nicole?'

'My wife. She just needed to put her car in the shop today and then . . . Thanksgiving . . . she needed to run some errands. She had my car back before lunch, just as she promised. That really has nothing to do with . . . it's just a coincidence.'

'Tell us about it anyway,' I said. 'Your wife phoned, did she? And said what?'

'Said, "My car's getting its window fixed and I just remembered I need sweet potatoes and those little pearl onions. My mother will have a fit if I don't have creamed onions the way she always fixed them". Something like that.'

'Very good,' I said, thinking it probably took a lawyer to remember details like that. 'So she came and got the keys from you?' He was shaking his head. 'What then?'

'She has her own set of keys for everything. We both do. She said, "I'll send one of the yard men for the car", and hung up, and I remembered she had a crew there today, trimming the trees and bushes. So I went back to work and forgot about it because Nicole, you know, is quite capable of arranging things to suit herself.' The usual whiff of rancor blew through as he talked about his wife, and for a moment he sounded restored.

'Keep going,' Ray said, 'you came down for lunch and the car was back, just as she promised.'

'But with a man I didn't know sitting in the passenger's seat.'

'You're sure you never saw him before?'

'To tell you the truth he looked vaguely familiar, but I couldn't place him. Maybe he's somebody who's worked for one of us, a lot of people have. Anyway, he had no business sitting in my car, so I opened the door to tell him to get out of there, and—'

'It wasn't locked?'

'No. Is that a clue?' His health was coming back fast; he got great contempt into his voice and upper lip when he asked that question. 'I pulled it open and—'

'You opened the door for a man who was holding a gun?'

'He wasn't holding it. I didn't see the gun until I opened the door and he began to fall out. Then I tried to close it again quickly, but I couldn't because . . . he must have been leaning against it—'

'The gun?'

'No, the door, the door! As soon as I opened the door he began to fall out, and the gun was coming out with him . . . sort of on top of him. And this is where . . .' Looking miserable, he said, 'Oh, God, I should have told you this before.' It burst out of him like an eruption.

'What?'

'I told you I never touched him but that isn't exactly true. His head and shoulders fell sideways out of the car and the gun slid out on top of him, but . . . see, he didn't come all the way *out*. He was hanging upside down with his feet in the car and I didn't know – how could I know? – whether he was dead or . . . I thought he might be injured, or drunk, and he certainly shouldn't be hanging there like that, so I – I tried to pick him up to put him back in. But he was so *heavy* and kind of . . . *slidey* . . . if people aren't helping they're very hard to pick up, did you know that?'

Ray and I both nodded.

'Yes, I suppose you would know that. Policemen know all kinds of wretched things, don't they? Anyway, without thinking I finally just pulled him all the way out, so at least he could be lying flat. And so I suppose' – he was sweating now and almost weeping – 'I bet those lab people are going to find my DNA all over him, aren't they? And then think I killed him!'

'That's quite a stretch. Why would anybody think you killed a man you don't even know?'

'Because of Owen! Everybody thinks I killed Owen and now they're going to think I'm some kind of a crazy . . . Hannibal Lector or something, just killing people for the fun of it.'

I wanted to reassure him that nobody would ever think he did anything just for the fun of it, but I suppressed that thought and asked him, 'Have you talked to your wife since you found the man in your car?'

'No. Why? You think I should have phoned and asked her, "Oh, by the way, love, did you leave a body in my car?"'

It was wonderful to see what malice did for him. He sounded almost like his old self.

Ray, not amused, said, 'Maybe not, but I'd like to talk to her about it. Let me have her number.'

Ethan shoved his card across the little table. 'The bottom one of those home numbers is the only one she'll answer. But I strongly advise against calling her this afternoon, Detective. She'll be having her annual cream sauce tantrum about now.'

Ray's phone rang. He excused himself and went outside to answer it, came back in and said, 'Will you excuse us for a minute, please, Mr Kester?' He nodded to me and we stepped outside.

'His uncle's here to pick him up. We need to decide right now if we have enough to arrest this guy.'

'It's all very circumstantial, isn't it? And I don't read him as a flight risk at all. Why don't we squeeze his toes a little and let him go, see what we come up with in the next few days?'

'That's what I think too. And then . . . You know it's almost four-thirty? We'll have crews back in here in a few minutes. And as soon as we get them debriefed,' he said, in a voice that expressed my feelings exactly, 'I guess we all have to face Thanksgiving, ready or not.'

Ray went back inside and let Ethan sweat for a few more minutes, made him beg for his freedom over Thanksgiving and promise that he would not even think about leaving town.

'If you do,' Ray said, 'I'll put an ankle bracelet on you and you can check in with my office twice a week till this case is settled.'

While he finished up with Ethan, I went out and had a word with Jonas Robbins. He was courteous as ever but 'very distressed about this bizarre cluster of misfortunes that's being visited on our family'. He hoped we could quickly find whatever 'pernicious agency' seemed to be 'bent on doing us harm'. With the serenity I'd begun to recognize as breathtaking self-confidence, he simply assumed no one could possibly suspect a Robbins or Kester of criminal intent.

In front of his uncle, we thanked a pale and quiet Ethan for his help. Then Jonas tucked him, almost literally, under his wing, and wafted him out of there on clouds of self-assurance. *The poor sod has a lot to measure up to*, I thought as I watched Ethan trying to grow more magisterial in his uncle's shadow.

Ray never really got around to debriefing his detectives about what they found at the farm, though. And Thanksgiving eve had to wait a little longer than our families might have wished, because Clint and Rosie, as they walked back to the oblong conference table where everybody had clustered, saw the picture Ray had put up on the computer monitor and said, with one voice, 'What's up with Maynard?'

ELEVEN

Everybody talked at once. Ray said, 'That's Maynard?'

Bo, walking in just then, said, 'Who's Maynard?'

Andy said, 'Is that the guy Clint calls "My Pet Gossip?"'

I said, unreasonably, 'Now you tell us, when we're all ready to go home?' The question was way out of line since they had just walked in. But the need to go get Benny was pulling at me like a magnet.

Rosie gave me a withering look and turned to Ray. 'Why do you have his picture up?'

Winnie said, 'He looks dead!'

'He is dead,' Ray said. 'I guess you never heard about this out at the farm, did you?' He told them where we'd just been and why Maynard's picture was there.

Clint said, 'Holy cow, Maynard,' and they all sat down. Every synapse in my brain pleaded, *No, No, don't sit down!*

Ray told them about calling Pokey, getting him there in time to rescue the body from the ambulance, get it looked at, certified, put away. 'So we can all go have Thanksgiving instead of spending the night making phone calls.' He felt quite proud of his achievement; he wanted some gratitude.

Winnie said, 'Funny thing, you know, I never saw that guy out there at the farm.'

'No, because while you were all out there he was dead in Ethan's car.'

Rosie said, 'That makes no sense at all.'

'I know,' Ray said, 'but it just happens to be true.'

'And it's too late to do anything about it tonight,' I said. 'And we are definitely not going to put in any double overtime talking about it tomorrow when everybody's off in the labs so we can't accomplish anything. So let's get everything put away here and come back Friday morning ready to work.'

That sounded pretty reasonable when I said it, but it left out some things.

To begin with, Doris and Henry heard the news from Ethan. They both phoned Ray and then me, wanting to know what had *really* happened. (We were cops, they thought we should know). Doris had a predictable reaction when I told her I didn't know who killed Maynard.

'There, you see?' she said. 'Aggie said this was going to spread and it's spreading. I can't make Thanksgiving for my children here with this black cloud hanging over us! I'm going to get my mother to take them home with her. Including Alan, if he'll go.'

'What about you?'

'Somebody has to take care of all the animals. Charlie Blaise says he'll stay and help me. And Elmer, of course.'

'Why do you say "of course"? Is Elmer on a chain?'

'Elmer lives here. Always has. But nobody else wants to stay, they're all quitting. For me, actually, work is better than sitting idle. I'll be fine.'

As soon as I was off the phone with her, Henry called to ask, 'Have you figured out yet what that tramp was doing in Ethan's car?'

'No,' I told him, 'and we can't get to work on that until all the lab people come back from Thanksgiving, Mr Kester.'

'What, you don't work on – oh, I suppose it's the damn unions, isn't it?' He knew, he said, that the damn unions were always trying to turn us all into godless Communists.

'Gotta give lab technicians the holidays off, yes, sir,' I said, walking a neutral line. 'Pretty strict rules about that.'

I knew better than to wish him a happy one. He said he was going out to Home Farm now to see if he could help Doris.

'She keeps saying, "Don't worry, Dad, Charlie and I will get it all done". She's a strong, clever girl but she still can't be in two places at once, so I'm gonna try to convince her I ain't quite old enough to be useless yet.'

'She said Elmer's staying too.'

'Well, sure. Where would he go? When will any of them scientists get back to work?'

'Friday,' I said. 'I'll let you know on Friday how the autopsy went.' With that, he got off the phone and let me drive the rest of the way home in peace – or as much peace as Benny would allow me. My son had rediscovered Father Torture as a hobby. Even a teething ring wouldn't get him to stop complaining.

Trudy was not inclined to be forgiving, either, about my late arrival with Benny.

'I thought at least tonight you could make an effort,' she started, but I leaned across my ferociously chewing child and cut her off with a big warm kiss on the mouth. She came out of it grinning, saying, 'What was that for?'

'For being a reasonable human being who is not named Kester,' I said. 'And' – I took a deep breath and jumped – 'for being an intelligent professional who is going to understand when I say I have to go back to work.'

'What?' It took her a while to get her expression to the right degree of horrified shock. 'You have to do what?'

'I have to go back to work. Maybe for quite a while because there's nobody to help me. But we just got a fresh body dumped in our laps. Possible suicide or overdose but we don't know for sure. There's a gun with the body but he wasn't shot . . . it's freaking bizarre, and I just can't walk away and let all the evidence deteriorate for thirty-six hours while I fool around out here preparing to eat fat birds and sing stupid songs, can I? Believe me, you would not want to be married to a Chief of Detectives who would do that.' She was still standing in front of me with her mouth open, evidently shocked speechless. 'Trudy?'

Ben quit chewing suddenly, let out an eardrum-piercing roar and dropped his teething ring on the floor. His bad behavior did wonders for his mom, who snapped back into focus, took our son out of my arms and dumped him unceremoniously in his high chair. 'I'll call my mother,' she said, above his wails, 'and my sister. They'll help me, we'll get it done. Shouldn't you have a snack before you go?'

My footsteps sounded loud as I walked into the darkened detective division, debating with myself about where to start. When I turned on the lights I saw rows of neat desks with covered computers. My own office was the only one with piles of work sitting around – in my haste to get Ben I hadn't stayed to tidy up. *Fine*, I thought, rummaging through a pile. *I'll find a notebook and a pen, and make a list.*

Then Ray's voice behind me said, 'Ah. You are here.' When I turned to face him he said, 'I saw your pickup. Is this all right with Trudy?'

'She doesn't love it but she knows it's what I do. But your new bride, are you—'

'She said, "I knew you were kind of a nut when I married you". Where do you want to start?'

'I . . . with Nicole, I think. But since you're here . . . you're good at all this searching business, too, and I wonder . . . do you think you might be able to dig up some skinny on Maynard?'

'That's what I was thinking,' he said. 'The labs are all closed but the Internet's still working.'

'Exactly. So why not start with Been Verified for the basics of who he is, and go on to CriMNet to see if he'd been in trouble hereabouts before he offed himself. If he did.'

'Good. After CriMNet go for NCIC, huh? And . . . Matt Kester too, while I'm at it?'

'Why not? He's been gone for a lot of years – first thing, why don't you see if you can find enough prize money to live on? Because otherwise—'

'What was his ace in the hole? Good point.' He chuckled. 'Digging for dirt about the Kesters – feels kind of radical, doesn't it? But fun. How about old Ethan? You think I could find something to hang on him?'

'I don't expect him to turn up on CriMNet but if there's a note anywhere about how he sneaks an extra cookie at Chamber of Commerce meetings, I'll be on him like a swarm of bees.'

I began loading my body – first with recorder, notebooks, pens, camera . . . Strapping on my Glock, I wondered: was Nicole the intellectual going to refuse to speak to me if I was packing? Hell with it, I decided; if she does I'll handcuff her and bring her downtown.

Then footsteps sounded in the hall and Winnie walked in.

She said, 'I was passing and saw your cars. Where do you want me to start?'

'Winnie,' I said, 'I can't let you – the rules—'

'I took two sick days earlier this pay period,' she said. 'You make up the payroll lists; show me as working those days.'

'But your family, won't they—'

'Jake, Thanksgiving is not a Vietnamese holiday. My sister's children love all this business with the Pilgrim hats and pumpkin pies, but I guess I was just too late getting started. I have never been able to find anything attractive about turkey with cranberries. Please don't tell immigration.'

I laughed and asked Ray, 'What else do we want most?'

He said, 'Get Doris to say exactly what Maynard didn't do before she fired him. Maybe we can figure out what hours he could have been doing something else, see if they fit any blanks in those diagrams we been making.'

'I can certainly do that,' Winnie said, and turned to go.

'I said, 'Take your Glock. And your Taser.'

'Oh? I'm only asking a few ques—'

I stopped her with a raised palm. 'The Kesters are going through a bad patch. From now on, when you deal with them, go armed.'

Before we left, I got Ray to run off several copies apiece of the picture he still had up on the monitor in the meeting room. 'Every place you go for the next few days, show this to the people you talk to,' I said. 'This guy's been working around here for some time, somebody must know him.'

Then Winnie got into her dinky Prius, and used maybe a cupful of gas to drive to the extreme north edge of town, previously known as 'country'. I turned up the heater in my apple-red Ford pickup with dualies and tool chest, and burned through a couple of gallons getting across Rutherford on flawlessly paved streets. Americans, even quite new ones, have always used their means of transportation to express themselves, and it's going to be a hard habit to break.

Ethan Kester's house was on Mercer Street, in a section of town where all the houses were large and substantial. Ethan's had the extra elegance that characterizes houses built by well-to-do people in the first two decades of the twentieth century. They have features any sensible person would want but nobody builds any more, like pantries and second-floor sleeping porches.

The house was dark in front but I saw blazing lights and move-ment back where the kitchen must be. I rang the bell and watched while somebody, coming forward, turned on a hall light and then the light over my head. I held my shield up by my face while the person scrutinized me through a dark sidelight. When the deadbolt slid back and the door opened a crack I said, 'Good evening. Jake Hines, detective division, Rutherford Police Department.' I didn't smile, and neither did she – just stood in her barely-open door and said, 'Ethan's not home. He took the boys to a movie so I could do my holiday cooking.'

'No problem. I came to see you.'

'Oh? What about?'

'I have some questions about the body in your husband's car,' I said.

'I don't know anything about that,' she said, 'and I'm very busy tonight, so . . .' She started to close the door but I was standing on the sill and pushed back. We were standing almost nose to nose now. 'I can't talk through the door,' I said. 'If you won't let me in I'll have to take you downtown.'

She watched me quietly, deciding whether I was bluffing. 'I know you're busy,' I said. 'And if you'll let me in I won't take any more of your time than I have to.'

'I have things cooking in the kitchen that have to be tended to,' she said. 'If you'll come back there and talk to me you can take all the time you like.'

The air inside was warm and smelled wonderfully of spices and sugar. I followed her past a shining mahogany staircase that turned at a landing with an elegant carved newel post. She led me along a wainscoted hall hung with family portraits into an octagonal dining room with windows lining three sides. I got an impression of small-figured wallpaper and shutters. We passed a round table, went through a swinging door into a pantry and through another swinging door into a large kitchen with a great deal of stainless steel, where the wonderful smells got more intense.

She wore a large white no-nonsense apron like the ones Trudy uses, mousy hair pulled back in a ponytail and large, thick glasses with heavy rims. Despite her lack of physical charm, something about her erect figure and assured voice led me to believe the assessment her husband had delivered earlier that day: 'Nicole, you know, is quite capable of arranging things to suit herself.' I did not doubt that she had done exactly that in this perfect house, and wondered if Ethan realized he was living with a major talent.

She went back to work at a chopping block, a big range and a couple of ovens. The granite counters were crowded with high-end appliances, and shiny pans and spoons hung from an overhead rack. One shelf held a row of cookbooks with famous chefs beaming from their covers. Except for Nicole's nondescript appearance, the whole scene might have been ripped from the pages of some glossy home magazine.

Admiring her work wasn't going to get me where I needed to go, though. I laid one of my Maynard pictures on the counter and asked her, 'You know this man?'

She took her time measuring eight cups of water into a pan and setting it on a burner before she glanced at the picture and said, 'No.' She set the heat control carefully, thinking about it. How hard could it be to hit 'High'?

'Sure? He's the man your husband found dead in his car this morning.'

She made a face and said, 'Ugh.'

'He worked at the Kester farm. But you didn't know him?'

'No. I never go there; I don't know any of those people.'

'You never go to your family's farm?' She shook her head. 'Why, you have allergies, or—?'

'I do not share the Kester passion for the revered family farm, that's all. The sacrosanct acres that suck up all the attention in any room where Kesters gather.'

'I suppose those conversations do lack variety.'

She laughed a humorless little bark. 'You might say that. Unless you're fascinated by plans to buy cows with registered tits and train horses with names longer than European kings.'

'Looking around this house, I'd guess you have somewhat different interests.'

'Uh-huh. I'm the funny-faced wife that reads *books*, of all things. Likes to talk about movies and listen to music. All total conversation-stoppers at a Kester gathering, where the pressing need for more cows and horses never leaves any money for anything the homely intellectual might fancy.'

'Like what?'

'Like a sweet little home decorator's shop with a small inventory and high fees for consulting. You got the picture?'

'Yup. Clear as day. What was wrong with your car?' She filled a measuring cup exactly to the brim with sugar, poured it into the pan of hot water on the stove and gave it a stir. 'This morning, Nicole? When you put it in the shop?'

'Oh . . .' She shrugged. 'The locking mechanism on the front passenger door wasn't working right.' She measured out another cup of sugar, dumped it into the pan, and stirred some more, giving it her full attention.

'It wouldn't lock? Or unlock?'

'Both. Either. From the driver's side. It's supposed to be, you know, controllable all around from the driver's side.' She cut open a sack and waited. When the sugar water bubbled, she tilted the sack above it, and cranberries poured into the boiling water with fat, satisfying little plops.

'But they fixed it? Where'd you take it, by the way?'

'To the dealership where I bought it. The Lexus people out there on the Beltway.'

'Spielman's?'

'Um . . .' She was watching the cranberries rise. 'Yes, I guess . . .' She stirred the frothy mixture with her long-handled spoon.

'And they fixed it?'

'No. They said it was something electrical so they'd have to take the whole door apart and it might take all day. So I said, "Well, I can't be without a car all day today". I took it back and had the yard man return Ethan's.'

'He was following you, was he? The yard man? What's his name, by the way?' I had my notebook in front of me now.

'Good heavens, I don't know.'

'You don't know the name of the man who trims your trees?'

'It's a service. They hire, I suppose, all sorts of people. From the looks of them, I doubt they all have documentation, but I deal with the company, I don't have to care who . . . Why?' She looked at me coldly with her eyebrows raised. 'Are you going to check up on me?'

'That's the way the system works, yes. We verify answers. What's the name of the yard company you use?'

'I . . .' She peered into the pink froth in the pan, gave it a couple of stirs, picked out a couple of berries and slid them onto a small plate. 'I have their card there . . . on the board somewhere.' She waved at the framed corkboard by her wall phone.

It was bristling with colored thumbtacks holding cards and reminder notes. She blew on the two berries on the plate, tasted one, dumped both in the sink. 'I'll find it for you when I have time. Or you're welcome to look for yourself.' She flashed a little sideways smile.

'I'll count on you to find it for me. After you took your car back from the dealer you went on to the store and got your onions, hmm?'

'Good heavens, you even know about the onions?' Her little mocking laugh was so like Ethan's – did they line up and hold contests in this family, I wondered? See whose tiny laugh could hold the most effective sneer?

'Which store did you go to, for the onions? No store near that Lexus dealership where you could buy those little pearl onions, is there? And the sweet potatoes,' I said. 'Your husband mentioned them too.'

'He's got a remarkable memory,' she said. 'You too.'

'But you don't, I guess. Hmmm? If you forgot to buy the two classic items that every housewife in America includes in her Thanksgiving dinner menu?'

'Do they? I haven't been cooking it that long. Thanksgiving was always my mother's feast to prepare, till she had a stroke last year and—' She turned to face me suddenly, her face flushed from the steam she was bending over. 'Did my husband's remarkable memory yield up the name of his Saturday secretary yet? Have you talked to her? Patti the Playmate? Pretty Patti, the peter licker?' Maybe it wasn't all because of the steam – her cheeks kept getting redder as she talked.

'I don't believe – is there something in particular you think I should ask her?'

The laugh wasn't small this time. It burst out in a big guffaw, rage and contempt boiling out of it. 'Oh, you bet there is, Mr Pussyfoot Detective, there's one particular question I'd love to hear her answer! Ask her' – she leaned across her beautiful granite workspace, her gray eyes gleaming with hate – 'if she's really simpleton enough to think she's ever going to get her slimy hands on this house and my beautiful boys and the money from that filthy bloated farm they're all so proud of. Does she actually suppose I'm so dim I can't keep her from making that snatch?'

The pot on the stove boiled over with a great crackling as the liquid hit the burner, followed by an awful stench of burning sugar. Nicole gave a little strangled cry, banged her long-handled spoon down on her cutting board and turned the heat off under the pan. 'There! See what you've made me do? Talking to me when I'm cooking? Now my stove is a stinking mess, damn it! And the cranberries are ruined – I'll have to throw the whole fucking thing down the drain. Ah!' She slapped her forehead. 'How will I ever get everything done?'

She seized the pot full of cranberries and sauce, bubbling hot, off the burner, and swung it in a dangerous arc toward the sink. A few drops of the boiling sauce flew off the pan as she passed me, and hit my arm. They burned like the fires of hell. I got up from the stool where I was perched, scrabbling at my burning arm with a dishtowel I grabbed off the counter.

She had her back to me now, bent over the sink, turning the water faucet on high. Then she turned on the DisposAll and tipped her boiling panful of berries toward the drain. While they poured in a crimson tide into the growling maw she turned her crazed face toward me and screamed over her shoulder, above the grinding noise, 'Get out of my house, you fool!'

I had already retreated as far as the pantry door. Clearly there was no use trying to talk any more to the enraged termagant at the sink, so I retraced my steps to her front door. As soon as I got outside I grabbed a handful of snow off her lawn and slapped it on my sticky, suffering arm. I held it there till it melted, and it helped, a little. I did it again, standing at the curb panting with pain, on the way to my pickup. When I could breathe evenly, I crossed the street to my truck and climbed in.

Before I got my lights on, a pale green Lexus slid past my window and paused in the Kester driveway, waiting while the garage door slid up. I watched as Ethan Kester parked his wife's car in the left-hand bay.

The right-hand bay was empty tonight, since we had his Cadillac in impound. So I could see, as I eased past the end of his driveway in my darkened vehicle, how the two little boys sprinted heedlessly away from the Lexus, calling out, 'Mom!' as they climbed the steps and opened the kitchen door. And how their father, systematic and careful as always, turned off the car's lights, got out and pushed the button that locked all the doors electronically from the driver's side, before he let down the garage door and followed his children into the house.

Ethan had sent me the name of his Saturday secretary, just as he'd promised, and included all the necessary numbers. Her name was not Johnson or Carlson, but Peterson, and she lived in student housing. But she had agreed, two hours ago, to meet me in a café on campus whenever I called. 'It's no trouble,' she said. 'I'll be right here studying.'

I found a booth near the front, ordered the strongest coffee they offered and called her. The place was about half full of students peering at blinking screens (even the ones holding hands). Otherwise, one tableful of exhausted-looking faculty staff and a couple of building-maintenance guys – I figured I wouldn't be hard to spot.

Patti Peterson picked me out even before she saw my badge, and slid into the booth after a quick handshake. She was soft all over: soft brown hair, pillowy lips, plenty of meat on the thighs. Plump and pretty but not stylish – I pegged her as probably top of her high school class in one of the small towns around Rutherford, hoping to study her way up to a better life than her folks had.

She debated her order, said she really shouldn't but oh, they made the best fruit smoothies here.

'Better have one,' I said, 'keep up your strength for all that studying. Let me buy and I'll have one too.'

I thought I was playing Good Cop to put her at ease, but when my smoothie came it tasted so good I promised myself never to work late again without one.

I started with the picture, again, and got the same indifferent response as from Nicole – no idea, never saw him before. When I said, 'He's the man Ethan found dead in his car,' she said, 'Oh, my, he told me about that. Must have been an awful scare.'

She'd answered a notice on the bulletin board in the Admin building, she said, to get the Saturday job. 'Just right for me – I'm a business major. I already type well and I'm good with spreadsheets, now I want to build up my math skills so I'm ready to hit the ground running when I graduate.'

'You're ambitious.'

'You bet.' Her eyes were pale blue and clear and her smile

was polite, no more. If Patti the Playmate was living behind that smile somewhere she was not beckoning to me.

'Is one day a week enough? Can you live on that?'

'No. I got a scholarship that covers registration and books, I saved all the money from my last three summer jobs and my folks are helping a little with the first two years. If I want to go on I'll have to get a government loan.'

'Worth it, I guess.'

'We'll see.' She watched me over the top of her glass as she sucked up the last of her smoothie. 'Something you want to ask about my schedule, Captain Hines?' She had read my card.

'You have somewhat flexible hours, is that right?'

'No. I work eight hours, every Saturday.'

'But not always the same eight hours, is it? Sometimes you start early so you can get away early?'

'Oh.' For just a few seconds she looked a little ruffled. But then she said in that placid voice, 'My friends tell me I don't know how lucky I am to get hired by these nice lawyers.' I tried not to look surprised. 'My hours were eight to five with an hour off for lunch, but when I found out how early Ethan comes to work, I asked if I could sometimes come at seven also and work straight through. That way I'm done by three and have the rest of the day to study or do laundry – it makes Sundays so much easier!'

'I bet. You call him Ethan?'

'Yes, because he asked me to. He's the youngest one in that office and – he seems almost middle-aged to me, but I think he likes to emphasize the difference between him and his partners, who are really old.'

'And he agreed? About the hours?'

She nodded and beamed. 'He said, "Looks like I found another early bird like me!" And the two older attorneys, bless their hearts, they said, "Whatever's best for Ethan – he's such a hard worker!"'

'So last Saturday,' I said, getting anxious to wind up this child's garden of verses, 'you came in at seven?'

'Yes.'

'And worked straight through, and left at three?'

'Yes.'

'And Ethan was right there in the office with you, until he got the call from the farm?'

'All the time. Yes.' She didn't have to scrutinize the corner of the room while she said it, I noticed – it seemed to be just information, to her.

'About what time was that?'

'I can tell you precisely, as it happens. We were working on the Esterhazy account and I was keeping track of billable hours. So . . . I logged us off at . . .' She flipped open a little notebook. 'Eleven-ten.'

'Hey, go to the head of the class.'

She smiled, politely.

'OK – he went out to the farm then. And came back about when?'

'I didn't write it down, because I wasn't sure we were going back to work on the contracts, but I remember it was shortly after one. He came back very upset and made a call to . . . I think he called police headquarters first, and got another number, and called – I think he said one of your detectives—'

'Yes. And left again?'

'He left to go out there to that hunting field, where they had found the – the bod—' She couldn't quite manage it. After a few seconds she said, 'His brother.' I finished my coffee while she collected herself. 'Poor man. He came back just before I left, and he was just . . . blown away. I asked him, "Is there anything I can do for you?" and he just shook his head. He couldn't speak.'

'Do you know Mrs Kester?'

She looked puzzled.

'Nicole? Ethan's wife?'

'No. She came in the office one Saturday with the two boys, but nobody introduced us and she didn't speak to me.'

'You think they're happily married?' Sometimes if you ask the most offensive question you jar something loose.

Patti Peterson looked at me wide-eyed, shaking her head, and said, 'Oh, I wouldn't have even the foggiest idea about that, Captain.' Then the implications of what I had asked her grew clear, and her face closed up. She waited five seconds and added: 'And if you ask me that again a year from now, I don't expect to know any more about it by then.' She put her little notebook back in her purse and said, 'Is that about it? Are we done?'

We stood. I thanked her for her time, and she left without a backward glance.

Ray was in his office under a single light, hunched over his monitor, typing in fast little bursts. When he saw me ease into his visitor's chair he raised one finger and finished a sentence, sat back with a sigh and said, 'Maynard Phelps doesn't exist.'

'I know,' I said. 'He's dead.'

'Doesn't seem to matter. He left no footprints even when he was alive.'

'Oh, come on, he had to have payroll records. Unless you think the sanctified Kester Corporation was paying him under the table?'

'Doubt it. But maybe he's only worked there a couple of quarters and the state's that far behind in filings. I haven't found any entries for this year.'

'And no arrest records, no detentions?'

'Not even a speeding stop.'

'So he wins the Careful Drivers' plaque. But he never went to school in Minnesota? Or voted here?'

'Or got married or divorced or bought a car or renewed a driver's license anywhere in the US.' He turned a take-no-prisoners Bailey frown on his yellow legal pad, where a whole row of possibilities had been neatly entered and systematically crossed out.

'You saying he doesn't even show up on Been Verified?'

'No. There's a Maynard Phelps in Brainerd who's seventy years old. A bright kid who just won a spelling bee in Albert Lea, but he's eleven.'

'How does a drifter living under the radar get hired on a farm?' Then I answered my own question. 'Probably about as tough as getting the dishwasher slot in a greasy spoon, huh? For which you need a social security card and a heartbeat.' I worked my way through school at jobs like that. 'So who's the local forger?'

'Don't know. Maybe Bo can tell us Friday. Or maybe he's not local.'

'Did you tell Winnie to ask who hired him and when?'

'Yeah, I caught her just as she was finishing up out there. She'll be here shortly.' He stretched and groaned. 'You do any good?'

'Oh, indeed, I managed to increase the confusion quite a bit. Wish you could have been there, Ray – you'd have been proud.' I told him how cleverly I had escaped from the Mad Housewife on Mercer Street, and how adroitly I'd infuriated Ethan's secretary just a few minutes later.

'While you were fleeing from those ladies, did you get any impression of their characters?'

'Nicole Kester is suitable punishment for every sin Ethan has ever committed.'

'Oh? A real ball-buster, huh? Does he seek the comfort of sex outside the home, then? In the arms of his secretary, maybe?'

'If he does I'm afraid he's wasting his time.'

'Tsk. No fun anywhere for Ethan, huh?'

'If that young woman is a playmate she is also an actress of great skill.'

'Well, my night's been just about equally valuable,' he said. 'One thing, though – I've got new respect for those scientists I so often bad mouth. They may be too slow to suit me, but goddamn, it's frustrating trying to prove anything without them. I could search till hell freezes over,' he said, angrily stacking papers into a pile, 'and it wouldn't prove what one good autopsy report would show you in a couple of hours.'

'Well, but sometimes an interview can be pretty helpful,' Winnie said, behind me.

'Easy for you to say,' I said, 'I bet you weren't dodging any boiling cranberries, were you?'

'What?'

'Wait.' I carried in the captain's chair from the meeting room and told her, 'Sit,' before I described my interviewing prowess.

'Well, you're right, mine went better than that,' she said. 'Doris says Maynard turned up at the farm this spring just as calving was starting,' Winnie said. 'They were short two hands, needed help badly. He said he'd lost his social security card but he remembered the number, so Owen put him to work and told her, "if he does the jobs all right we'll run the records check later". But calving ran late and haying started early this year, so she thinks maybe they just forgot about it.'

'His work must have been good enough in the beginning, huh?'

'Yes. Nothing complicated, she said, mucking stalls, feeding stock and hauling hay. She never paid much attention to him – he was just one of Owen's hands, and she was busy with her own jobs.

'She was annoyed that the stalls never got cleaned the day Owen got shot. She remembered Owen saying he was leaving Maynard at the barn to do chores while he took supplies to the fence menders, so she knew he had time to get the stalls clean. But then Rosie came and told her Owen was dead, and that just blew everything else out of her mind. In the end, she let it go.

'But in the days that followed she began to be aware that Maynard simply wasn't following orders – he was sneaking around, leaving other people to do his jobs or just leaving them undone.' She waved a couple of handwritten sheets. 'I've got her estimates here, of the times when he skipped out. She didn't know where he went – said she didn't care, he wasn't where he belonged and that was all that mattered – but now she knows why it's important, and she'll try to find out.'

Winnie sat cross-legged, curled up in her big chair while she described her visit with Doris. 'She said, "I can't stop what I'm doing, but we can talk if you'll follow me around". The four of them, Doris and Henry and that foreman, Charlie, and his little old sidekick Elmer, are doing all the work on those two big farms. Doris still has that one part-time woman in the kitchen, but that's all she does – housework.

'They've shipped off most of the boarding horses and put the rest out to pasture. But the cows, God, twice a day to milk and feed – she said, "Henry and I are joined at the hip now, I guess that's a plus". Her mother took all her children up to their place – she even persuaded Alan to go, for a day or two.'

'The foreman will stick, huh?'

'He has a vested interest – he earns a share a year in the corporation. The part-time woman, Aggie, lives in the neighborhood and says nobody's going to scare her out of a job with the hours she needs. And Elmer stays because it's the only home he's got – did you know that?'

'No. Is it important?'

'Maybe not, but it's a remarkable story. Elmer arrived at the farm with his father, so long ago that nobody remembers the year. Get this – it was Henry's father who hired Elmer's father, and gave them both a place to sleep – some little corner of a shed at first, I gather. He lives in Charlie's house at Dairy Farm now.

'Elmer's father worked at Home Farm till he died, but that was years and years ago – and Elmer has never had any other home. Doris said he only got a year or two of schooling at a one-room school that used to be kept in the neighborhood – he can barely sign his name. She said he's too old for most farm work now, but he's so good with the animals that she and Owen never regretted keeping him on. She says he's wonderful at calving season, and he can calm an excited horse like nobody she's ever known.'

'OK, Charlie and Elmer and Doris. Henry still hanging in there?'

'Barely. Very tired.'

'But no Matt around, helping?'

'No, she's adamant: he can't come on the place. He pulled that stunt, hiring Maynard back after she fired him, and then came over to Home Farm and started giving new orders to Charlie Blaise – did you hear about that?'

'No. Who told you?'

'Aggie. The talker in the kitchen. I guess he thought he was really going to take over, shove the widow aside.' She shook her head in wonder. 'You could almost feel sorry for the poor schlub, not knowing where he stood with people better than that. Charlie just laughed at him, Aggie said, and his own father told him to go back to the river and behave himself.'

'So it looks like Doris won't have to fight to keep her place.'

'Well, not with Henry, anyway.' She gave a little wiggle of dissatisfaction. 'Something else is going on, though.'

'What?'

'I don't know. The old man, Henry, looks . . . apprehensive. Keeps looking into corners. Like he doesn't think the killing's done. There's a ton more places on that farm to look for weapons and ammo.'

'Winnie, cut it out,' Ray said. 'There's really nothing more we can usefully do till we get this holiday behind us and get everybody back to work.'

She looked at me, raised her eyebrows.

'Ray's right,' I said. 'That's what we were talking about when you walked in – we need the labs up and running. Working like this, it's like one hand's tied behind you.' I yawned. 'What time is it? Almost midnight. Let's all get some sleep, play nice about gravy and dressing tomorrow, and go after this again Friday when we can do it right.'

Winnie said, 'But I've got this whole list—'

'Me too.' I leaned toward her small, dissatisfied face that loved her job and had no use for cranberries. 'We'll deal with our lists on Friday, Winnie.'

My house was silent and dark, but smelled like a gourmet restaurant at the peak of rush hour. My stomach growled as I walked across the kitchen, but I resisted the impulse to turn on a light and help myself to some classy snacks. Who knew what perfect arrangement of gherkins I might wreck? I poured a big glass of milk in the light from the refrigerator, and left a note on the island that read, *Wake me early, I got plenty of sleep!*

I undressed in my dark bedroom to the gentle snoring of two sound sleepers, and slid into bed. Trudy turned over but didn't wake up. I still have a street cop's ability to go to sleep fast when I get the chance – I heard the hot water pump turn on in the cellar, listened to hot water gurgling through the radiator under the window, and was gone.

Trudy woke me with a tweak on the elbow, and handed me coffee. Bright sunlight streamed in the windows. My watch said seven. 'If you meant that note,' she said, 'how about helping me get turkeys in the oven before you shower?'

'Sure,' I said. 'Soon as you kiss me.' I held her close a minute after and said, 'Let's make up our minds to enjoy this party, shall we? It's not life or death, is it?'

I spoke from recent experience, and I guess my conviction showed.

'You're right,' she said – words that any sensible husband would walk barefoot over broken glass to hear. She led the way to the kitchen where Benny was chewing the hell out of a couple of crackers. 'Two teeth are all the way through, see?' I praised him extravagantly and he roared and smashed a cracker to celebrate.

Trudy's sturdy clan of Nordic settlers would never stoop to using prepared dressing, so Trudy's mother Ella and her sister Bonnie had come to our house last night and endured the boredom of tearing several loaves of two-day-old bread into small bits. They had also chopped several onions and left them in plastic baggies, so all we had to do now was mix the two in a tub, and add spices and butter and hot water. I mashed it all into a thick gooey sludge that looked like a mistake that should be thrown out at once, and stuffed it into the carcasses of two huge buttered turkeys. We slid them into the ovens by eight o'clock, 'Right on time,' Trudy said, beaming.

I got cereal and a shower and then the day took on its own momentum. I peeled buckets of potatoes, both white and sweet, since Hansons, on holidays, require both colors. Before I'd finished, Ella swept in with her frosted pompadour and the holiday delicacies that only she can be trusted to make: the filled cookies, the pickle relish, the cranberry mold. Attention had to be paid, items moved to make room in the pantry and refrigerator. Then we took a coffee break with some of Ella's cookies before the big crunch over table settings.

The Hansons had found a couple of Carlson uncles and a new trio of cousins, and Bo and Nelly were coming, so Ella had brought her good silver. It put our stainless in the shade but we segregated by tables and Trudy was pacified when Ella showed her the fan-fold for the napkins that tied the whole room together.

Bonnie came in bringing her specialty, Waldorf salad, and she and Trudy held their usual debate about flour versus cornstarch for the gravy. I managed to tune out most of it but my impression was that Trudy's cornstarch carried the day. Then everybody else began arriving with casseroles of veggies, many breadstuffs, and more pies than I had ever before seen in a home kitchen at one time.

Carving and eating took a long time, enlivened by many toasts. When we could not get outside of one more bite of pie we cleared the tables and, to head off the threat of Uncle Elmer's Sven and Ole jokes, played Screw Your Neighbor. It's a card game that Hansons play for kitchen matches, yelling and slapping down cards as passionately as if matches were five-dollar bills. We had a short table for the kids where Nelly taught small Hansons to play Crazy Eights. Eddy kept score till he got bored and played spy on the floor behind two couches, wrapped in the solitary gravitas he still sometimes retreats into.

Benny had a good time for most of the party, waving and high-fiving the guests when he wasn't too busy drooling and chewing. When he got tired we heated up a bottle and he got passed from lap to lap while he drank it and took a snooze.

Best Thanksgiving ever, everybody agreed as they walked out the door into the chilly dusk, taking their dirty casseroles with them. Most of the cleanup had been done by the guests. When we finished the pans Trudy poured out the last of the chilled white wine. I touched her glass and said, 'I give thanks for you every day, babe.'

'And for our life together. Yes.' The wine tasted very good now in our quiet house. 'It wasn't so bad today, was it? I thought you seemed a little . . . more at ease with my noisy relatives.'

'I think I'm getting the hang of it,' I said. 'But how did they ever produce you, I wonder?'

'Families are very . . . mysterious.'

'Amen. I believe the Kesters have cured me of wishing I had one.'

'Well. So long as it wasn't Hansons that did it.'

TWELVE

Most of the crew had a look, Friday morning, about halfway between 'second-helping-mistake' and 'Friday-work-stupid'. Ray introduced our new recruit, Josh Felder, who formed the one bright spot in the room – pleased to be working homicide, he had that ask-me-for-anything look.

Frowning with concentration, Ray pushed them briskly through the day's assignments. He was hurrying because he knew Pokey would want to do the autopsy as soon as he could get a room, 'and I'll have to be there, since I was the officer on scene'.

He told them he'd been searching for records on Maynard and coming up empty. 'Did he ever mention to you,' he asked Clint, 'where he grew up, went to school?' As Clint kept shaking his head Ray said, 'Nothing at all about where he's ever worked before?'

'Maynard was full of tall tales, but they were all malicious little items about the Kesters,' Clint said. 'Funny, now that you ask me . . . I don't think he ever said where he was from or any of that. Most of our conversations were on about the level of seventh-grade gym class – little dirty digs at the women on the place, always suggesting Doris was "looking to get a little extra".' He blinked thoughtfully. 'If I'd known we were going to want to know more about Maynard, I could have been digging a little. But I thought he was the least interesting person on the place, just this malicious little scut dishing lies about the boss's family, so I let him ramble on.'

'OK. Who's got holdover work today?'

Bo said he supposed he should go back to the jail to try to talk to the Mad Dad, 'if he's sobered up enough by now'.

'Yes,' Ray said. 'And the friend – let's get them charged, today, if we can. Think you can get a high enough bail to keep them inside until trial? You've got a couple of priors on the dad, don't you?'

'Yes. And it's Judge McGee, so I can probably do that.'

'I think I got all I'm going to get from that farm Wednesday,' Rosie said. 'And it wasn't much. Everybody was leaving; I was mostly talking to the backs of people as they packed. How are they going to run that farm with no help, I wonder?'

'With great difficulty, I suppose,' I said. 'By working their butts off.' Winnie hadn't told anybody about her visit to the farm Wednesday night, because I'd asked her not to. We'd stretched a rule that I didn't want stretched very often, and I certainly didn't want to argue about it right now.

'It's the strangest thing,' Rosie said. 'They all claimed to like and admire Owen Kester, but when he turned up dead they stuck by Doris a hundred per cent, kept asking her how they could help. Now this roustabout they didn't even like, that they were glad to see get fired – somebody finds him dead in a car and they're totally spooked.'

'Who's "they"?' I said. 'Who'd you talk to?'

'Well . . . the women in the kitchen. And one of the field hands who came in for some water.'

'What did they say about it?'

'That this was one of them. So somebody's after the staff now.'

'Ah. That's what Doris was afraid of. She said it's going to spread.'

'Yeah. They seem to think murder might be catching – like a bad rash, or an alien plague. Maybe they all read paranormal lit. Anyway, they're threatened, so they're quitting.'

'I know,' I said. 'The kitchen help first, except Aggie – she seems to be sticking. And then the field hands. By evening, Doris had only her foreman and her father-in-law.'

'Oh, you checked with her later?'

'Um, yes.' I didn't look at Winnie. She had her eyes on me this morning. I could tell she was looking for a chance to corner me, so she could campaign for searches she wanted to do with Rosie at the dairy and River Farm. I was determined to stay out of the lineup today and let Ray assign them to whatever plan he'd mapped out.

And he was doing that now. 'Visit the Lexus dealer on the Beltway,' he told them, 'and find out when Ethan's wife Nicole brought her car in. And what work if any they did on it.'

'What's this all about?' Rosie asked. 'I haven't heard anything – is Ethan's wife in trouble now?'

'I'll let you know after you bring me this information,' Ray said.

'Those elite dealers . . . they're not going to want to—'

'I know. Flash your badge. Use the dread word "homicide". Insist on precise answers, and make them show you work orders! When you're done there I want you to visit Ethan's office, get him to show you the computer Patti used on Saturday and confirm the log-in and log-out times on the Esterhazy contract. Make copies.'

'Let's have everybody carry a couple of these pictures from now on.' I grabbed them off the stack of Maynard portraits. 'Show these to everybody,' I told the room. 'Ask if they've ever seen this man.'

'And while you're hanging around that office, get acquainted with the other secretaries there, will you?' Ray said. 'See what they think of Patti's work.' He shrugged. 'Or anything else they'd like to say about her.'

'And try to get back here around two,' he added. 'Because I should be getting back from the autopsy about then, and maybe we'll have' – he made a wolfish face – 'some clues!'

'Clues – wow,' Andy said. He told us Clint had gone after a warrant so they could search all the buildings at Dairy Farm, still looking for a murder weapon and/or anything that would give them any idea how Owen's body ended up at the wrong end of the pasture.

'That's fine. He can take Josh along. OK, Josh? And while you're searching he can tell you about this case, which will be quicker than the long explanation I don't have time for.'

Ray asked Andy to go back out to Home Farm and take up where he left off when they all got called to the domestic disturbance, get Charlie and Elmer to show him the break in the fence, and explain how they fixed it without the tools that Owen never brought. He said, 'Try to get them to remember the times when they did each of those jobs and when they got back to the house.'

Ray just about got all that out of his mouth when Pokey phoned and told him to hustle his butt down to the lab at County where he had just procured a room.

'I know perfectly well,' Ray told me as he loaded up his kit, 'that I shouldn't be this hands-on, and you shouldn't either, but what else can we do?'

'Nothing. Let's just take it as it comes.'

'OK, so will you anchor for me here again today?'

'Sure. I'll put on my headset so I can bring my stats up to date and start the payroll while I talk on the phone.'

'You can do that?'

'Of course.' I thought I was bragging a little, but actually that was the way that day worked out, for me. I got almost all my outstanding dog-work done while I fielded the steady stream of calls that came in – because they were all essentially the same phone call over and over. I could have cut and pasted the answers.

Everybody in reach of a phone, which these days is everybody breathing, wanted to ask if it was true we'd found Maynard Phelps's body in Ethan Kester's car. Some of the callers didn't even know his name – it was the second death that got their attention. When the chief walked in just before noon I told him, 'I feel like the boy who kicked the hornet's nest.'

He was just as curious as everybody else, so I asked LeeAnn to hold calls a minute while I told him where we stood. That conversation got a little awkward, because where we stood was in a widening gap between what we knew and what we needed to know.

It looked as if the man in the car might have overdosed on something, I told him, but we didn't know yet if that was true. Was Pokey's autopsy going to tell us? We hoped so but couldn't be sure. If it was true, he asked me, why would he climb into Ethan's car to off himself? No idea. Were they particularly close? On the contrary, Ethan claimed he didn't even recognize him.

'This is kind of ridiculous,' the chief said. 'You got any theories?'

'The one thing I know about him,' I said, 'is that he seemed to sort of spy on the Kester family and liked to talk about what he knew about them. So he might have been killed over something he knew – or said he knew.'

'So again, that would point to someone in the family.'

'Well, yeah. But if Pokey shows us he committed suicide, then that theory's out the window.'

'If he did kill himself we don't need to care why he did it, do we? He's just a hired hand – he could be responding to something that happened at the last place he worked.'

'That's a comforting thought. Why do I find it so hard to believe?'

'Because it's been a hard week and you're not by nature a very optimistic fellow,' the chief said, getting up. 'Keep me posted.'

'Sure. You talked to the lab lately?' He gave me a blank stare and I reminded him, 'You were going to try to expedite the DNA report from that cooler room, remember? Did you talk to them?'

'I certainly did. And that's been, let's see . . .'

'Tuesday, I think. Of course they all took Thursday off, but . . . would you mind giving them a nudge? If we could be sure that was Owen's blood, we'd at least have proved one thing.'

'And maybe the tide would turn? Sure, I'll call them.'

The information flow did seem to reverse for a while after Ray got back from the autopsy. He was tired and tense from standing on a cold floor in a cold room watching two cold scientists carve up a human being. He had learned to tolerate autopsies and respect the information gained from them, but no amount of talk about their intellectual value could teach him to enjoy one.

The doctors, on the other hand, he said, had all sorts of zesty fun with this autopsy, because Maynard's carcass proved to be such an accurate catalog of his heedlessly greedy life. Ray had flinched and quailed as they competed with each other to identify the symptoms: the herpes sores and gonorrheal scars that signaled plenty of careless sex, the cirrhosis of the liver left by a lifetime of hard drinking, the yellowing eyes and high blood sugar of diabetes that indicated heedless over-indulgence in sweet and fatty foods.

When they got to deciding the cause of death, though, they got a little more anxious and whiny.

'You're serious? Pokey whined?'

'Well, he wasn't happy,' Ray said, 'because the signs were all kind of . . . subtle, I think he said.'

The clinic doc was also anxious to come to a conclusion, Ray said, but cautious about deciding if the damage he saw was more likely homicidal or self-inflicted. His name was Mason, and he was young and kind of keen, Ray said. Seemed like he might be leaving any minute to go into rocket science.

'The hyoid bone wasn't broken,' Ray said, 'but they talked a lot about,' he read from his notes, 'being pretty sure they saw a line of ecchymosis around his neck.'

'What's that?'

'I finally got them to tell me it means bruising, discoloration. Like from a garrote? Then Pokey pointed out what he said were petechiae in the eyes, those are blood spots, and they looked and said they thought they saw one or two in the mouth too. And later on they claimed they saw evidence of,' reading again, 'cerebral hypoxia.'

'I'm impressed,' I said. 'What does it all mean?'

'They're about ninety-eight per cent certain he died of strangulation. For some reason, they couldn't decide whether somebody offed him or he did himself. Either one is possible, they said, and agreed they'd seen examples of both. They had a high old time, for a few minutes, telling stories of the ways they'd seen people asphyxiate themselves. "You'll have to get that information some other way", they said.'

'Oh, for Christ's sake,' I retorted. 'That's their job! Don't we have enough to do?'

'That's what I said. But the docs said, "We can only tell you what we know".'

So the autopsy report was going to confirm that Maynard Phelps died of strangulation, inflicted either by himself or another person. The doctors did not, of course, care to speculate on the presence of the shotgun, except to state that it hadn't killed Maynard Phelps. 'Who doesn't, at least on the Internet, exist,' Ray said.

Winnie and Rosie had returned, as Ray had asked, by two, and were listening to the verdict.

'Ethan was right,' Rosie said. 'He's in the weeds.'

'Except the motivation is crazy,' I said. 'Why would Ethan Kester kill a guy he didn't even know?'

'He *says* he didn't know him. We don't know that's true.'

'Well, good, so add that to the long and growing list of things we don't know about Maynard, including his real name. How soon,' I asked Ray, 'are we going to know anything more?'

'Well, I already know one more thing about him than I was looking for,' Ray said. 'Remember the hands you were so anxious to have me bag? The docs were taking a swab for a firearms residue test, and Pokey said, "Maybe we oughta make a swab for cocaine residue, his nose looks a little sore to me". And Mason said, "Hell, we still got some urine from this guy, haven't we? I'm pretty sure we've got one of those quick tester kits here someplace". He rummaged around in a cupboard and found it, and bingo.'

'Maynard had coke in his urine?'

'Yup. Tox screen will confirm, they said, and maybe other goodies as well. This guy was really pleasure-bent. Pokey's sending blood and tissue samples to BCA today. And fingerprints. The chief is already on the phone with the director up there, begging for a rush order. Probably have to wait in line for DNA and tox, but might get a speed-up on prints – if we could even get a match there, we'd at least have an identity to work with. I'll send his photo to the five-state area. I'm reaching out to guys I know to get it into BOLOs. We might get lucky.'

'And pigs might fly,' Rosie said. 'You ready for the news from the Lexus dealer?'

'In a minute,' I said. 'First I want to ask, how does a farm hand make enough money to buy cocaine?'

The whole table answered at once, 'By selling cocaine.'

'Isn't it fun the way this keeps growing? Now we need the name of his supplier and a list of his customers and oh, what else? The locations where he was moving it, I guess.'

'I'll ask Bo to help,' Ray said.

'Right. Now, Rosie. The Lexus dealer, tell me.'

'They never saw Nicole Kester on Wednesday. They haven't heard about an electrical problem with her car. If they do they're sure they can fix it. If it means the vehicle is disabled for any length of time they will certainly furnish a loaner, since she is a premium customer whose comfort is their first consideration.' She watched us thoughtfully. 'What nice smiles you both have.'

'We do when you bring us good news,' Ray said. 'What did you learn at Ethan's office?'

'Precious little, because those lace collar ladies are a little, um, precious. They understand, Mr Robbins and the Messers. Kester made it clear to them that they must cooperate in this police investigation. But they want to be sure *we* understand they are not accustomed to sharing the confidential business of the firm with *outsiders* . . . I now know exactly how it feels to be an outsider, don't you, Winnie?'

'I come from people who fled Vietnam on a raft,' Winnie said, 'I already knew that. But I agree, that lady with the brooch gives it new meaning.'

'What is this, sensitivity week?' Ray said. 'Did you get the log times or didn't you?'

'Of course we got them,' Rosie said, slapping down copies on his desk.

'But they said they don't gossip about fellow employees,' Winnie said. The corners of her mouth twitched.

'So I told them, "Good, neither do we",' Rosie said. ' "But we ask very pointed questions in a homicide investigation, and one way or the other we always get answers".'

'After that,' Winnie said, 'in response to some very pointed questions, they told us Patti types very well and leaves her desk neat but they wish she'd use something so the whole office didn't smell like sex after she works there. "First thing we have to do Monday morning", Mrs Waycross said, "is air out the office".'

'I have to ask,' I said. 'What did you find for a log-in time on the Esterhazy contract?'

'Um . . .' Rosie picked it up and studied it. 'Eight-thirty.'

'Ah,' Ray said. 'So Maynard gets an hour and a half of happiness a week. How like him to keep it brisk.'

'And Jake Hines, sad to relate,' I said, 'gets the booby prize for letting himself be fooled by a little newbie girl from the sticks.'

'Oh, put a positive spin on it,' Ray said. 'Patti Peterson gets the award for Best Actress in a Sordid Story.'

Ray's phone rang and he got into a long dumb-sounding conversation with Clint, mostly grunts and denials on his end. 'Yeah. Uh-huh. No. No. You be in soon? Oh? So no. OK, bye.' He folded up his phone, made an impatient noise, and said, 'They're having too much fun out there, admiring the milking machines. I think I'll put Josh Felder to work with somebody else tomorrow.'

'They find anything useful?'

'No, he says that place is just too damn spread out and open to search with any hope of success. Acres and acres of *cows*, he keeps saying. What else was he expecting at a dairy?'

Bo got back to the station around four-thirty. He poked his nose into Ray's office, where I was sitting while we mapped out strategy for the next week, and said, 'Done.'

'You got them both charged?'

He nodded. 'The arresting officers showed the judge their scars. And two social workers came from the hospital to tell what they'd done to the kids. After that McGee wouldn't even set bail for Big Bad Dad. And his friend can't raise any money so it comes to the same thing. I think the friend actually wants to stay in jail so Mom can't get at him. I probably should have arrested her too but' – he sighed – 'then the kids wouldn't have anybody. That older social worker, that Delia Delaney, you know her?'

'Yeah, good head,' Ray said.

'She's going to try to get somebody assigned to that household.' He got up. 'Best I could do.'

'Sit a minute,' I said. I told him about the dead farm hand with cocaine in his urine. 'You ever hear that name, Maynard Phelps?'

'No.'

'Or see this guy?' I showed him the picture.

'No.'

'Well, could you make us a list of his probable suppliers?'

'Sure. I better make a couple of calls first. If I just give you what I remember, half of them will be behind bars or gone back down the river since I quit working that beat. Things change fast in the drug trade.'

On that happy note we all went back in our workstations to type reports and answer email. The section was a hive of quiet taps and hums when Andy walked into it at four-forty-five a.m.

'No need to stop for me,' he told us all. 'I got no surprises, just a few notes about times.'

'Good,' Ray said. 'Come in here.' He pulled up the spreadsheet and I watched while they put in the times and events Andy had brought back in his recorder: 'Four-forty a.m. to the road where the dead horses lay by the truck. Five-oh-five a.m., swap vehicles with Owen and go looking for the break in the fence. Riding the fence line looking for the break, maybe half an hour. Found it, called the boss shortly after six a.m. He said he'd bring supplies to fix it.'

'It's fitting right into what we had, isn't it?' I said.

'Yup. They agree with Doris's story right down the line,' Andy said.

'And all the physical evidence supports that story,' Ray said.

'"Waited by break".' Andy was reading again, '"shooed off horses twice. Waited over an hour, finally decided to jury-rig a mend".

'I asked them, how'd you do that without any supplies? and Charlie said, "Times like that is when you need an Elmer along", and they both kind of chortled. This old guy, Elmer Hisey, who they say has lived on that farm since about the Hoover administration, has built or mended every yard of fence on that place, many times over. So he knows all the places where they left a little coil of extra wire around a post, and he has some hidey-holes under rocks where he keeps a pickle jar or tobacco can with a few nails and staples. And when it comes time to hammer in a staple, he says, "nothin' wrong with usin' a boot-heel".'

'There,' Andy said, as Ray logged off. 'Made it by quitting time, by Jimminy.' He laughed. 'See, I spent the afternoon with those farmers, now I'm talking like them.'

'Sounds like you kind of enjoyed it,' I said.

'Yeah. I worked for guys like that, summers when I was in high school. Great kidders but they'd work you to death and not even notice. They were just so *strong* from working all the time; they didn't get tired when I did.' He thought a minute, sitting with his hands on his knees. 'That Elmer, you know . . . Charlie says he's almost illiterate, barely can sign his name. But they all agree he's a genius with the animals, he can get them to do what he wants with nothing but a little cluck and a nudge now and then. And he knows all kinds of canny little survival tricks, like that fence-mending caper. Ways to make do with whatever you got. We hardly even grow people like him in this country anymore.'

He sighed and stood up. 'Good news and bad, I guess.' He laughed out loud again, a gusty bark. 'Charlie says Elmer's favorite TV show is *Dancing With the Stars*.'

THIRTEEN

The drive home was a pleasure Friday night, with my cheerful son crowing and waving at birds behind me. He had two fine white teeth growing on his lower front jaw; he was pain-free and had glimpsed a life beyond pablum. Untold flavors of crackers and cookies waited, on his horizon, to be reduced to soggy pulp. He was ready to share some joy.

Trudy had apple sauce and a bottle for him and a plea for me. 'I know all the bad jokes by heart but can you please put up with leftovers tonight? I am way too beat to cook.'

'Leftovers are the one part of turkey dinner I like,' I said. 'Sit here and enjoy the boy. I am a whiz at taking dishes out of the refrigerator.' To prove it I slid out a big platter of turkey parts, double-wrapped in yards of aluminum foil. 'Wow, did we think this bird was still trying to run away?' As I unwrapped the bird, the smell of dressing reached my nostrils and greed took over my soul. Dressing is so much better the second day! 'Why are you so tired?' I asked her, picking shamelessly at morsels. 'Something go wrong at work?'

'No. I guess it's just let-down. Yesterday was kind of . . . large.'

'And you worked so hard at it because I had to run out on you. You were a real champ about that, did I thank you?'

'Five times at least. Have we got anything left in the house to drink?'

'Trust me.' I went and found the bottle of Shiraz I had hidden in the cellar. While we sipped the first glass we debated the relative merits of the microwave versus the toaster oven for reclaimed dressing and turkey parts.

'Actually I kind of like it cold,' I finally confessed, eating some more of it cold. 'Don't you? And then we could finish off that apple pie with some cheese.'

When Ben finished his bottle I put him in the high chair with a couple of spoons, and he practiced his pounding and throwing while he watched us eat. I let him try tiny nibbles of this and that – he felt so-so about dressing, thought Mamie Carlson's mashed sweet potatoes had some merit, and threw cheddar cheese on the floor with a look that said I had to be kidding.

When the phone rang I said, 'Tell me that's your mother, wanting to recap yesterday while I put away these dishes.'

'Let us hope,' she said. She answered it, made a face and handed it to me, saying, 'Ray.'

'I'm at Methodist ER,' he said. 'Winnie called me because Doris called her—'

'Since when,' I said, 'is Winnie taking the calls for detective division?'

'Oh, they kind of bonded, you know, after Owen . . . just listen, OK? Doris Kester called Winnie and said, "I know I shouldn't bother you at home but you said if there was ever anything you could do . . ." Long story short, Doris just brought that old guy named Elmer in here. Charlie Blaise found him in a stall unconscious.'

'And she thinks we take accident calls?'

'The docs here are trying everything to resuscitate but Charlie thinks any minute they're going to pronounce him DOA. And the thing is, Jake, the way Charlie found him in a stall, it looks like he got kicked by the horse that was in there with him. But Charlie insists that's crazy, says no way does Elmer ever get kicked by any horse, but especially not that old brood mare that he has known and fussed over for almost twenty years.'

'So if Elmer makes it we'll be looking to prove assault?'

'And if he doesn't I'm going to call Pokey and try to take charge of the body right away, because Charlie is positive somebody beat his head in.'

'Let me know which one happens,' I said. 'I'm going to get on the phone with the chief right now. Because either way, we've got to get somebody out there to isolate that stall and sequester whatever we find there.'

'What about overtime, is it—'

'I'll have to get authorization for it. And . . . is Charlie Blaise still there?'

'Oh, sure. He wouldn't think of leaving till he finds out how Elmer's doing.'

'May I speak to him, please?'

The foreman's voice, when he came on, was steady but subdued. 'H'lo?'

I said, 'Jake Hines here, Charlie. Sorry about your trouble.'

'Mmm.'

'Is the animal still in that stall?'

'Yeah, I didn't dare take the time to change her – anyway I thought you'd want to see it . . . the way it was.'

'Good thinking.'

'But as I told Ray here, I'm sure old Bessie didn't do this. That horse and Elmer was like best friends.'

'I understand. When I can get somebody out there, will he be able to get in the barn?'

'Yes.' He described the location and markings of the stall. 'I'll help you all I can later on, but . . . I kind of want to stick here till I see how it's going with Elmer.'

'Of course. Is Doris there with you?'

'Yes. You want to talk to her?'

'Not necessarily. Just tell her not to be surprised if and when she finds our vehicles in her yard.' I punched off, dialed McCafferty and caught him at home on a rare night with no meetings.

He said, 'Never mind the money, Jake, I'll squeeze some more shoes and get it. Something very bad is going on with this family, isn't it? Are you getting any closer to knowing what the hell it is?'

'I'm beginning to think so. But I better tell you about it later because I got about a hundred things to do right now.'

Trudy was watching me as I closed my phone. 'I hate to do this to you,' I said.

She waved me off, saying, 'I am a whiz at putting dishes back in the refrigerator.' She watched me carefully gearing up, checking my Glock and my Taser, putting an extra clip of ammo in a pocket and settling my jacket over my vest. 'It's getting a little hairy, isn't it?'

'We damn sure need to get it stopped,' I said. 'But don't worry. I'll just be supervising and we probably can't do much tonight anyway.'

'Good. I'll be right here, not worrying. So keep in touch when you can, will you?'

'You bet.' I called Ray again, because I was waffling about where to go first. He said the ER team had just called time of death on Elmer, and Pokey was on his way.

'I'm on my way in too.'

'Good. Andy just got here, too,' Ray said. 'He said, "You don't need to time me in – I just wanted to be here".'

'How'd he hear about it?'

'Um . . . Winnie called him. She knew how he felt about Elmer.'

They were all together in the waiting room, Ray and Winnie, Andy and Charlie, clustered around Doris. To my surprise the silent boy, Alan, was with her, sitting close to his mother but not touching. I raised my eyebrows and Winnie whispered, 'He was getting too anxious so her mother brought him back.'

Then Pokey was there, all business, no time to talk to us until he had made his deal with the attending physicians. He wanted to stake his claim, 'get my body moved to County right away', I heard him saying in the curtained enclosure. He had been lucky enough to find a room open at County Medical, had a van coming to transport and was anxious to examine what was left of Elmer Hisey before anybody else laid a hand on him.

It's one of his big concerns, the reason he gladly endures freezing in a field the way he did at Owen Kester's crime scene. He hates the loss of information he faces on a body that's been treated in a hospital. 'So much washing and disinfecting,' he told me once. 'Good for patient maybe. Big loss for me.'

He let us in, for a minute, while he waited for his driver. We stood in a row a careful three feet from the gurney, an odd group painfully aware we didn't belong together. The body on the gurney looked shriveled, ancient, abstract – like a less-than-lifesize impression of a man, made by an artist whose skills needed work. It was hard to believe he had recently been the busy, useful person everybody was already describing.

'First time I ever saw him not smiling,' Winnie murmured.

'He was kind to everything,' Doris said. 'Even the cats loved him.'

'Because he always brought them milk,' Charlie said. 'Elmer was the best hand with a sick animal I ever saw.'

'And the newborns,' Doris said. 'He'd hold them and he could seem to feel what they needed.' She gave vent to a long, sad sigh. 'I'm going to *miss* him.'

Amazingly, it was still only eight o'clock when they wheeled the gurney out to the van. Ray and I had walked out with Pokey, and stood beside him as the driver slammed the big back door and drove away. Pokey said he had time now and the lab was available, so he thought he'd go ahead with the autopsy 'soon as I can scrub in'.

I said, 'Pokey, isn't two in one day kind of too much?'

He looked at me as if the question was too lame to deserve an answer. Nodding brightly to Ray, he said, 'Whoever's coming, better be quick.'

When he was gone I told Ray, 'Whoever you give it to is going to log considerable overtime – why not assign the person who wants it most?'

'You mean Bo? Good idea.' He pulled out his phone.

'One thing before you start that – I think we should take a look in that stall tonight before time changes it any more, don't you?'

'Absolutely.'

'So while you call Bo shall I go see if Andy's free to go along?'

'Sure. Winnie too, if she's still up for it. She should know that place pretty well by now – she and Rosie have spent more time there than anybody. So now,' he began to punch buttons, 'let's see if I can find Bo. He and Rosie are kind of all over the place right now; they found a house to move into together and they're—' Somebody answered one of the numbers he had punched, and his voice took on an unnatural sweetness. Must be Nelly, I thought, and as I walked away I heard him say, 'Hi, honey, this is Ray Bailey. Is your dad there?'

Back in the waiting room I caught Andy's eye and then Winnie's, nodded toward the door, and stepped into the hall to wait for them. Standing in the harsh light of the cold, busy corridor, getting nudged and poked by busy people carrying bulky objects, I told him, 'I just got authorization from the chief for as many overtime hours as we need for this case. Ray and I think we ought to take a look in that barn before time changes it any more. You up for it tonight?'

'You bet,' Andy said, and Winnie nodded emphatically.

'OK, you're on the clock starting now. You got all your gear with you?'

'In the car,' they both said, then looked at each other in surprise and laughed.

'The way things have been going,' Andy said, 'I just try to stay prepared.'

I went inside to make sure Doris and her foreman were on board with this decision. They both endorsed the idea and offered to help. Ray and I held a private intense conversation in the hall about the pros and cons of accepting their offer.

'It's not exactly kosher, is it?' he said, all his long face screwed into pondering knots. 'Officially they're still on my list of suspects.'

'But we don't know the layout,' I said, 'or the animals. And it's night.'

'Yeah. Let's do what works and fix it with the rule book later.'

We all got busy with prep, then bought fresh bottles of water from one vending machine, energy bars from another. Ray had a cache of flashlight batteries that he shared around. Winnie went out to her car to check her weapons and armor, and came back in carrying a half-dozen printouts of Maynard's picture, which she scattered around the room, saying, 'Might as well put every location to use.'

Doris and Charlie got into her big SUV to go home, saying they would meet us at the barn and show us anything we wanted to see. There was no more mutual suspicion now – we were all on the same team. Even Alan, who was always, quietly but insistently, by his mother's side, seemed less alien than before.

We followed them in a caravan of our own cars – not efficient, but we all wanted to be prepared to go home from there without coming back to the station to check out cars. It was a clear, bright night – after we passed the last lights from gas stations and C-Stores, we could see many stars.

At the farm, there was one light on a tall pole in the yard, another beside the front door of the Kester house, and light streaming out of ground-floor windows. Doris came out of the house as we parked, carrying a big flashlight, and Charlie was waiting by the barn door with a battery-powered lantern. He turned on overhead lights that provided dim illumination in the aisles of the silent barn.

Most of the stalls were empty, Doris explained. 'I turned out all the stock except the two horses we sometimes need to ride, and this one brood mare, because she's close to foaling.'

'Isn't she a little out of season?'

'Oh,' she made an embarrassed face, 'she didn't take when I bred her in the winter, so I thought she was getting too old and didn't try the next month. Left her out in the pasture with some yearlings and one of them turned out to be a little . . . precocious. So Bessie's having a catch-colt, after all these years. My bad.'

We stood by the box stall where the dark mare stood quietly. 'Doris and I were just back from milking at Dairy Farm,' Charlie said. 'Late – but Henry had been working over there most of the day and he looked beat, so at about five we persuaded him to go home and let us finish up. Anyway, we finally got the milk put up ready to ship in the morning, Doris went up to the house to warm up whatever Aggie had left for her and Alan to eat, and I came in here to drop my gear and take Elmer home. He's lived in my house the last ten years, and my wife had supper ready.

'I passed him in the aisle here as he was just going into Bessie's stall and I told him to be ready to go in ten minutes. He said, "All right, just going to check on Bessie's feed and water and I'm ready too". He went in there humming one of them nonsense songs he sings to calm animals down. I was down at the end of the aisle there putting my tools away. Then I heard—'

I had been watching the mare while he talked, and also looking around the stall. When he didn't go on, I turned to look at him and was stunned to see that he was weeping. I said, 'Oh, here' and reached out for him but Doris got to him first, supporting with her hands under his elbows, pulling a stool into place with her foot.

'Sit here,' she said, and eased him down.

'God, Doris, he was right here, and,' he pointed with a shaking hand, 'I was right . . . down . . . there. Wouldn't you think I'd have brains enough to come up here and help him? But I just went on putting my tools away, my gloves in the drawer,' he looked around at all of us desperately, 'as if any of that mattered more than saving Elmer,' he said, his voice getting all soggy and muddled now as the tears poured down.

The reality of this terrible week was all catching up with him at once. Right through the other deaths he'd been stolid and kept it all in, doing his job, helping where he could and making no waves, and now with the death of this kind old man he had reached the end of his very tough rope and was breaking down.

'You didn't know,' Doris said, bending over him. 'You did all you could.'

'Charlie,' Ray said, 'I know it's hard but can you tell us what you heard?'

'I—' He choked, turned his face away, fumbled and found a handkerchief, swabbed his face. We all waited. When he could speak again he told us, 'He was singing to the horse . . . and then he said – something. It wasn't very . . . it was hardly even a word. If it was anything, it was, "No". Or maybe just, "Oh". And then I heard a thump.' He thought some more. 'So I said, "Elmer, you OK?" And when he didn't answer I said again, "Elmer?"'

He turned sideways on his stool, then again so he was facing down the aisle toward where he had been standing. I saw his shoulders heave a couple of times while he fought for control. When he had himself in hand he turned back to face us all, raised his hands and shoulders in a big sorrowful shrug and said, 'About then I realized something was wrong and came running over here – and oh, Jesus,' he said, looking up into Doris's face, 'you should have seen how that mare was behaving. All lathered up and rolling her eyes—'

'*Bessie?*'

'Yeah, Bessie, old Lady Placid. But boy, was she agitated. I thought maybe a snake – so I pushed her aside and got into the stall and there was Elmer—'

Ray asked him, 'Can you show us?'

'Sure.' He stood up, thought about it, and told Doris, 'I believe I'd just as soon move the horse before I let all these people in there.'

'I'll do it,' she said. The mare, very pregnant and clearly back in placid mode, waddled after Doris to another stall and began munching up a fresh serving of hay. Charlie carried out a couple of forkfuls of manure, said, 'There now', and we all filed in.

'Bessie was way up at the front of the stall and leaning on

the gate like she wanted to get out. Which she never does – she's not a horse that fights the stall. And Elmer was right alongside of her, with his feet toward the rear of the stall and his head just about right here.'

We shined all the lights we had on the spot in the straw he indicated. Looking for dark spots that might be blood, looking for *anything* . . . but there was only the nice, clean straw Elmer had been spreading. We pushed it carefully aside, looking for anything that shouldn't be there. There was nothing under the straw except dirt.

Winnie was looking up, asking, 'His head was right here under the trapdoor?'

'Mmm, yes.'

'But the trapdoor's always closed, isn't it? Except when you're pulling down hay?'

'Yes.'

'How does that work?' Ray asked him. 'Don't you run out of hay that's close enough to grab?'

'It's a two-stage job. Somebody goes up once a day and loads the chutes. Twice a day somebody pulls a feeding down from here for any of the stalls that are occupied.'

'Where do you go up?' Winnie asked. 'Through the chutes?'

'Hardly.' Too sad to laugh, he made a small ironic sound. 'Well, *you* could do that, easily, but . . . Most of us would find it pretty snug. There's a stairway in the back that drops down.' He pointed. 'You come back in the daytime, I can show you all this better.'

'We'll do that,' Winnie said. And then, embarrassed by having spoken out of turn, asked Ray, 'Won't we?'

'Yup. Not much use trying for fingerprints on this rough lumber, I guess,' he was looking around, 'but we could try swabbing for DNA maybe . . . I'll talk to BCA in the morning. Has anybody got any crime scene tape?'

'I have,' Andy said, and went to get it.

'I know I could just ask you to leave it alone,' Ray said, 'but somebody else coming in . . .'

'It's all right,' Doris said. 'Business is pretty much at a standstill in this barn right now anyway.' Andy came back with the tape and he and Winnie wrapped it around the stall a couple of times.

'That's probably about all we can do tonight unless . . . Who're you calling on the phone there?' he asked me.

'Oh,' I folded it up, 'the chief asked me to call after we got here. He's concerned about your safety,' I told Doris. 'He wonders if you wouldn't like to move to town for a while.'

She was shaking her head before I finished. 'I can't leave my place empty; I won't leave my animals. I'll be – we'll be – fine.' Her eyes darted to Alan as, I realized, they had been doing all evening, and he flicked his glance a little sideways – the nearest he could come, apparently, to making eye contact. One of the most amazing things about this indomitable woman, I was beginning to realize, was the calm and soothing way she cared for a child who desperately needed her but could not bear to be touched.

'The security guys we hired will stay on patrol,' she said. 'They're out there now; did you see them on the way in?'

'One,' Jake said. 'I think.'

'Well, if you're not sure,' she said, 'they're doing their job right.'

'The chief is talking to the sheriff about this case,' I said, 'and asking for his deputies to ride some extra night tours around here for a while.'

'They can't patrol on city property, can they?' Doris said.

'Well . . . not exactly but . . . we help each other out once in a while,' I said. 'Since we're both short-handed,' I added lamely, justifying an old practice that went back through many eras. Come to think of it, when had we not felt short-handed?

It seemed wrong to leave, but everybody needed to rest, especially the two who were staying behind. Charlie had regained his rock-solid control but looked exhausted; Doris was calm but her beauty had lost some luster since I had first seen her. Only five days ago, could that be right?

Rolling out her long driveway behind the string of other car lights, I scanned right and left, but never saw a guard patrolling. *You better not be scamming her, you bastards.* The world was full of enemies tonight, all of them unseen.

By morning the weather had turned sullen, with a stiff, knife-edged breeze and full overcast of clouds that looked heavy with snow. BCA said they would respond to a demand for help if the autopsy indicated a strong likelihood of foul play. Lacking that, they said politely, they were always ready to help with advice.

Without denigrating the value of their counsel, I sincerely hoped Pokey's suspicious nature was in full play today. I told the chief I understood exactly how those dinosaurs felt so many years ago, when they realized this shiny black stuff they'd wandered onto was a tar pit.

'Feels like we're up to our necks in this case,' I told the chief. 'And any minute we're going to sink without a bubble.'

'God, you can be a whiner,' he said. 'I already said I'll take the old man off your back today – what more do you want?'

'If I thought you were serious I've got a long list. But don't worry,' I said as he raised a protesting hand, 'I just came in to tell you why Henry's coming to visit.'

'His oldest employee getting killed out there last night. Yes, I suppose that did hit him pretty hard. But who's running the milking machines while he's in here talking?'

'Well, Henry explained this morning that he put his foot down yesterday with his lawyer son, Ethan. Said it was by God time he earned some more of the money his shares were bringing him. Told him he had to get his butt out there to the farm and help out for a change. Said, "If I can do it you can do it".'

'Ethan tried protesting that he couldn't be spared from the law firm, but Henry checked with the uncles and they said, "Oh, sure, we can spare him for a few days". So to stave off going back in the barn with Dad, Ethan went down to the unemployment office, found some Venezuelans with green cards sitting there all happy because their corn crops were in the silos and they were looking forward to getting on the dole for a while.'

'Can they do that?'

'I guess they can if they've been working long enough. These two won't find out though, because Ethan told the desk people there he had plenty of work – send me the next five guys who walk in, he said. Then he talked his father and the foreman at the farm into believing they can start the gauchos on mucking out and feeding, and they'll work up to running the machines in no time. I think maybe Ethan's ready to go into politics.'

'Or anything else that keeps him from getting stuck in a stall with Dad again, huh?'

'Right. Anyway, that gave Henry a much-needed day off so naturally he wants to come in and review the case with me. Which I have not got time to do so I said I have good news for you, Henry: the chief is going to go over the details with you today.'

'How much does he know about that latest casualty in his barn last night?'

'Doris told him all she knew, he said. So I hope you can show him some pity, Frank, because underneath all the bluster Henry's a pretty good old skate.'

'Uh-huh. When he's not chewing on you. But now, tell me that the new victim got kicked by a horse, unless he didn't. Where are you with that? You went out to the farm last night?'

'Yes.' I told him about it. 'I'm depending on Pokey to deliver a verdict that's at least ambiguous enough to get BCA into the case, because I don't have any idea how to distinguish a horse kick from a blow on the head from a weapon I can't find.'

'You haven't searched much yet, have you?'

'No. Ray's sending a crew out there now. Speaking of searches, how are you doing with BCA? Any chance of speeding up some of that Maynard information we asked for?'

'They said they'd try on the prints. I'll check with them again this morning. But your crew might find something in the barn on a daytime search, right?'

'Yes. And Bo will be in pretty soon – he worked so late on the autopsy, he asked for an hour off this morning to get Nelly settled in her new school. You know he and Rosie are moving into a new house together? So – when he gets in here, we'll ask about the autopsy. Pray for horseshoe marks!'

'Don't believe I've ever done that before. But the Lord is still merciful, as we know because my youngest daughter passed her math test yesterday in spite of those happy days on the slopes. Let me know what Bo says.'

My phone was blinking when I got back to my desk, and the message was from a number I didn't recognize. I called it and Doris answered in the middle of the first ring. She said, 'Captain Hines, a strange thing – an unprecedented thing happened this morning.' Her voice sounded like tin pans banging in the wind.

I said, 'Doris, do you need to take a breath before you tell me? You sound pretty excited.'

'I am, but . . . I'm all right. I need to tell you this, will you just listen?'

'Yes. Go ahead.'

'My son Alan *talked to me.*'

She said that much and stopped, as if that statement was striking enough to stop traffic. I listened to her ragged breathing. After a few seconds I said, 'You said he does that sometimes.'

'A word or two. This morning, he said a whole sentence.'

'What did he say?'

'He had a copy of that picture – the one your detective Winnie was leaving around on tables in the hospital? Evidently Alan picked one up last night. This morning he held it up to me and said, "That man carried Daddy".'

'Maynard? He's saying Maynard carried your husband?'

'That's what he said. Yes.'

'Where? Were you able to ask him where?'

'Yes. I asked him if he could show me, and he made his little come-along sign . . . it's one of the signs he only does with me. So I followed him and he led me to the walk-in cooler.'

I was breathing funny myself by now. I asked her, 'Doris, did you ask him where Maynard carried him from there?'

'Sure. And he tried to answer but . . . he was getting tired. His attention span is very short, so staying on one subject exhausts him. But for just a second he made that rum-rum noise that he uses to mean a vehicle.'

'So you think he's saying Maynard carried your husband from the cooler room to the pickup?'

'I think so. But his concentration was gone by then, so when I asked him, "Did he carry Daddy to his pickup?" he just nodded his head once or twice and looked away. But he must have meant the pickup – that's what Owen had there.'

'It would have been right there nearby, wouldn't it? Where Owen meant to load it with supplies?'

'Yes.'

'Doris, this is very exciting – this is more of a break than we've had. But listen, who else knows about this?'

'Nobody. Alan and I were all alone here; we'd just gotten out of bed when he showed me the picture. And I haven't told anybody else yet.'

'Good, then don't.'

'OK, fine.'

'No, Doris, I mean be totally certain you do not tell another living soul about this until I say it's OK, understand?' I could hardly explain to her that the buildings at her farm seemed to be leaking information. I didn't believe that myself, literally, but something was going on that enabled this killer to stay one step ahead of us. I could feel it in my bones, and I was beginning to think it put her and Alan in awful danger. 'Promise me,' I said.

'*All right*, I won't! But . . . you do believe me about this, don't you?'

'Absolutely. And we're going to go to work on it right away. We've already got a search going for Maynard's records, and now we'll . . . accelerate the search.' The last sentence sounded lame to me even as I said it, but luckily I was able to fold up my phone before Doris told me I was talking baloney.

I hurried over to Ray's office and found him, of course, on the phone. But he was wearing a look that said his caller was telling him something extremely interesting, so when he pointed to the chair in front of his desk I sat down in it and waited. 'Good, good,' he said, and, 'fine.' Buoyed up by those pleasant words, and the fact that he was making rapid notes while he said them, I waited some more, even though waiting made me want to jump out of my skin.

Finally he said, 'And you're faxing all that down to me? That's great, Doug. Thanks.'

He hung up and gave me a most un-Bailey-like smile.

I said, 'What?'

He said, 'Maynard Phelps's real name was Artie Pritzer, and he was one naughty boy.'

'Tell me.'

'Arrests stretching back twenty years, three convictions . . . the first one for assault, as a juvenile.' He read from his notes. 'The other two for dealing, in ascending order of magnitude. Artie was pretty big in the drug trade, a little farther down the Mississippi. Mostly down around Saint Louis, looks like.'

'So what the hell was he doing on a farm in Minnesota?'

'A whole lot that wasn't in his job description, I bet.'

'Including one very puzzling thing I just heard about.' I told him about Doris Kester's phone call.

Ray said, 'I feel like my brain's going into gridlock.'

'Me too, but we can't freeze now, because I can feel this coming to a *point*, can't you? Something's going to pop and when it does we need to be ready to – oh, shit, that phone!'

But he was already answering it, and this time his face was folding into the old familiar Bailey gloom. 'Andy,' he said, 'I don't have time to . . . wait, what?' And then his face changed, a little, and he said with more respect, 'Wait a minute, Andy, I never said . . . OK, yes, I *hear you,* Jesus, don't get so – I'll be right there.'

He hung up the phone and got up in one move. In the next he was clipping on his Glock, pulling his vest out of the console. He looked a little pale.

'Ray,' I said, 'what did Andy say?'

'He said, "Quit being such a shithead and get out here. Winnie found something".'

'So now you're headed for the farm?'

'Yup.' He patted himself all over, nodded, and walked out of his office.

I opened my mouth to say that I would field his calls when the rogue thought surfaced: *He's going where all his calls would come from.* I darted into my own office and repeated most of the moves I had just watched Ray make. Glock, Taser . . . I couldn't find a can of Mace, but I took my Streamlight and an extra clip for the Glock. I reached the top of the stairs just as Ray was going out the door. Bo was on the other side, reaching for the handle. I saw Ray say something, without breaking stride, and Bo turned and followed him to his car.

A skanky wind was raising dust and ice-crusted snow off the parking lot, as the first flakes of the coming storm drifted down. The sky was a dirty puce color. I pulled on my lights and turned into the street, where everybody else had their lights on too. I shivered and turned up the heat, and at the first stop light I zipped my jacket and pulled on gloves. Minnesota was getting ready to show us her ugly side.

Three department vehicles were parked in the yard at the farm. Ray and I pulled into line beside them and the three of us walked to the barn, where Winnie stood waiting for us. Doris was there, too, with Alan in his usual position, near her side but not touching.

Winnie said, 'The others are waiting for us in the loft.' She led us down the aisle, past stalls that were suddenly all occupied. The small arena in the center of the barn was filled, too, with unhaltered animals eating hay out of haysacks hung from the posts, and I noticed that the building was a lot warmer than outside, thanks to the body heat of so many animals.

'I've been moving them in all day,' Doris said. 'It's going to be too cold outside for a few days, especially for the ones that have been in the barn and don't have full winter coats.'

We walked on, to the back of the barn where a long wooden trapdoor was pulled down and tied off to bolts at the side of the aisle, so the steps built onto the back of it formed a stairway up.

Up in the fragrant loft we found Andy, Clint and Rosie kneeling around the trove of evil treasure Winnie had found.

'There's the package of . . . Andy thinks it's cocaine,' Doris said, pointing to a tight-wrapped white brick, well taped. Doris's voice was muffled; she spoke in the hushed tones of a person at a wake. And every time the barn timbers creaked in the rising wind, I noticed, she looked around. The fearless farmer lady of yesterday was a little spooked now.

'Well, it stands to reason,' Andy said. 'It isn't pot, and the autopsy showed coke in Maynard, right? And this, I think, is the short-handled crowbar that killed poor Elmer.' He was wearing spandex gloves, as were Clint and Rosie – they were getting the items packed in cartons, ready to move to town.

'But this . . . elegant little blue rope,' Winnie said. 'What is it good for? So nicely finished on both ends, see? Almost looks like a lariat except it's too small.'

'Ah, so you used to ride horses but you didn't ever try rodeo riding, huh?' Clint held it up, and I felt a little balloon forming over my head. I looked at Ray. He looked as if he felt a balloon growing too.

'A piggin string,' Ray said.

'Of course,' I said. 'Perfect.'

Clint looked up from the carton he was holding. 'For what?'

'For a garrote. I believe we're going to prove it killed the felon named Artie Pritzer.'

'That's the no-good formerly known as Maynard?'

'Yes, indeed.'

'Ray, you look downright happy,' Rosie said. 'Is that appropriate at this time?'

'Maybe not, but I can't help myself. A piggin string, is that a hole in the boat or what?'

'It is.' I knelt by the group. 'What about this twine gizmo? Looks like it might be a plant holder.'

'Probably was,' Andy said. 'Looks like it was adapted by some clever climber to help him up and down through those hay chutes.'

'Winnie,' Ray said, 'where'd you find all this stuff?'

'Up in the eaves under the roof,' she said, 'where the swallows roost, and the owls. You want to see it now?'

We followed her across the hollow-sounding floorboards of the hayloft. The front rows of hay bales had been used up, so there were bare spots to walk in, next to the front wall of the barn. All the rest of the space was packed tight with clover-smelling hay.

When Winnie stopped, she said, 'These pieces of wood nailed onto the uprights here, they make a ladder to climb up on, see? And there's a kind of cubby built up there. You can see the bottom from here.' She pointed. 'Almost like a child's tree house.'

'I think that's what it was, once,' Doris said. 'Owen said they used to play up here when they were kids. Pirates and explorers, games like that.'

'How'd you find it, Winnie?' I asked her.

'Alan showed me,' she said. The boy was standing by his mother but, at the mention of his name, when everybody turned to look at him, he shrank back.

'He made a little gesture that I took to mean, follow me,' Winnie said. 'And when we got over here he shinnied up this hand-built ladder. So I followed him up . . .'

Doris's face was filled with conflicting emotions: jealousy that he'd shown someone else one of his secret signs, fear for his obvious vulnerability – and then pride won out. 'I've always let him wander all he likes when we're out here in the barn together,' she said. 'I guess he knows this place better than I do by now.'

'How'd you get all that stuff down, though, Winnie?'

'Well, I couldn't, by myself, so I went down and told the

others, and everybody gloved up and followed me.' Behind her hand, she giggled discreetly. 'Rosie climbed right up behind me. The others came part-way and we passed things down.'

A big gust of wind shook the sides of the barn suddenly, followed by a bullet-like sound of wind-driven sleet.

'The weather's closing in,' Andy said. 'We'd better pack up and get this stuff downtown.'

'Doris,' Ray said, 'we would all like to urge you to move into town until this is over.'

'No. I've hired two more security guys to stay in the house and barn with me at night. They'll be inside, and the other two outside – we'll be fine.'

Sure. Just like Elmer was fine here last night. It was in my mind to say it, and when I looked around I saw all the other detectives thinking it too. But she owned this place – it was her call. So we all turned toward the back.

Bo led down the stairs, Andy and Clint and Rosie coming behind him each carrying a piece of the evidence Winnie had found. Doris came behind them looking at her watch, saying to Winnie, 'I've got to get over to the dairy now, and help Charlie get the milk ready for the haulers.'

I was last, coming down those noisy wooden steps into the yeasty-smelling barn where the crowded animals fed and the barn timbers creaked in the wind. Halfway down I heard the cry – was it an owl? But Doris turned toward it and said, 'Alan?' And then screamed, 'Alaaann!' and pushed Rosie ahead of her down the last two steps. Then all the detectives dropped what they were carrying and streaked out of the barn with her.

We reached the yard in time to see Alan's terrified face in the rear window of a gray Silverado pickup I'd never seen before. As we reached the yard it drove out the gate and disappeared into a white cloud of whirling snow.

We all ran to our vehicles and set out in pursuit of a vehicle we couldn't see any more – all but Bo, who ran to the little open-air Jeep that was parked by the front gate. He must have noticed when he came in that the keys were in the ignition. He climbed in and started it now, and roared out the driveway at the head of the pack, directly behind the pickup.

We could see each other, intermittently – the snow would let up a little and we'd see Bo in the Jeep just behind the dark gray truck. Driving fast into a white-out, surrounded by other vehicles doing the same thing, felt like every bad dream I ever had.

The next time the storm lifted I saw Bo in the ditch along-side the driveway, pulling even with the pickup and then a little ahead. Then I saw nothing but white-out for a terrible couple of seconds that felt like a week. But just as we reached the main road I saw Bo ahead veering the Jeep broadside in front of the pickup, which rammed into it and took it aboard.

Bo disappeared across the top of the Silverado into the ditch on the other side. But even a high-powered pickup with snow tires wasn't going far in a snowstorm with a Jeep draped across its windshield. It slowed to a crawl and then we were all there, swarming the pickup on both sides, tearing the doors open, pulling the driver out. Andy had him, holding him aloft like a newborn calf squealing and kicking. Not cool at all anymore.

Winnie had Alan almost out of the backseat, turning to give him to his mother. But Doris wasn't beside her any longer; she had stooped to take something out of her boot and now was running full tilt toward the viciously struggling figure of Matt Kester, who was clamped in Andy's iron embrace. Doris's face was terrible now, she had the knife raised and she was going to reach him before any of us could get there to stop her.

But Winnie dropped Alan and pushed her body quickly in front of Doris. Standing fearlessly under the knife, she said softly into Doris's face, 'Your children need you.' Her words made Doris pause for one critical second, and in that tiny interval, Ray and I reached her.

So we were on either side of her when her strong raised arms seemed to lose all their power, and she melted, weeping, into our arms. We held her tenderly, as the knife fell out of her hands. We helped her to her car and strapped her in. We held the passenger door open so that her silent needy son could climb in beside her and sit where he needed to sit, close by but not quite touching.

FOURTEEN

I t took all winter to get Matt Kester's case into court. Ridiculous amount of red tape, I kept saying – we caught the guy red-handed, what more proof does anybody need?

'Maybe a credible explanation?' the chief suggested, on a frigid day in late December. He was cranky from listening to the Christmas carols wheezing out of every storefront, and taking it out on me. 'Motivation that a reasonable person can understand?'

'You want reasonable murderers now?' We still had a week of fa-la-la to get through, and I was just as sick of it as he was. 'No whacked-out sociopaths need apply in Rutherford, is that it?'

'You know what I mean – quit pretending you don't. Get your ass in gear and connect the dots so it makes sense for a jury – how'd he do all this damage and why?'

I had most of the how typed into the case file by then, but building a coherent storyline that explained the why wasn't all that easy.

I thought then, and I'm still convinced, that Matt Kester's basic problem was that he started from a false premise. He thought his place in the family was as secure as his mother said it was, that he was such a star, admired by all, that any little glitches could be waved away. He brushed aside Ethan's jealousy and Henry's stern disapproval, totally discounted Doris's mastery of all the jobs he'd never bothered to learn at all, and believed he could get his father to forget his earlier treachery.

So he thought he only had to clear away a few obstacles – a brother who had been kind to him but wasn't going to change his mind about sand mining, a crony he'd brought along with him from his cocaine-dealing days on the rodeo circuit, who now wanted a bigger cut and thought blackmail would be fun to try. Just get rid of these speed bumps, Matt thought, and his dreams would come true.

He had always felt entitled to the top spot on the team, we learned by talking to some of his old buddies and ex-girlfriends. Wasn't he the handsome one, the brilliant, admired one who could sing and play the guitar and ride anything on four feet – wild bulls, crazy horses, whatever? But for some reason the other males of the family kept putting him back to the end of the line – treating him like Little Brother, the goof-up.

'All that guff he threw at us about Kesters sticking together, that was just pure hot air,' Ray told me after he'd interviewed Aggie, the talkative cook. 'Aggie told me Matt was always out for himself first and foremost, and everybody on the place knew it.'

Ray figured out another little piece of the scenario too. Both the pictures of the pickup that Tom Baines took the day Owen was found and Andy's own examination of the scene made it clear there were no fencing supplies in the pickup. But Owen went back to the barn to load them – why didn't he start?

'He must have seen the doors open on the smokehouse and the walk-in cooler,' Ray said, 'when he drove in the yard. So he must have bypassed the barn and gone right to the cooler.' And found Matt there, starting to lay a track of lighter fluid from the smokehouse into the cooler. We had found the can and lighter on a shelf behind the meat. 'That started the fight.'

'And Maynard must have been there with him, helping,' I said. (We had all gone back to calling him Maynard because 'that Artie guy we've all known as Maynard' was too cumbersome to live with.)

'I'm sure that's how it went down,' Ray said. 'Owen would certainly have confronted his brother, and I believe Owen started dialing nine-one-one to report the attempted arson to police. That's when Matt went and got the shotgun he was carrying in the pickup from River Farm. We know Dispatch got an interrupted phone call from Owen's phone, but we've never found it – Matt must have thrown it in the river.'

All the physical evidence says that Matt pulled the insulated door shut on the cooler to mask the noise and shot Owen. Then Matt cleaned up the cooler while Maynard carried Owen's body to his pickup and took it to the field near the goose hunt. That's what Alan saw that day, and later told his mother. He's a poor sleeper so he often gets up very early and wanders around the farm watching the birds and animals wake up, Doris says.

Ray was indignant about the fact that we could have found some of this earlier if we'd had more staff to put to work on the case. 'Hell, we hadn't even found all the vehicles on those three farms yet,' he said. 'Let alone get a real handle on everybody's whereabouts that day. I told you, Jake, we've been totally snowed under with this case from start to finish.'

'Have to try to get our homicides done in smaller venues from now on,' I said, and he gave me the special Bailey look that approximates a raised middle finger.

Josh Felder turned out to be key to understanding the conflicting motivations in that family's story – he really was a canny nerd, as Kevin had claimed. Though I wasn't exactly blown away when he announced, early on in his first morning of searching, that the piggin string Winnie had found in the loft was called 'Lyle's Blue Gunslinger'.

'That's fun to know,' I said, 'but maybe not essential to the prosecution.'

'He's just getting started,' Ray said. 'Give him time.' And by an hour later he had found Matt's prison record, which put a stop to any misgivings I'd had about Josh's searching talents – in fact, I wanted to give him a Master Nerd award on the spot, because it blew the doors open on the whole case.

Matt Kester had done his time in Fulton State Prison, and his sentence coincided with one of Arthur Pritzer's, whom we all briefly went back to calling, 'the no-good formerly known as Maynard'.

So it was pretty easy to establish that they had known each other there. Matt was still not talking, at that time, about the deal they made. But Josh found Arthur Pritzer's mother, who said Artie told her he was going to Minnesota 'to hook up with an old buddy from his rodeo days'.

'I think he meant an old buddy from Fulton Prison days,' Ray said.

I asked Josh, 'How come you never found any of this criminal record before, though?'

'I was only searching in Minnesota,' he said. 'All those records said they were a founding family that never left Minnesota.'

'That was before. This is now. You didn't look far enough.'

'You didn't even want to hear all of what I did find,' he said. 'Don't you remember? You all kept falling asleep.'

'Because you only read us the dull parts. If you'd put the juicy parts first—'

'Oh, for the love of God,' Ray said. 'He's found it now, be grateful.'

The county attorney kept complaining to the chief that we weren't bringing him a coherent narrative. Somewhere he'd read an article that convinced him 'good stories win cases'.

'Chief,' I kept saying all winter, 'we're not fucking novelists, we're cops.'

'He wants a story,' the chief said. 'Give him a story.'

Henry finally gave us the plot we needed. 'Anna Carrie told Matt we were buying the River Farm,' he said. 'I think Matt and that Maynard guy decided a farm with river frontage would be a perfect place to receive drug shipments.'

'And they were getting started with that,' I told the chief. 'We found the corner in the barn down there where they were breaking down product – they cut it with baking soda.'

'But after Matt got here and heard about all the silica sand offers,' Henry said, 'I believe he decided he'd rather get his share of that money.'

'But he said he didn't care,' I said. 'He said whatever Owen wanted—'

'Jake, haven't you seen by now that Matt can never do anything straight up? He likes everything to be a little tricky.' He stared morosely into his coffee. 'Like when he left that first time. If he'd of come to me like a man and said, "I hate farming, I want to get my share now so I can follow the rodeo full time", I'd have set him up with everything he needed. Hell, he wasn't ever much use around the place anyway. But he enjoyed stealing it from me.' He shook his head mournfully. 'I don't know. You raise three boys, think you treat them all the same, and one turns out to be a crook. Go figure.'

I took that sad story to the CA, feeling quite proud of myself. He said, 'OK, I understand that part. What doesn't make sense to me is the extreme resistance of this one couple, Owen and Doris, to the sale. Why would they turn their backs on all that money?'

'They had the same objections to the sand mining as hundreds of other people in those small towns along the river.'

'Which are what?'

'Oh, hell,' I said. 'You haven't heard any of these arguments? Watched any of the hours of TV about it?'

He was shaking his head.

'Tell you what,' I said. 'I'm going to have my man send you a short movie which will explain it much better than I can.'

I turned Josh Felder loose on that task. 'Make sure it's no longer than an hour,' I said. 'The Second Coming wouldn't hold the CA's attention any longer than that.'

Josh found me when he had it ready, and asked, 'You want to take a look before I send it?'

'Maybe I better,' I said. It was February, the chief was on my back to get this case wrapped up, and I knew we'd never get the CA to sit through a second viewing. So I had Josh set it up at the conference table, and got Ray and Rosie to watch with me.

He opened on an almost-empty scene of a middle-aged man in shirt sleeves reading from a folder. He says, to someone off camera, 'Sometimes the information about sand mining is so confusing it seems to create its own Wonder World. Listen to this from the Wisconsin codes: "More research is needed to determine concentrations of acrylamides in frac sand wash water when mines are using polyacrylamide polymer flocculation products".'

'That's beautiful,' said a voice off camera. 'What does it mean?'

'I have absolutely no idea.'

Somewhere out of sight, people laughed. But the man said, 'There's a great deal of information like that about frac sand mining on the Internet, but you need an advanced degree to understand it. So people often just give up.'

Josh followed that with some rather horrifying footage, in which ordinary people in small towns along the river showed pictures of their hills and bluffs disappearing. Some of them cried.

Then he cut to four people talking about spills out of settling ponds into their pristine creeks and rivers, about hundreds of dead fish: 'You can call it an incident if you want to,' one lady shouted at a company official at a meeting, 'but hundreds of fish are dead in my creek and to me that's not an incident, that's a tragedy.'

The worst for me was a video featuring half-a-dozen people in the village of Maiden Rock, Wisconsin, talking about the ways in which their beloved community was being rendered unlivable. They talked about huge trucks running twenty-four/seven, wrecking the roads, spreading dust – 'and this is silica dust: you breathe it and your lungs are full of tiny pieces of glass.'

'We used to have a bed and breakfast in this town,' one of them said, 'but it failed because who wants to pay for a bed where nobody gets a rest from the noise?'

'It all happened so fast,' they said, 'nobody knew what to do. Pretty soon they were just there, ripping up the earth.'

'It's not just us we're worried about,' one woman said (she was blonde and handsome, like Doris), 'but what have we done to our children? This place we love so much – will there be anything left for them?'

The whole segment took less than forty-five minutes and when it ended, the three of us were almost too horrified to talk, but we agreed that yes, this video ought to do it. I took it to the CA and told him, 'If you need more than this, Doris Kester will be glad to explain.'

We had a heavy snow that afternoon, so I did a lot of shoveling before dinner. Ben and I had a very short playtime that night, and I was soon snoring loudly in my sack.

Somewhere in the pre-dawn hours the prehistoric lizard in the depth of my brain got fully rested, I guess, and began to amuse itself with a replay of the evening's games – but with a twist, of course. I was tweaking Ben's pink toes, crying happily, 'This little piggy went to market,' as we wiggled and chuckled our way through the digits. But when I got to the end of the counting game, oh, woe! There was one more toe there, that hadn't gone to market, or come home, or made roast beef – hadn't done squat, this toe. Was just an eleventh toe sticking out there, an extra pink toe I had never seen before.

In the dream, I looked into Ben's face, which had been smiling as usual, but now looked worried. He explained – in the magical way of dreams, my pre-verbal son was somehow able to explain to me – that too much frac sand washing solution had seeped into his aquifer and now babies were being born with extra feet, hands, heads – 'I was really lucky not to get one of those,' Ben said thoughtfully, 'because you might not love me if I had two heads.'

Trudy woke me when I began hugging my pillow and protesting that I would always love it no matter what.

I sat up and said, 'What? I didn't hear the phone.'

'It didn't ring. You were dreaming.'

'Oh. Did I wake you? Sorry.'

'Yes. And I thought you might like to stop yelling before you woke Ben too and destroyed your pillow.'

'My . . . Oh.' I detached from my soggy crumpled pillow and groped my way to the bathroom, where I pissed, splashed cold water on my face and muttered, 'Shee, what a crazy dream.' I went back to bed and told Trudy, 'Must've had too many spare ribs.'

I even went back to sleep that night, but on subsequent nights the dream came back. It took slightly different forms each time – sometimes Ben was short a digit, or even a whole limb, and once after we played horsey, his new favorite game when he rode on my back, he turned up in my dreams with a hoof, saying, 'I don't know, something spilled again, I guess.'

The next day at work, Ray said, 'Are you all right? You look a little green around the gills.'

I told him about the bad dreams that had been disturbing my sleep. He laughed out loud, which he doesn't do often, and confessed he'd been having his own ecological nightmare, which featured crumbling landscapes – whole mountains tumbling into rivers. He went and found Rosie in her workspace that day, and came back laughing with her story about grotesque dreams – in Rosie's, the rivers began getting thicker and thicker till they were turning to cement, 'and somehow,' Rosie said, 'in the dream I always know without a shadow of a doubt that it's all my fault.'

We all knew the sand mining process wasn't causing disasters like the ones in our dreams, but the overnight unease fit in with our feeling that we had stumbled onto an improvement with unknown downsides. So we were all as anxious as the chief was to get this case wrapped up and put away. 'We're close,' I told Ray. 'But it would help if we could make it clear that all those so-called accidents on the farm were Matt's doing.'

'We haven't proved them all,' I told the chief. 'The lame horse, the vet says he could go either way on that. But the tree falling on the house, yes – we found some marks from a cross-cut saw on the down side.'

'I haven't heard you say how they got Owen to the field without leaving any blood in the pickup.'

'That butcher paper that's hanging up there in big rolls, it has to be that they wrapped him in that.'

'And then trotted all the way home carrying the paper?'

'Or stashed it somewhere and went back later and burned it. We've built a time line that shows they had time to do all this – that call of Owen's was recorded at a few minutes before six – they still had more than an hour before daybreak.'

'And that works with when Matt arrived at the Burger King nearest River Farm.'

'He went and had breakfast while his partner planted the body?'

'Yes. Ordered a big breakfast and stayed there an hour and a half, talking to everybody so he'd have an alibi for the time. We've established that part with the owners. They were wondering why he was so friendly that day – he usually wasn't.

'It isn't hard to figure the next moves. Maynard probably said he was going to need a bigger cut of the money from the sale or he might have to come clean about putting the body in the field.'

'But the help from Nicole with the car – you're absolutely sure about that?'

'Oh, you bet. Jealousy turned Nicole into a real Wicked Queen of the West. Have you seen any of her interrogations? You should take a look – you'd be proud of how Ray got that job done. Slow and steady – he just gradually cornered her behind her own answers.'

'But in the end you offered her immunity.'

'Because we knew exactly what she had done but it was going to be hard to prove. We could never get her to admit that she was having sex with Matt – it was Matt who bragged about that. He got a little screwy after he got sick in prison and had to ask for drugs to help with withdrawal. That's when he finally explained the fire starter we found in the cooler. He said Owen came back in the yard and caught him and Maynard getting ready to set fire to the cooler. That was supposed to be the final big calamity that would convince Owen to quit farming and sell out. Matt claimed he never meant to kill Owen, "But he got so mad when he realized I caused all those accidents, he started calling the sheriff right then to turn me in. So I had to shoot him, don't you see? To shut him up". Nicole's wrecked anyway – Ethan's getting his divorce on very favorable terms, and I think she's going to see her worst nightmare come true: the secretary installed in her place. And we needed her testimony to make certain we nailed Matt. Because his crimes kept getting crazier, it was hard to convince anybody who wasn't there that it could have all happened the way it did. There's a lot about Matt's last two crimes that's pretty . . . uh, far-fetched? Even though I was there and saw what he did.'

'Henry thinks Matt killed Elmer mainly because he thought it would be the final straw for his father – that Henry would be hurt so much he'd just give up and sell the place for whatever he could get.'

'I think that was Matt's plan – as near as he came to having a plan by then. He was still concentrated on revenge against his father, and reckoning without Doris – I think he always reckoned without Doris.'

'Yes, well, his mom still calls her "the pushy Kleinschmidt girl".'

'Mom's a dear lady, isn't she? If Matt had been thinking rationally he'd have to know that we couldn't just walk away and let a whole string of murders go unsolved. But somehow he convinced himself that if he could get the family to sell out he could just take his share and go play on a beach. That's a Kester family characteristic, you know – that way of thinking, "If I want it, it's got to happen".'

'I guess we all do that sometimes, don't we? For instance, lately I keep thinking that any minute somebody will come and tell me I can quit worrying about the budget, the economy's all fixed.'

'And that will happen soon, Chief. We've been careful, and better times are coming.'

'Yeah, yeah, yeah. Not fast enough to suit me. Every month I have more gray hair, and we are still in the weeds on the budget.' He looked at me curiously. 'You seem to be holding up quite well in spite of the long hours. What's your secret?'

'I tell myself that if I do this exactly right, Matt Kester will get nothing lighter than life without possibility of parole.'

'Will that be compensation enough?'

'It will certainly help. Every hour of overtime I have to work till the budget gets fixed, I'm going to think about Matt Kester in the pokey in an orange jumpsuit, while his white hat and his fancy belt buckles sit unused in a closet. And that will help.'

'Uh-*huh*. Little vengeful streak beginning to form up there. Probably inevitable, but try to keep it selective, will you?

'You bet. Bad guys only. Are we done?'

He waved me off. 'Time to go get the boy, huh? How's he doing?'

'Pretty good. Two weeks till his first birthday, and he's almost ready to get up off his grubby knees and walk.'

'Enjoy every minute. Running away comes soon enough.'

Ben was crawling around Maxine's house, looking for something unsanitary to stick in his mouth, when I came in out of a howling March wind that slammed the door behind me.

'Sorry about that,' I said. 'Getting a little wild out there.'

'Sit a minute,' Maxine said. 'I've got something for you.'

'For me? It's not my birthday.' I don't really know my birthday, but I've always accepted October the fifteenth, the day Maxine says I was found in a dumpster. She got that information, along with a small plastic sack of clothing and a worn Teddy bear, from a tired elderly black woman named Bernice, who said she was my first foster mother.

Bernice was sorry to let me go, she told Maxine, but, 'He's speeding up and I'm slowing down, so I think I better do this while I can.' She left an address and phone number, but when Maxine tried to call her a few months later to celebrate my third birthday, she had gone without leaving a forwarding address.

'Forget your birthday – we've got something else to celebrate. You're always fretting about not knowing your family, so a couple of months ago I contacted the agency that arranged your transfer from Bernice to me.

'I've talked to them several times and last week they found one of the nurses that worked at that hospital in Red Wing. Where the cops took you after the night janitor at the Holiday Inn found you, you remember that part? OK. Mavis Schwartz is her name. She was a trainee then, thirty-seven years ago. She's retired now but still in good health, married and divorced, goes to the Gulf Coast in the winter.'

'What color hair dye does she use?'

'Don't be smart. We just visited a while, she's a nice person. And she told me that some of the nurses were eating lunch the day after you were brought in, and one of them said they should give you a name, so you wouldn't just be Baby Doe – it would give you a better chance of being adopted.'

'Is that true?'

'I have no idea. But they all thought being left in a Dumpster was a kind of rough start in life. She said they wanted to give you a little boost. They couldn't tell what race you were, so they said, "Let's give him some straight American name that will work no matter what he turns out to be".'

'All these years later, she remembers they said that?'

'That's what she told me. So one of the other nurses, Gloria, said, "Listen, I have a cat that's the best natured, most lovable pet I've ever owned. I'd be honored if we could call this baby after him – could we?" They all said maybe if it's not too weird and Gloria said, "Not weird at all, his name is Jake".'

'Oh, good, a cat.'

'But the *best* cat, don't forget. Lovable! And then they looked at the condiment tray and saw the ketchup bottle and one of them said, "Well, there, what could be more American than that?" But by the time they went to fill out the form on your registration somebody had moved the tray and Mavis wasn't a very good speller, so your Hines ended up being phonetic.' She beamed at me. 'There now, isn't that a good story?'

'Maxine, you guarantee you're not making this up?'

'Why would I do that? And I could never have found all this information if you hadn't given me that computer. So you see, your generosity has already been rewarded.'

'Benjamin Franklin,' I said, picking my dirty son up off the floor and grabbing whatever he was chewing out of his mouth,

'I think you and I had better be off home before the bullshit in this room gets so deep we have to shovel our way out.'

'Honestly,' Maxine said, 'you'd think a person would get a little appreciation for a long tough search like that. See you tomorrow, Benny.' She held up a hand and he high-fived it and gave her his crooked-toothy smile. His front teeth were crossing exactly the way mine do, but we were going to straighten his; they would soon be perfect like his mother's.

We went out into the gale and fought our way along a disappearing highway toward the oncoming blizzard. Nothing daunted, I shifted my apple-red pickup into four-wheel drive and clung to the slick pavement like a leech. I had been named after a cat and a ketchup bottle, unless I hadn't, and I had the goods on the black-hearted villain we would take in chains into court in the morning. We were having a little setback with the weather here at the moment, but it was March, almost Benny's first birthday, and better times were just around the corner.